IN THE NATIONAL INTEREST

Bernard McGrath

Fisher King Publishing

IN THE NATIONAL INTEREST

ISBN 978-1-910406-03-8

Published by
Fisher King Publishing
The Studio
Arthington Lane
Pool-in-Wharfedale
LS21 1JZ
England

First published in 2010 by Fisher King Publishing
under the title Operation Leprechaun

In loving memory
of my parents:

Charlie McGrath
1915 - 1992
Born Virginia,
Co. Cavan
Ireland 1915.

Rose McGrath
1917 - 2002
Born Loch Gowna,
Co. Cavan
Ireland 1917.

Contents

Prologue

'You can't put it there,' he said in a cantankerous grumpy tone.

'Why not?' they asked sulkily. They were both hot and tired and had had enough of being messed around.

'The lads won't stand for that place there, how about nearer the River Boyne, sure the sun rises over there and it'll shine on the yoke you're after building,' he said with an air of finality.

'Well I suppose so,' they muttered, both disgruntled at an offer they clearly couldn't refuse.

'What are you going to call it anyway: Hill Top or River View is it?' he asked the two of them pleasantly. Diarmid and Peadar exchanged glances; they hadn't thought of a name, presumably he had an idea. 'We don't know, what do you suggest?'

'How about Brú Na Bóinne or Newgrange, either of them have a nice ring to them.' This came more as an instruction than a suggestion. Diarmid and Peadar were a bit put out, this was the second time they had chosen a spot for the graves and this little interfering shite was trying their patience. They nodded and turned, walking back towards where the rest of the tribe were hard at work. As the two of them negotiated the closely packed trees, Peadar turned to Diarmid. 'What did gobshite say his name was?'

'He said he was called Ruairí; he's just a bully who thinks he can boss us around. You mark my words, that one will be trouble.'

'Ah yes, but one of these day Diarmid, that leprechaun and the sídhe will push their luck a bit too far. A great hero of the Fianna will arise and then they'll get what's coming to them'.

Pisa Cake

'… and then I persuade the little people to go Cavan. How about that for a stroke of genius?'

Niamh nearly choked on her coffee, little people had he really just said the little people or had she imagined it? She regained her composure and looked nonchalantly around her for any reactions from the other customers, nothing, they hadn't even noticed. She eyed him suspiciously, perhaps it had all come too late, without any fuss or a bit of bother on him; he'd just gone over the edge. The warning sign had been there, had she but known it, when she found him in the hotel bathroom poking about in the toilet with a coat hanger, allegedly trying to retrieve his watch.

'Cavan is a grand idea Donal, lovely, but can I just check I've got it right?' He looked at her expectantly. 'When you say little people, do you mean those Revenue Commissioners who've been asking those awkward questions, or is it those Gardaí with the faulty speed gun we met up with after your nieces wedding?' She laughed nervously, 'I mean you can't be referring to fairies, you know, bean sídhe's, leprechauns and all that jazz?'

'Of course its fairies and all that jazz, I've had enough of it Niamh, interfering in things, telling me what I can and can't do. It's about time I told them to pack up and shove off. '

Dear God, she thought. He means it! Perhaps he was having some kind of kind of breakdown, he had been under a lot of strain lately and perhaps it had all just proved too much for him. Work had been horrendous for both of them, but particularly for Donal. Being Taoiseach of Ireland wasn't a nine to five walk in the park. There were always going to be those against the government, but there was now a groundswell of mutterings and discontent amongst the party faithful. Donal had appeared to be weathering the storm and simply dismissed his critics as hurlers on the ditch but Niamh knew it was more serious than that. What he needed was a break away from everything, hence the holiday they were now enjoying in Tuscany.

She glanced around the Piazza Firenze; up until a couple of minutes ago it had been so perfect, the cafe tablecloths flapping lazily in a warm and gentle breeze, the hum of quiet conversation, a church clock chiming somewhere in the distance. Heaven she had thought to herself. Niamh suddenly noticed the guy at the next table; he had a large red face, ill-fitting jeans and a Green Army on Tour - European Championship t-shirt. An appreciation of Medici architecture was certainly not something he'd been soaking up; the stains on his top showed ample evidence of that.

She turned her attention away from the apparition next to them and back to Donal; she decided it might be better to humour him until she worked out what to do next. Niamh gave him a look of concerned sympathy and an I know what it's like smile.

He looked at her with an earnest expression. 'I mean it's

not as if De Valera is Prime Minister of Ireland, I am. This is the 21st century; try dancing at the crossroads today and some four wheel drive will splatter you all over the ditch.'

Well at least he wasn't developing megalomania, which was something. Donal might look like the young De Valera, but at least he didn't think he was Dev. She could just imagine what the media back home would make of all of this; Niamh could see the headline now: BONKERS BRADY - SAYS HE ISN'T DE VALERA. She suddenly caught movement out of the corner of her eye: the Green Army on Tour guy at the next table stood up, swayed slightly then lurched across the pavement.

'Howya Taoiseach yer bollix,' he said with a smile of recognition on his face. Niamh froze as he tripped, head butted Donal's nose and promptly threw up all over her.

Getting a willing taxi to take them back to the hotel proved a problem. Donal's nose was enlarging by the minute and you could smell Niamh from a distance of three metres. After paying twice the rate and being made to sit in the back carpeted with carrier bags and newspapers, they set off. Roberto eyed them warily in the rear view mirror, for all he knew the guy might puke up all over her again, and she might land another punch on him if he did. Donal stared mournfully out the window whilst Niamh tried to make small talk with Roberto.

Once back in their room Donal inspected his bruised nose in the mirror, wincing and feeling sorry for himself. Niamh went for a long soak. What a day, she thought to herself. You couldn't make it up if you tried. She closed her eyes and lay back in the bath. The sound of Donal surfing T.V. channels filtered in through the bathroom door, then it suddenly went quiet. The ominous silence was not a good sign; Niamh never liked it when it went quiet. It usually meant he was doing something he shouldn't. She came out of the bathroom and glanced over to the right to see him lying on the bed reading one of his books on Nazi Germany. As a hobby it was definitely weird, no matter what he thought. She took a look at the title of this one, The German Post Office at War 1939 – 1945. She despaired, she really did; when he was first running for election to the Dáil, she had asked him about his choice of reading matter.

'Why can't you read books on normal things? '

'What do you mean normal things?' Donal had appeared genuinely puzzled by the question. 'There's nothing abnormal about Nazi Germany.'

'Brilliant,' she had retorted at the time. 'We should put that on the election posters, *VOTE BRADY No 1, THERE'S NOTHING ABNORMAL ABOUT NAZI GERMANY.*' Whilst she sat on the edge of the bed drying her hair, Niamh thought about what Donal had said before the fracas at the cafe. She had to know if he was he really bonkers; it was hard to tell, he was behaving normal enough, well normal for him at any rate. Only one way to find out, but how? She decided the subtle approach might be best. 'You should write a book,' she said, trying to sound as relaxed as possible. He closed his German Post Office at War and looked at her suspiciously; this was definitely strange, thought Donal.

'A book about Nazi Germany you mean?' he asked incredulously.

'Well it could be I suppose, but how about something more interesting; how about the little people?'

A broad grin spread over Donal's face, 'Well now isn't that an idea. I wonder what they'd make of that. If the best kept secret in Ireland appeared in print they'd probably go ballistic!'

'And what secret would that be?' enquired Niamh. This wasn't proving as bad as she thought it would be.

He looked at her conspiratorially. 'They are real you know, sure some of the stories are made up, but not all of them. Do you remember I told you about seeing the big leprechaun in the G.P.O. on O'Connell Street buying stamps, about two metres tall he was? I was with my mammy at the time.' She had heard this tale before, 'But Donal you were only five, and anyway you've told me even you and your mammy didn't think he was really a leprechaun.'

He gave her a withering look, 'Of course he wasn't real, and doesn't everyone know they're only small? Anyway the point is that the real ones dress pretty much like he did: the breeches, stockings and the whole caboodle. That's for formal occasions of course.'

So he actually believes in leprechauns it wasn't the end of the world. Didn't The Minister for Defence believe

Achill Island was Atlantis, and what harm was there in that? As Donal had never shown any interest in the little people before, Niamh wondered why now. Even obsessional irrational mania had to come from somewhere.

'So when did you first realise they were real? '

A devious look overcame Donal and he glanced around the room, lowering his voice to a whisper he said, 'It was when I first met Ruairí; it was when I became Taoiseach. Ruairí lives in Leinster House, he's one of THEM.'

Niamh had thought she'd been making progress in this area, but he was now clearly regressing. 'Donal the term is gay; there's nothing wrong with being gay, after all you yourself said this is the 21st century.'

'NO OOO. He's one of them, the little people, the sídhe.'

Niamh considered this new delusion: so fairies living in the Irish Parliament building were in charge of government policy. 'I see, so you have meetings with this Ruairí do you?' she asked.

He nodded, 'You see, that's the point Niamh, not only do they exist, they interfere in things; they're always at it, had a say in Government since the foundation of the state. If you believe Ruairí these shenanigans go back even further. It was O.K in the old days, but not anymore. You know W.B. Yeats?'

'What about him?' she said, trying to remain calm.

'He was their man in the Seanad a sleeper working on the inside!' Donal smiled and winked. She wasn't absolutely sure, but was fairly certain that conspiracy theories were symptomatic of paranoia. The noise of the traffic outside their window began to impinge on her consciousness. What to do now was the problem, he was clearly certifiable. Niamh closed her eyes, took a deep breath and started to count slowly, 'aon dó, trí, ceathir… '

She was completely unprepared for what came next; opening her eyes she stared transfixed. 'Niamh, I'd like you to meet Ruairí, he's just dropped in on a surprise visit.' The figure on the bedside table was about half a metre tall, and was wearing Bermuda shorts, a flowery top and deck shoes.

Ruairí looked to be in his late forties and was balding, in his young days Niamh could imagine he would have been really good looking. 'Howaya Missus,' the diminutive visitor said. All she could manage by way of reply was a fish impersonation, her mouth opened and shut but no sound came out. Ruairí and Donal both nodded at her, and then moved over to the window. The discussion was clearly heated, even if it was in low tones. At one point it sounded like Ruairí addressed Donal as amadán, and waved a piece of paper at him. After about ten minutes things went quiet; she glanced around and Donal was alone.

Niamh looked at him. 'He… HE… was wearing Bermuda shorts.'

'I know, I keep telling him he looks stupid in them, but he won't listen. You should have seen what he had on when he went on holiday to Norway, a total disgrace to Ireland he was.'

Trying to look as relaxed as possible, Donal closed the windows to the balcony. She knew him better than that though, when he was tense and tried to appear in control he always looked shifty. It was now Niamh's turn to try and seem serene. Fighting the rising hysteria in her voice she asked, 'Just a social call was it?' She didn't really know what to say, a leprechaun drops in and, and... she could hardly run around the room like a mad thing.

'No it definitely was not a social call. I am not having a bunch of gobshites up Ben Bulben telling the government and me what we can and cannot do. I'll get them sorted out once and for all; I'll really give the bean sídhes something to wail about.' Donal paused dramatically, 'You see Niamh I have a plan.'

Thank God we're going home tomorrow, she thought to herself.

Donal's idea to sort out the little people had come to him during the wrangling at the E.U. Heads of Government meeting in Moscow. The formal business was bad enough, but the back stairs horse-trading put that in the shade. The arguments over what colour the new E.U. Passport was to be, was clearly a matter close to the heart of some people, but what came next upped the ante. Donal had lost the thread of the argument, but the French guy was clearly upset about the U.S import quota on Pyrenees Moose Antlers. Donal suspected all was not as it seemed, the Moose Antlers were most probably a Trojan horse. He looked wistfully at the Minister For Foreign Affairs next to him, listening intently through his headphones. Years of practice meant Tom always looked as if he was following every twist and turn of these meetings with real interest. This time it was the Ireland – Spain European Championship football match being relayed to him through the headphones. How much longer The Minister for Foreign Affairs could get away with this sort of thing was a matter of speculation; there was a rumour of a sweepstake by those in the know. He shuddered when he thought about the close run thing at the party Ard Fheis, state of the art graphics, a revamped Mansion House and the best sound system money could buy. He had reached the crescendo of his keynote address, '... and what reply had the opposition, to the success of our Fiscal policies?' (Rhetorical question – pause for dramatic effect!)

'You cute hoors', whispered Tom, (picked up by the multi million euro sound system, it was relayed around the hall). On that occasion it had been a late goal by Italy. Fortunately the delegates thought it was part of the script.

Donal tried to refocus on the proceedings. It might be minus eighteen outside the Kremlin, but in the conference room it was warm and soporific. His mind began to wander; Got to try and stay awake, get the auld brain in gear, he said to himself. How about the alphabet name game? That should get things moving. It was when he got to R that things did indeed start to move. R for Ruairí also meant resentment and it swelled like a high tide in Donal's mind. To the Taoiseach and indeed his predecessors,

Ireland's economic development and the little people were as interwoven as a page from the Book of Kells. While the country had been predominantly agricultural, there hadn't been any real problems. There had been the odd spat here and there, but as times changed, so did the country. A modus vivendi had developed, but now it was becoming more and more like a veto. God knows the months it took to sort out the LUAS route to Howth, with Ruairí pouring over maps, and then there was the spat over the new airport terminal. In Donal's mind the really big R stood for roads. Ireland needed roads, lots of them! Dual carriageways – motorways – ring roads – interchanges – slip roads – hard shoulders. The more he thought about it the more excited he became. Ireland needed motorways, and as Taoiseach, Donal was determined Ireland would get them. It was then the stroke of genius hit him, extend the M3 and move the sídhe to the Cavan - Longford border; there was feck all else there apart from bogs, lakes and English fishermen. The more he thought about it the more he liked it.

Come off the new section of the M3, drive a few miles up the road, and its Fairy Land in Lakeland. He sniggered to himself; how about that one for a Fáilte Ireland advertising slogan? He began to ponder his idea, then producing a pen from his top pocket began jotting down the outline of his scheme. He couldn't go public on this one; his Cavan scheme for the sídhe had to be kept within a tight circle. What he needed was a carrot and a stick approach if Ruairí and his friends were to be relocated, but what could he offer them? A broad grin spread across his face, that was it, offer them… he scribbled furiously. Next question, where exactly in Cavan to put his supernatural friends? What he needed was a front man, someone kept in the dark but doing the dirty work, a sacrificial lamb to be thrown to the wolves if it didn't work out, but who?

Mick McCarthy looked up at the leaden sky from beneath the sodden brim of his hat. The field sloped gently away from him and to the right; a small herd of damp cows surveyed the scene forlornly. He knew how they felt. It was at times like this he had to remind himself why he was doing this job. He looked down at his feet, slowly oozing and vanishing into the mud, and then looked up at Pat McGrath; the last time he had seen anyone resembling Pat, it was a character played by Sir John Mills in the film Ryan's Daughter. The old farmer smiled at him manically, 'I had yer man from The Western here yesterday, and that gobshite from Castlebar the day before that, and today it's yourself. Aren't you the great garsún coming all the way from England to see this,' Mick mused on his present situation. He was in a Connaught bog hole, or more precisely a trench, with a mid-fifties bachelor who was clearly unhinged. Fighting the urge to cut and run he looked around him. Mick could just see the Basilica at Knock over to the left, it was clearly a couple of kilometres away, but with a head start perhaps he might just make it. He wasn't sure if you could still claim sanctuary, but maybe it was worth the try. It was at times like this he wondered if opting for the E.U. Civil Service exchange programme had been such a good idea after all. It hadn't all gone according to plan in the first place; his exchange partner was currently on the run, fighting extradition from Slovenia, having been caught red-handed selling Irish passports to some very dodgy individuals. Anyway, here he was and he better make the best of it, 'Mr McGrath, as I have explained, I am not from England, I have come from Dublin to make an initial assessment of your claim.'

Pat looked at him as if it was trying to pull a stroke, 'If you're not from England, why have you got an English accent?'

Mick considered his options: get involved in a lengthy argument, lie, or ignore it altogether. 'Finally Mr McGrath, one last question, can you say why you are so sure these remains are a Roman Signal station?'

Pat regarded him as if he was some kind of simpleton. 'It's as plain as the nose on your face boy, so they could contact the other signal stations, what other kind of yoke do you think they'd build here?'

Mick fought the sudden urge to say, maybe it was an underground chariot park. It was now getting dark so discretion took over; he decided it might not be best to push this one and anyway, it was a long drive back.

When he reached the N17 junction at Knock he paused, the city of the tribes if he went right, Sligo if he went left. It was raining and time was getting on, but Mick couldn't just pass by. Ghosts would be too strong a word, but the memories couldn't be ignored. Ahead of him he could see the outline of the Domain buildings in the gloom. Crossing the junction he turned right into the main car park and picked a spot in the far right corner. Wandering up towards the Cross commemorating the Pope's visit in 1979, he wandered past the Blessed Sacrament Chapel and the closed book shop. Crossing the Domain he headed for the old church to say a prayer. He knelt down at the back and gazed up at the mural of Our Lady Queen of Knock - Queen of Ireland; he closed his eyes and recited the Salve Regina. The church was dimly lit and had a slightly damp, but comforting smell; the sanctuary lamp giving off a dim red glow. Despite the nearness of the main road it was surprisingly calm and quiet, the traffic a faraway muffled hum. Sitting back on the hard wooden bench, he remembered all the times he'd been here with his mother and Kathleen. It was his aunt's craze for Holy Water that came to mind, that and the muttered inaudible Rosaries she said as they circled the old church. Mick remembered once being dispatched in the pouring rain to fill up the six or seven two litre bottles with Holy Water, and meeting that woman from London way. She was prim, proper, had black wavy hair fringing her glasses and was dressed for the weather. She had eyed him warily, only a true religious fanatic would venture out in a Mayo monsoon to fill up on 14 litres of Holy Water. Smiling uncomfortably, she had helpfully pointed out a round circular object on the wall,

'You press that to get the water.' No wonder he was baffled, last time Mick had been here it was all taps.

He sat there a little longer lost in his thoughts. First it was his father, he had died in 1992, then his mother in 2002, and now Kathleen was gone. With each passing, part of Mick's Ireland, the Ireland he had grown up with, the Ireland he had known and loved, had died with them.

He slowly walked back to the car; at least the rain had stopped he thought to himself. The quickest way back would probably be cross-country through Castlerea and via Roscommon down towards Dublin. So long as he kept well clear of the Cavan - Longford border he was probably safe enough. Thoughts of that unfortunate incident with the Garda squad car on the road to Granard still made him shudder. One thing for sure, the cops weren't going to let bygones be bygones, if the sergeant hadn't dragged him off, officer Murphy had been determined to do something with a police car aerial that it had definitely not been designed for. He settled himself down for the drive to Lucan; if he put his foot down there'd be loads of time to get back to the house, grab a bag and catch the flight. Tomorrow was another day, and he had a weekend break back home to look forward to.

'Ladies and gentlemen we are now commencing our descent to Wykeford International, please return to your seats and make sure the tray is stowed and your seat is in the upright position.'

Mick looked out over the Pennines, and far below him he could see the lights of Halifax twinkling in the darkness. The setting sun cast long shadows behind the wind turbines whirring silently above Ogden water. Car headlights could be seen, snaking along the thin concrete ribbon that was the M62, weary commuters hurrying home for the weekend. In the distance was the orange glow from the streetlights of Bradford. The plane took a sharp right then a left and he heard the landing gear going down and lock into position. He looked at his watch, only another ten minutes or so and they'd be on the ground.

He always had a strange feeling of sadness and longing, tinged with relief when he came back. This sensation was something he had felt even as a child. He was leaving his homeland, his people, and what had helped make and shape the man he was. He was going back to a land that had also shaped him, it was the one he had been born and brought up in. It was a land of ambiguity; Mick's parents had brought him up in an Irish cultural environment and imbued him with Irish values and attitudes. He had gone to school with other children the same as himself. When at Primary school the class had been given the choice to draw whatever they wanted, the second-generation Irish kids always divided the paper into three parts. One third was shaded green, the middle left white, and the last third was coloured orange. It apparently drove his class teacher mad that Irish kids wanted to draw and shade the Irish national flag. It was considered bizarre that English born second generation Irish children saw themselves as Irish. He often felt, identity wise, like a stateless person. He glanced at the unopened Evening Herald on his lap: *PUNCH UP AT PISA PIAZZA – DUBLIN MAN ASSAULTS TAOISEACH* ran the headline. From what Mick had heard about Donal Brady he probably deserved it.

After collecting his bags, he switched on his mobile; there was a message from Clare saying she'd pick him up at the airport. He was never quite clear about his relationship with Clare; they had been great friends for donkey's years, but is that all it was or would ever be? He spotted her coming out of the airport shop and waved. They headed down the concourse towards the check in desks until they got to the car park pay machine, then out to the short stay parking area.

'Anyway, you're looking well Clare, what's new with you?'

'Not a lot really, job is still the same, kids don't listen to you, golden boys and girls get promotions. Same old craic, the Calvinist principle of predestination when it comes to getting on, you have to be one of the elect to get anywhere. The headmaster has a dream, more like a frigging nightmare if you ask me. Never mind Latin for the gifted and talented kids, its Feng Shui, Gregorian Plain Chant and Hieroglyphics, as from September. I don't know why he doesn't go all the way with this one. The Egyptian angle offers huge possibilities. Interior design your own pyramid, or extracting brains through noses prior to mummification would be a great one for them to get their teeth into. I don't know if you can sing the Rosetta stone in plain chant, but it's worth a try I suppose, cross curricula as well. How about your job Mick, still enjoying Dublin and the rare old times?'

'Yeah, it's O.K.' They turned onto the ring road and towards Penn, when they got to St.Jude's Road she stopped outside his flat.

'I won't come in, have to go and see my da. Then up to the Centre, there's a Dinner Dance on. Oh, by the way, Lech is back, I said you'd be here for a few days and he thought you could both meet up.' Mick thought about it, and what harm?

Lech was one of his old friends; they had been in the church choir together and gone to the same secondary school. He was, as they say, something of a character, but even his decision to become a priest had taken them all by surprise. Being as proudly second generation Ukrainian as Mick was proud of being second generation Irish, Lech had opted for a seminary in Lvov. They had kept in contact and whenever the two of them were back in Wykeford they usually went out for the night. Mick dialled the number and waited. Lech sounded a little worse for wear.

'Yeah no problem, be nice to see you. I have to meet a parishioner first though, meet you afterwards. Seeing her downtown.' Mick was surprised; it was unusual for Lech to go anywhere apart from the Ukrainian Parish Club. As he was back in Wykeford, it was probably some kind of pastoral work. He knew Lech was expected to help out in the Parish when he came back.

'Well how about I meet you down town, where are we going anyway?' A muffled grunt of agreement came from Lech's end of the phone. When he heard the pub name Mick knew he'd definitely better go too; he'd only heard of it by reputation, but it wasn't the best place for Lech to go on his own.

The clientele of the Laughing Duck had looked at the two of them suspiciously when they'd first come in; it was that sort of pub. The bar was one long counter, and the interior was a little dark. A group of burly looking characters with close-cropped hair and tattoos were gathered along the bar. Furtive figures lurked in dimly lit corners clutching carrier bags, which clearly did not contain groceries from Tesco. So long as you didn't ask any questions, you could get cut-price bargains at knock down prices. It was a pub where everyone knew everyone else, and Mick and Lech clearly didn't belong. Having got a couple of pints they stood next to the wall, closely examining the smoke stained floral wallpaper and trying not to be noticed.

'What time are we back on duty at Mill Garth? ' Lech asked.

Mick froze, he knew Lech had downed a few before they met up, he hadn't realised just how many. Playing policeman in a pub like this was like asking Ian Paisley to say Mass for a special intention.

'Not here,' Mick hissed back, hoping no one else had heard. Thankfully Lech went quiet and then suddenly announced he was going outside for some fresh air. Mick began to wonder, what had happened to this mystery parishioner? All he'd wanted was a quiet night out, but he doubted it would stay that way. His train of thought was interrupted by an altercation around the door.

The woman was smallish and had sandy coloured hair; she was wearing a smock and was clearly livid. Her language was colourful to say the least, and the object of her attention was coming into the pub with her. She stepped past Mick and went into the Pool room. Through the outside doors came the sheepish figure of Lech; he sidled up to Mick and picked up his pint. Conversation in the pub began to subside, as the other customers shifted attention onto the developing floorshow, a loud and constant stream of obscenity emanated from the Pool room.

Mick looked at Lech, 'What the Hell did you say to her?'

'Nothing.' he replied nervously and unconvincingly. Mick thought he'd better try and repair the damage, establish good relations. His mistake was to think he could smooth things over. Sandy hair was not alone, her companion was taller, had black hair, and was wearing a white trouser suit and black boots. The foul-mouthed diatribe from sandy hair continued unabated. Mick decided he'd better try and calm things down.

'Look, I don't what he's said, but he's pissed. He's no

idea what he's saying and I'm taking him out of here, O.K.?'

Sandy hair, brown smock paused and then asked, 'Why's he been taking car numbers then?' He knew well what Lech had been up to, but it was definitely not a good idea to try and explain why he'd been playing policeman. The two of them had once done it in order to speed up some chips at a takeaway, but that had been another time and another place.

'I have no idea, he's pissed, ignore it.'

It was at this point that black hair, white trouser suit stood up and spoke, 'And we're going to f****** have you as well,' she said. It was at this point that he became aware the two lovelies opposite could quiet easily block his line of retreat. He was on one side of the pool table; the door and two women were on the other. He raised his arms in the I surrender position and edged towards the door. Walking backwards out of the Pool room he glanced at Lech and nodded towards the outside doors. Walking backwards out the door they just managed to avoid the two-pint glasses thrown by sandy hair and black hair.

'Come on, let's go to the Corn Exchange and get a bus home.' Lech said nothing but just followed him. Standing in the bus queue, Mick thought, it was bad but could have been worse. At least they hadn't been followed out of the pub, and Lech's mystery woman parishioner never turned up. Had she done, things could really have turned interesting.

'Fancy some chips on the way home?' asked Mick.

Lech nodded, they usually did. The bus took them down through the Calls and over the Aire, past the expanding belt of penthouses and riverside apartments. Where the money came from to build these things was a mystery to him, an even bigger mystery was where the people who bought them got their money. The bus continued its journey to Penn, crossing Langcliffe Avenue and onto Dewsbury Road. When they got past The Halfway House they got off and crossed the road to the chip shop. The wit and repartee took its usual course.

'Been out for a few beers lads?' It was weird that Les always managed to say lads as if it ended in a z. They nodded in unison, and waited for the next question.

'Get any women then lads?' Normally they just smirked with a knowing look combined with a wouldn't you like to know expression, but not this time.

Mick looked at him, 'Not as such no. My friend here, who is by the way training to be a Catholic priest, nearly got us into a scrap with two hoors; however we did manage to get out of the pub before they went for us with pint glasses. How's your night been Les?' No reaction at all, nothing, he just ladled out the chips onto the newspaper.

'Is it the normal special with the chips?' asked Les making a statement of a question.

They left the shop and wandered up towards the traffic lights at John O'Malley's. It was the only pub in Wykeford named after a person, and there were various stories as to who he was and why he was now immortalised as a pub name. Mick was dog-tired and he just waved as Lech crossed over the road towards Whitecotes. Mick turned right towards Penn, wandering down St Jude's Road. He fumbled for his keys, fell through the door and went straight to bed.

The phone rang waking him up, and for that he was mighty thankful. He had reached the point in his dream where the women in trouser suits waving pint glasses had just about caught up with him. A fully battle dressed Roman soldier just looked on, grinning and shouting good girl yourself as a sandy haired woman emerged from the mob carrying a car aerial. He lifted the receiver to hear Clare's voice, 'Get up you lazy sod, it's a beautiful day and I want to take you away from all of this'.

'Well it sounds like an offer I can't refuse. To which intoxicatingly romantic idyll do you intend to transport me?'

'Malham. I'll pick you up in half an hour. We're going there with the kids from school in September and I want to check it out.'

'But I haven't come prepared to go Malham.'

'For God's sake Mick we are not going to climb Mount Kilimanjaro. It's the Yorkshire Dales.' The honking of a car horn alerted him to Clare's arrival, and true to form she was on time. The journey out was uneventful. Clare didn't say much, not like her at all.

'You're very quiet, anything wrong?'

'Nah, just a bit hung over. Went to the Irish Centre last night for The Westmeath Association Dinner Dance. I made an exhibition of myself after The Siege of Ennis. I managed to sneak up on the stage when Sean South started and decided to sing along to it .You can't keep a good girl down you know.'

Clare with a good few down her was hardly what he would describe as a good girl. He remembered the time at the Irish Centre staff Christmas party, she got so drunk she started taking all her clothes off. Mick always found it hard to visualise her standing in front of a bunch of kids. If only they knew what Miss, got up to in her spare time.

'How are all my friends at the Centre?'

'You know the score, same old craic and the same egos running the same things. Joe Murphy was there last night, same speech he always does. He thanked everyone and his dog for making the night what it was. I swear to God that one of these days he'll thank our parent's for conceiving us. If that hadn't happened none of us would be there at all, listening to his blathering. How was your night out with Lech?'

Mick didn't really know where to begin; Clare was a bit traditional when it came to the clergy.

'He was on good form,' at least that was accurate and fairly innocuous. They were speeding past Menwith Hill and on towards Skipton. 'Why do you think those radar domes are that shape?'

'Fylingdales isn't, it's a pyramid.'

Clare glanced over at him with a here he goes again look. 'Maybe it's symbolic, a load of balls.'

Mick looked out the window, watching the countryside shoot past.

'Oh, by the way Mick, I got you a ticket for the Concert tour tonight; I could do with some stimulating company.'

They turned off the Skipton bypass and headed towards Gargrave. Fifteen minutes later the car turned into the car park. As soon as they got out of the car Clare presented him with a clipboard.

'Now make yourself useful and fill in that bit I've put a circle around. All you have to do is write down what the buildings are used for. I'll meet you back here in half an hour and we'll go for a pub lunch.' Knowing Clare as he did he wasn't late. After they had both sat down Clare took a look at Mick's map.

'Well it'll do I suppose,' was all she had to say. High praise indeed!

'If they're going to do this when they come with you, what's the point of doing it now?'

'You can't trust the little darlings; over half of them don't bother and about 25 % of them make it up. If you're lucky the remainder plot it as it really is.'

After lunch, they wandered up to the top of Malham Cove. Clare gazed in the direction of the village.

'I must have been here on school trips about a dozen times. You know the first time I came here I nearly sent about twenty of them to an early grave. I'd been told the steps were in the corner, so I assumed it was left, it's thataway, I said. When they saw the warning sign about the dangerous drop they all thought I'd done it on purpose.'

Mick looked across at Clare; she was intelligent, funny, her own boss and a good looker. She was petite rather than small, and had beautiful brown eyes you could just sink into. Mick had long held a notion about Clare but held out little hope. He had loads of women friends; it was the getting a proper girlfriend department he had the problem with. Clare had made her opinion clear on his last one; non-too subtle references to bunny boilers had come up. For some reason he always seemed to end up with the lunatic fringe.

'What are you thinking?' Clare asked him.

Mick looked up at the sky, 'I think it's going to rain, and we'd better be making tracks anyway.' It did indeed start to rain. Mick never liked the steps down the front of The Cove, and he was doubly cautious going down them this time. They managed to make the car park before the deluge began.

The Irish Centre was a large, mostly single story building by a dual carriageway on the north eastern side of Wykeford. It had opened in the late 1960s, and replaced the old Irish National Club that had been in the city centre. The downstairs part consisted of The Slane Suite, formerly just known as the concert room. Around the other side of the building and also on the ground floor was the Games

Room. Putting in a wall at the top end and creating a small oblong room had modified the Games Room. This new creation was accessed through an archway, and was universally known as The Chapel of Rest amongst regulars. Upstairs was the Canon O'Boyle Suite. It was so named after Canon Paddy O'Boyle who had been a major driving force in the Irish community over many years. The manager once famously informed a visiting R.T.É. radio crew that it was so named because, 'This is where he spent most of his time'.

Mick had mixed feelings about the Irish Centre. The Leitrim mafia ran everything, so you were either in or out depending on whether you were County Leitrim or not. Some groups and societies gave nepotism a bad name. It was also an odd place in more than one sense, preserving an Irish culture and value system you didn't find any more in Ireland. It was The Ballroom of Romance come to life. As a child, and indeed as a teenager, he had rarely visited The Centre. His family had lived on the other side of town, and it was hard to get to by bus. It was only when he got older and learned to drive that he started becoming something of a regular. Mick was even more conscious of the divergence between Wykeford Irish Centre and modern Ireland now that he was living and working over there. However, the Centre was the Ireland he had grown up with. To a large extent he had far more in common with the Ireland found within its four walls than the real thing across the water.

The concert tour was always held in the Slane Suite, so that's where they headed. Inside along the walls were framed photographs of W.B. Yeats, Sean O'Casey and Oscar Wilde, a passing drunk having once enquired of Mick, 'ish them the committee? ' Once inside they took a right past the manager's office, then left towards the lower part of the concert room. The Skellig Michael bar was over to their right, the Inishvichillane bar to their left. The room was fairly full already, but then there was only fifteen minutes to go before proceedings began. Clare and Mick looked around them for somewhere to sit. Approaching them from Skellig Michael, Mick could see the unmistakeable shape of Bridie Kelly.

'Keep your head down, it's that bloody woman,' he hissed at Clare.

'Where?' she whispered back.

'Just sit down here and hope she hasn't seen us,' but it was too late.

Bridie waved, and made her way towards them with single-minded determination. Bridie could never work out what exactly the relationship between Mick and Clare actually was; it was a source of great speculation to more than her. Sitting down she surveyed the two of them. What on Earth does Clare Comiskey see in him, she thought? A good-looking girl like her; for a start there was his hair, God Bless us she'd seen better-endowed toilet brushes. As for the clothes, well he'd no idea had he? If he thought that outfit was going to impress the ladies, well he was sadly wrong. She assumed the sweatshirt had once actually been a pristine white; it now appeared to have a kind of grey veneer. Her gaze turned downwards; it was hard to tell in this light, but to Bridie the jeans seemed flared. Mick had all the attributes of an Abba fan who still yearned for the seventies and had the clothes to prove it.

Bridie was no oil painting herself; she had on a blue velvet dress that had seen better days and Connemara marble earrings. Despite her best efforts, her shoulder length hair always had a half-finished appearance, and any makeup gave the impression of having been an afterthought. Bridie was an individual who had decided her intellectual horizons needed broadening, and that Mick was both her mentor and guide in this mission. Unfortunately most of what she read tended to be totally beyond her. Mick viewed any encounter with Bridie with a little apprehension, as he knew well what turn the conversation could take.

'Howaya Mick', Bridie nodded vaguely at Clare by way of recognition. 'Haven't seen you around these parts of late, hear you're working in Dublin now.'

'Yeah, Civil Service exchange programme, nothing too exciting.'

Bridie looked at him with an air of expectation, 'It must be a gas though, the craic just around every corner, the wit and banter of the Dubs, quiet strolls through Phoenix Park on sunny summer afternoons.' Clare looked at her, was this for real or had she been reading too many holiday brochures? Mick wasn't too sure where this conversation was going, but he had little doubt he would soon find out. Bridie was not best known for her subtlety. Following a disagreement with a member of the Wykeford Irish Camogie team she had referred to them subsequently as the Donegal B.U.S. (Big Ugly Shite).

'Anyway Mick, to matters more brainy, I've been doing some more reading lately, poems and the like. You know Synge and Yeats who wrote books and plays?'

'Not personally.'

Bridie looked puzzled, 'Well I wouldn't think you would, they've been pushing up the daisies for donkey's years. The point is, what do you think of them, do you think they were on something?'

'On something, what do you mean were they on something?'

Bridie tossed her hair and looked straight at him. 'Wacky Baccy, or...' she rolled her eyes in what she thought was a meaningful way. A strangled gurgling sound could be heard, and Mick glanced round to see Clare choking with hysterics.

'Soz, sweet went down the wrong way.'

Mick looked at Bridie with unbridled admiration; the very originality of thought was pure genius. 'So why do you think they were on something?'

'You couldn't write stuff like that and be right in the head could you?'

He really was intrigued now. 'Stuff like what?'

'The Playboy of the Western World for a start and as for Yeats, well! a grown man writing about fairies, it isn't normal is it?' Mick nodded his head slowly as if pondering this proposition as a serious possibility.

'And there's another thing, there's this painting by James Joyce.'

He looked at her in anticipation.

'I asked Wykeford Art Gallery about A Portrait of the Artist As A young Man but they said they'd never heard of it,' said Bridie in a challenging tone.

It was at this point that Clare just had to get up and go, she simply couldn't control herself anymore. The lights dimmed, the curtain opened and she was saved as everyone stood to attention for Amhrán Na Bhfiann

The concert ended about ten thirty and they went back to Clare's for a cup of coffee. She lived in Glenmoore Avenue, Chapelhill, a cosmopolitan inner city area, on the same side of town as the Irish Centre. Clare had been lucky enough to buy before property prices really took off, what had been a back to back worth £35,000 now sold for upwards of £85,000.Despite its reputation as a rough area, she liked living there. Apart from a sizeable Irish contingent, there were also West Indians, Philippinos, Asians and some East Europeans. The shops, bars and takeaways all reflected this ethnic mix. Next door to her were some African trainee nurses who worked at the nearby St Andrew's Hospital; this was universally known as St Andies in the city.

Clare lived about half way up Glenmoore Avenue, just around the corner from Chapelhill Lane, the main road that bisected the area east to west. It was an area where the uniform of baseball hat, trainers and jogging bottoms with a large shapeless t-shirt was de rigour. They parked the car outside the house and went up the few steps to the door. He noticed new security locks and a burglar alarm had been added since his last visit.

'I thought you said this area was O.K.'

'Well it is, but you still can't be too careful' Unlocking the door, they stepped straight into the living room. Apart from a T.V. and music deck, the only other contents of the room was a camping chair and beanbag. In the corner was a disorganised heap of C.D.s.

'Put some music on, sit yourself down and I'll get us a drink. Tea or coffee?'

Mick was trying to decide on the beanbag or chair. 'Err….tae will be fine.'

Clare looked at him and smiled. 'Going native now are we.? It's not tea anymore, now it's tae. Sorry about the state of the room, I've just finished varnishing the floor and painting the walls.'

Mick rummaged through the pile in the corner and picked out a C.D, as the strains of I Useda love Her rang around the room he heard Clare say in a mock teasing voice, 'Are you trying to tell me something Mr McCarthy?'

'You know a lot of people in Ireland can't stand The Saw Doctors' replied Mick. 'I was in a shop in Mullingar looking for their latest album and the guy behind the counter started giving out to me. The way he was carrying on you'd think I'd come in asking for it just to annoy him.'

Clare brought the tray in and put it on the floor. 'Wasn't it a great night when we saw them last.' Mick rested his neck on the back of the chair, and closed his eyes transporting himself back in time to the gig. In his mind's eye he could see and hear the crowd belting out stone walls and the grass is green, the band just standing on stage letting them get on with it.

'Sure was, did I ever tell you the tale about my brother Pete being big palls with them in their early days playing Wykeford?'

Clare ignored him having heard it all before, 'Come on, sit down here with me, you in that chair and me on a bean bag is hardly sociable is it.' Mick eased himself down against the wall. He could hear her rhythmic breathing, feel her warmth next to him; smelling her hair, he leaned over to softly caress her cheek.

'So, come on tell me all about the job in Dublin,' said Clare, suddenly turning to face him. Taken by surprise Mick lost the moment.

'Are you O.K.?' asked Clare seeing the look on his face. 'You don't seem O.K.'

'Grand thanks. Now about the job. I work for Teach agus Talamh. That's the Department's name and due to its initials as gaeilge it's often shortened to T.T, or as some guys in the office call it the Pioneers Department. I get to travel around a bit, so it's not just stuck in the office. I suppose I'm a bit like an archaeological insurance assessor. If someone thinks they've found something worth investigating, I go out and make a preliminary assessment. There's a special project I have to take on board, to do with an Iron Age ditch called The Black Pig's Dyke along the Cavan - Longford border; there's a proposal to preserve and conserve part of it.'

'Black Pig's what? Never heard of it, do you ever bump into my cousin?'

'No chance, she's in a different ball game all together. The closest I come to the Department of the Taoiseach is seeing him on T.V. with her stood behind him. Isn't she his P.A or something?'

'She's a bit more than that,' said Clare, her tone nuanced. 'I was thinking of going over to see Niamh later this week, so I could drop in on you as well.'

'Well, you know you're always welcome. Try the mobile if there's no reply from the house.' Mick looked at his watch, time to go. 'I'd better phone for a taxi.' They made further small talk until a knock at the door announced the arrival of the cab. Clare saw him down the steps. It's really bizarre, she thought to herself, I can tell he fancies me, but he's never made a pass. The way he looks at me says it all; will he just surprise me one of these days?

The Lovely County Cavan

Jim Ahern gazed out of his window and across the sculptured lawns and gardens of Dundalk Park; he loved this view, especially at this time of the year when all the flowers were out and blooming. The trees rolled and bucked in the breeze, and in the distance he could hear the lonesome call of a solitary cow. The rolling Meath countryside was slowly revealed by the clearing mist, and just beyond his gaze was the Hill of Tara. The question uppermost in his mind was how much longer this idyllic peace and tranquillity would last. The arrival of the M3 had been bad enough, but the attendant housing estates and factories now springing up along the Meath stretch were worse. Anyway, wasn't there now the threatened Boyne Valley link motorway from Drogheda to Navan to worry about? His eyes followed the sweep of the gravel path just below his office and towards the ornamental lake a few hundred metres away. Sitting on his usual bench just to the left of the lake, and in deep and animated conversation, was Peter Antheney.

'Who do you think the poor old crathur's talking to now?' Jim asked Tony as the latter entered the room.

'God knows, could be anyone, it was Dermot McMurrough yesterday, the guy who invited the English to invade in 1168. According to Peter we've got poor ould Dermot wrong for the past 800 years or so. He never actually invited anyone to come over here at all, all he was doing was trying to find a man to marry Aoife and things got out of control. There was no local lad to fit the bill in Ireland so he went over to Wales. Anyway, he's had this hard day investigating the local bachelor boy market and decided to go for a quiet drink. This bunch of lads in the same tavern take a shine to Dermot and all made a night of it. The craic was mighty and he was invited back to their place for a nightcap. The next morning he's nursing this sore head, the like of which he's never experienced before. In comes this Norman waving this piece of vellum, signed by Dermot, and says most of Leinster now belongs to some character called Strongbow and Aiofe's part of the deal. Dermot tells him he's never heard of yer man, and can't remember much about the night before anyway. When Strongbow gets to hear Donal's apparently reneging on the deal, he got all moody and in a fit of pique invaded Wexford.'

Tony gave a sigh, poor old Peter; he was never the same after that chaplaincy post with Club Espana 18 – 30. They should be grateful he'd only done a four-month stint, what he would have been like after a year he shuddered to think.

Tony craned his neck to look out the window. He could see Peter shuffling his way along the gravel path towards the main building. 'If you want to know who today's star turn was you can ask him yourself. He's on his way in, and I'd bet he comes up here.'

Tony began to edge towards the door.

Jim raised his eyebrows quizzically, 'And exactly where

are you running off to you coward?'

'I'm not running anywhere. I said I'd help the railway group with their leaflet rally in Kells this morning,' Tony replied.

'Well I'd get rid of that beard for a start if you're going out to meet the public, it makes you look like you've stepped off the deck of a Killybegs trawler.' Jim cocked his head slightly and with a smirk added, 'Those glasses don't do much for you either.'

Tony was absolutely right, a few minutes after he made his escape Peter did indeed pay Jim a visit. The one thing everyone gave Father Antheney full credit for was his immaculate turnout. It may not have been what people expected of a man in his position, but you couldn't fault him. His drainpipe trousers always had a crease in them you cut bread with, and his kipper ties complimented the colour scheme of his lumberjack shirts to perfection. Blue suede shoes and a hairstyle that owed more to the Teddy boy era than contemporary fashion, topped off the whole effect. Peter rarely bothered knocking, and today was no exception; he seemed a little agitated when he came into the room, yet was trying not to be making it obvious.

'Howaya Peter, would you have time for a cup of tea?' enquired Jim. Peter nodded his assent and settled himself down into the large leather armchair. He sought out a packet of twenty Major from his inside pocket, and as was usual on the occasion of his visits, offered one to Jim. Jim shook his head, Peter took one out and lit it.

'Well now Peter,' said Jim. 'This is an unexpected pleasure, what can I do for you, or is it just a social visit?'

Father Antheney sipped his tea and measured his words carefully before answering. 'Things are reaching a queer pitch Father and I don't think we should let the grass grow under our feet. Don't you agree?'

'Well now you could well be right.' It was as about as diplomatic and non-committal as Jim could manage. It was obviously something close to Peter's heart; he only ever used the formal address Father, rather than first names when it was serious. 'You see, things are rarely what they seem. Take this M3 motorway for example.' Peter took a drag of his cigarette and a short slurp of tea. Jim was relieved; at least he now knew they were on safe ground. The routing of the M3 close to the Hill of Tara had been very contentious. 'You can't stop progress Peter; the road system in this country is desperate to put it mildly.'

Jim leaned back in his chair, he was a little puzzled, and since when did Father Peter Atheney become interested in the M3? 'That's all well and good, but at what cost Father? We lost some of our own grounds when they built it, and here's the rub, why did it go so close to the Hill of Tara, why are they now mad keen to extend it to Cavan?'

Peter looked at Jim as if he had just scored some major verbal knockout blow. 'Well I don't know, probably because the Government and National Roads Authority thought it the best route.'

'Father, if you had heard what I had heard this morning,

and who told it to me, you wouldn't be saying that.'

Peter leaned forward in his chair and whispered, 'There's far more to this motorway extension business than you could ever imagine, but he swore me to secrecy. When the time is right, I'll tell you what he said and all will be revealed.' Peter stood up and headed for the door.

Jim was fascinated by the exchange they had just had. 'And who were you talking to Peter that you had to be sworn to secrecy?'

He turned to Jim and deliberated before answering, 'It was Brian Ború, he's raging mad about this motorway. Don't look so surprised; you can hardly expect the greatest High King of Ireland we ever had not to be mad about a thing like this.'

Father Antheney stood up and headed for the door. 'Anyway I must be going Father, I'll talk to you later.'

Father Antheney stood for a moment in the corridor pondering. He knew well what Jim and the others thought of him, not right in the head was the common consensus. Well they could think what they liked. He looked at his watch, nearly 11.30, time to drive into town and stock up on his week's supply of cigarettes, he thought to himself. He had yet to pack for his trip to Garryowen where he was filling in for a week, so he he'd better get moving. As he negotiated the gates out of Dundalk Park and turned onto the N3, he nearly collided with a fast moving Opel Astra hurtling towards him. He caught a glimpse of a balding man in a suit, glaring at him with an annoyed look on his face as the car swerved and shot past.

Mick took avoiding action when an old Volkswagen Beetle, driven by what appeared to be an elderly Teddy boy in a dog collar, apparently attempted to ram the side of his car. He shot him a withering glance as he sped past. The car Mick was driving wasn't his; it was on loan from work, so the last thing he needed was for some clerical maniac to wreck it.

Mick wasn't too sure about this special project he'd been asked to take on; he had a feeling that it wasn't quite what it appeared to be. He had come into work as normal, all set to head to the northwest once he had collected all his bits and pieces. Mick's boss, Brian Kelly, had called him into his office shortly after he had arrived; a summons to Brian's office normally meant a bollicking. It was therefore with a little trepidation that Mick had entered the room.

Brian was seated at his desk, which, whether by accident or design, was positioned so he had the light behind him. It meant of course, that at certain times of the day unfortunate interviewees sat squinting into sunlight and couldn't see Brian's face properly at all. A tall elegant woman in a dark blue pinstriped skirt and jacket stood with her back to Brian gazing out the window, she had shoulder length mousy coloured hair, and the collar of light blue blouse could be just made out. Brian had not introduced her, but who she was and what she represented soon became clear. Brian wanted to know had he read the briefing files on the Black Pig's Dyke, and what did he think? Mick had mumbled about 'Our Celtic Heritage...a national treasure...preserve and conserve.' All the meaningless neutral platitudes he could think of, to play safe. It was then the bombshell was dropped; the immaculately coiffured immobile female by the window slowly turned to spoke to him.

'The directive for this project comes all the way from the top. Your brief is to inspect the sections of the Black Pig's Dyke in South Cavan - North Longford and submit a preservation and conservation feasibility report. The plan has not yet been finalised, but the intention is to integrate the earthwork with a Celtic Heritage living theme park. An integral part of your brief is to examine the section bordering Cavan - Longford, with a view to its suitability, and whilst there consider the village of Duncarrick as a possible site for the interpretation centre. Whilst we appreciate the latter is somewhat beyond your remit and area of expertise, we would appreciate the opinion of the layman, so to speak. A general election is in the offing, so there are political sensibilities to consider. The Cavan - Monaghan and Longford -Roscommon electorate can't be allowed to get wind of this. They'll all think Christmas has come early and its jobs for the boys. It is therefore imperative no one knows the true nature of your brief. If anyone asks, you're a locations director for an English T.V. Company, who is going to make an Irish based drama, called Lakeland. Tell anyone what your real assignment is and you'll back in Britain faster than you can say Land of

Hope and Glory.'

At this point she ran a finger across the wall map of Ireland and carefully examined it; she picked out the southwest corner of Cavan using an immaculately manicured fingernail.

'Duncarrick is here; you are staying at the Crannóg guesthouse in the village. The Black Pig's Dyke is to the south.'

He didn't know who she was, but she clearly had clout; the tone of voice exuded self-assurance and authority.

'I understand you had a little difficulty with the Gardaí the last time you were down Longford – Cavan direction, is that right? Something to do with a squad car I believe.'

Mick had nodded at her; how on earth had she known about that he wondered?

'Any trouble this time just phone this number; you're now officially working for The Department of the Taoiseach.' She had taken an envelope from the inside breast pocket of her jacket and handed it to Mick. He opened it to see the name Gerry Forde and a mobile phone number.

'If you need to contact him just tell him that Niamh Comiskey told you to call.'

So that's who she was, Clare's cousin! Mick was tempted to say something but decided that now was probably not the time or place. With that he was give half a dozen maps, some surveying equipment and a set of car keys. Mick looked at the key fob, he had been loaned a newly registered departmental car, an Opel Astra. He could only assume that getting one of the department's best cars was down to Niamh Comiskey. Mick collected up his files and briefing documents and went to find the car. In the boot were a set of surveying poles, a theodolite and a digital camera. Slamming the boot shut he looked at his watch, time to go back to Lucan, pick up his bags and set off.

Within about an hour and a quarter of leaving Dublin, Mick was approaching Navan, having taken the N3 to avoid the motorway toll. He crossed the bridge over the Boyne following the edge of the river. To his left was the town centre, and beyond the railway viaduct was the Drogheda – Slane junction. Mick drove straight ahead through the traffic lights at the Slane junction, towards the fire station and onto Tara mines. The next place was Kells, about the only thing Mick knew about Kells were its high cross and the famous book in Trinity College.

Ahead of him Mick could see the town of Kells, a church spire giving him advance warning of the fact. He swept into the town, passed The Headford Arms and followed the road around to the right. A sharp left between brightly coloured houses and he was heading out of town. Just beyond the town and close to the new industrial estate, there appeared to be a roadblock. A bored looking Garda wearing the usual florescent jacket stood by a squad car as he spoke into a radio. Mick could see some cars stopping and people handing out leaflets to drivers. He slowed down to get a closer look. There was a trestle table by the side of the road with a banner attached; all he could make out were the words Train and No. An intense looking man with a beard, wearing a parka and brown horned rimmed glasses tapped on Mick's window, smiled, and indicated winding it down. Mick smiled back, he had no idea what was going on but decided it best to humour him, from Mick's experience of these people he could well be a header.

'And how are you today sir?' Before Mick could reply, he launched into what was an obviously well-rehearsed speech.

'We are Community 21, campaigning for more rail links in this country. Motorways aren't the answer; they just create more problems and look like the Government has a transport policy.' At this point he handed Mick a leaflet.

'Have a read of this leaflet, which outlines the case for the Navan – Dublin passenger line to be extended to Kells. Then once you've read it send the letter on the back to your T.D.'

Mick didn't like his tone and it showed; he put the leaflet on the front passenger seat without even looking at it. He decided to be non- committal. 'Well I shall certainly read it, and give it a great deal of thought.'

The bearded one guessed that Mick couldn't care a shite and, something finally snapped. He had spent an hour talking to people in cars who had evinced as much interest and sympathy as this one. Amongst the kindest things he had been called by some people was fecker. Well he had had enough of indifference rudeness and apathy.

'You're a tourist,' he said, enunciating the word tourist as if diagnosing a contagious and nasty disease. He was now definitely beginning to irritate Mick and had a belligerent tone.

'It's O.K. for yous, you only come here on holiday, we have to live here, and do you know what that's like, of course not. We don't all live in whitewashed thatched cottages digging turf, with an ass and cart at the back of the house, Ireland of the welcomes? My arse it is.'

Mick looked at him taken aback, where had all this come from? 'But...' was all he was able to get out before the diatribe relaunched itself.

'Come down the country on some big adventure from Dublin have you? I suppose you think it'd be great craic to tell your friends all about us Culchies.'

Mick now had a chance to say something. 'I'm not on holiday; I'm an Irish Government Civil servant.' Having worked himself into an apparent frenzy, beardy now seemed deflated and calm. 'Ah well and what harm, fair play to you. Thanks a million for stopping.'

The bored looking Garda wandered over; he glanced at Mick, and slowly walked around the car inspecting the tyres and lights as he did so.

As Mick wound the window back up the policeman turned to the bearded one. 'Is he giving you any trouble Father Tony?' Father Tony slowly shook his head and readjusted his glasses. Mick gave them both a fixed glazed smile, engaged first gear and drove away.

Niamh was looking at the new fiction section in Sheraton and Hughes when she became aware of someone sidling up behind her. She resisted the temptation to turn around, and studied the shelves with renewed devotion.

'Well now Ms Comiskey, fancy meeting you here, it must be fate'.

She instantly recognised the voice, it was Martin Adams. Niamh turned to face him, same old Martin. He was a man of indeterminate age, managing to appear permanently to be about forty-something and was impeccably dressed as usual. Martin had neatly cropped brown hair, and spectacles, which imparted an expression of permanent surprise on his rounded face. He looked more like a bank manger than the Cultural correspondent for The Irish Chronicle, Ireland's biggest selling broadsheet. He was the kind of journalist who never allowed truth to get in the way of a good story. He liked to think he could charm the birds out of the trees, and put his success down to his bonding ability with those he interviewed. What he believed to be his sympathetic manner merely came over as obsequious. Niamh however knew him of old, they were long acquainted through Government Press Conferences. He knew, and she knew that he knew that the Martin Magic cut no ice with Niamh Comiskey; she smiled at him sweetly and lightly touched his arm.

'Looking for a new book are we Martin. I heard you hadn't finished colouring in the last one?' Niamh's demeanour was icy and with an edge. She had things to do, and small talk with the like of Martin Adams was not one of them. It was clear he was after something, might as well find out sooner rather than later what it was. 'What do you want Martin?'

'I'd like your esteemed opinion on an affair of state, how about a chat, and a cup of coffee?' It was then Niamh noticed he was carrying a large A4 envelope.

'I was on the way to the paper when I saw you heading up Grafton Street. As I said it must be fate, I guessed you'd head into the Stephen's Green Centre and I was right.'

This piece of information set silent alarm bell ringing in Niamhs head. Martin was not the type to deliberately trail his quarry like this. He must really think he had something this time, but what was it?

'O.K. Martin.'

Niamh wanted somewhere that was open plan and very public

'How about Dunne's Restaurant?' If he was going to try a fast one, that might make him think.

Martin considered the proposed venue, unusual for a woman of Niamh's calibre, but so be it.

Once seated Martin opened his envelope and slid the photographs across the table. The first one appeared to be of a partially finished rockery wall and patio. The others were similar, but included an oldish man in a flat cap and opened necked check shirt pointing at something.

Niamh looked at them incredulously, what on earth were these supposed to be? She looked around her; fortunately no one else appeared to be taking much notice of him or her. 'You brought me here to look at your garden D.I.Y. photographs?' she said in a baffled tone.

Martin stirred his coffee lazily, and sucked his spoon. He sat back in his chair, removed his glasses and ran his hand over his eyes. 'What do you know about the Romans, or more specifically the Romans and this country?'

This was getting more surreal by the minute thought Niamh. 'Are you serious?'

She could see that apparently he was. 'Well there was probably some trade between Roman Britain and Ireland, but apart from that nothing else, they never came here.'

Martin leaned forward in his chair, 'Yes they did. It's been hushed up for years. Either the evidence has been deliberately ignored, or simply misinterpreted. You and your bosses are trying to cover this one up too. These photos show clear evidence that the Romans did come here, and it wasn't just to trade, these photos show the foundations of a Roman signal station, and it's in Connaught'

He really is scraping the barrel for news if he's thinking of running with this one she thought. Roman buildings in Ireland were right up there with Elvis Presley on Mars or London buses on the Moon. She pushed the photographs back inside the envelope and handed them across the table.

She looked at her watch, 'I have to go.'

She gazed past him and towards the household section. A family were looking at bathroom towels, the youngest child rolling around on the floor and screaming. Sometimes she just wished she could be like them, Mr and Mrs average with nothing more serious to worry about than colour schemes.

'So it's no comment then? Even though you are a part of this conspiracy?'

If she didn't know him better she'd have assumed he'd been drinking.

'Conspiracies! You've been sold a pup, and as for conspiracies, are you getting dementia in your old age?'

'The man in the photographs lives in Co Mayo. Prior to retiring he was Head of the Department of Classical Cultures at U.C.G. He always suspected something like it was there. This guy knows what he's talking about. When he found it, he followed procedure and contacted The T and T Department. They duly sent out an investigating officer who filed a report, one Michael McCarthy. No one at the Department knows anything about his report, absolutely zilch. In fact he's no longer at the T. and T. Department.'

Niamh wondered where all this was leading. 'And you are trying to say all this has something to do with me?'

Martin leaned closer to Niamh, 'When I contacted Teach agus Talamh to speak to the investigating officer I was told he was unavailable. In fact he's been transferred on temporary assignment to The Department of the

Taoiseach, and you transferred him. No one knows where Mick McCarthy is, or what his assignment is, either that or he or she is not telling. So what's going on?'

'Nothing,' said Niamh as she pushed back her chair, stood up and walked away. She began to think rapidly as she moved towards the escalator. What possible damage could accrue, even if he tracked down Mick McCarthy, what harm? McCarthy thought he was investigating The Black Pig's Dyke, when he was really checking the suitability of the site for the sídhe. As far as nosey parkers in Cavan-Longford were concerned, he was locations director for an English T.V. Company. Let Martin sort that one out! Niamh had to hand it to Donal, it was clever, and some might even describe it as devious and cunning.

Martin Adams finished his coffee; he had definitely pushed some buttons. It was the mention of Mick McCarthy that did it. A tiny imperceptible tremor had crossed the granite face opposite him when that name was mentioned. He was onto something for sure; time to make a phone call. He glanced around him, old habits die hard; he didn't want anyone eaves dropping on this conversation. Apart from the odd person dotted around the tables he was alone.

The time was when the approach to Irish county towns had some character about them, and Mick was sure that had once applied to Cavan. Crossing over the roundabout at the bypass he passed the now standard car showrooms, small industrial estate and the obligatory McDonalds. The latter a sure sign that somewhere had arrived. He was none too sure of where to go from here. Driving on he saw Brefnie Park G.A.A ground to his left, and an area of council houses to his right. Following the road around, he caught sight of a car park sign, and turned into it, time to consult the map. He was apparently at the quiet end of town. There were a couple of bars opposite, and one or two shops. In a corner of the car park, fronting the street was a fruit and veg stall. Plenty of time to explore Cavan some other day he thought to himself. Looking at the map, it seemed he had only another 30 km or so to go. Whichever way he went, it meant back roads would be part of the bargain. Things had got better in Ireland, at least there were now some road signs to help. He remembered once coming off the Ferry at Dublin Port with Clare, and getting hopelessly lost. They had ploughed on through the rush hour traffic, heading up towards Howth, when Clare had suddenly shouted, 'Look, a plane! That'll be going to the airport, follow that and we'll pick up the M50 don't lose it whatever you do.' With great restraint Mick had pointed out they were on the ground and it was in the sky. Clare had looked at him with wild desperation, 'Anyway, if you do lose it, it's no great shakes, there'll be another one along in a few minutes, so we can follow that one.' The amazing thing was that it had worked. Mick doubted he could try the same trick out here. If he went back towards Brefnie Park he could go towards Ballykillmichael and onto Duncarrick.

The choice was the new road or the old one to Ballykillmichael. Mick reckoned the old one might offer more promise for directions, at least he could always stop and ask someone.

Mick found Duncarrick more by accident than design. He had indeed got lost, and the directions solicited from the solitary figure he had encountered beyond Ballykillmichael had been less than helpful.

His enquiry, 'Is this the road to Duncarrick?' had elicited the cryptic response, 'It could be'. This was nearly as good as the advice he had once received for the quickest way to Limerick, 'It's a straight road, but watch out for the bends in it'. After listening carefully to the old man from Ballykillmichael, and then translating his instructions into a rough sketch, he drove on. Taking a gamble at the Drumduff junction he turned left. A signpost stood at an angle of forty five degrees. Mick stopped the car and got out to inspect it, he was really none the wiser. The road rose before him and the wind was on his back; the rain fell softly on the fields. Ahead of him was one of those never ending roads undulating as far as the horizon. He pressed on and took a sharp right down a hill. As he shot over a bridge that appeared from nowhere, he caught sight of a metal plate with Duncarick Bridge affixed to it.

Pressing on he passed some isolated farms and began to encounter much newer houses, which was encouraging. He turned sharp right, and Duncarrick came into view together with its network of lakes. He passed a small factory on his left, and to his right he spotted a handball alley and there was a general store with an adjacent bar just beyond it.

The village was clustered around a crossroads. Diagonally across from him, to his right, was the Post Office, on the facing corner was another bar and lounge. There were three pubs in total, a Post Office and two general stores. A solitary Telecom Éireann phone box stood guard at the crossroads. Cars were parked on all sides of the street and there was little sign of life. He decided to go left as this seemed to be where most of the village was located. Driving slowly he looked out for The Crannóg. He found it next door to the largest pub in the village, Dwyer's Bar and Lounge. That's handy he thought to himself. Manoeuvring the car into the only available space, he switched off the engine, took a deep breath and stretched.

The Crannóg was as quiet as the rest of the village. It was a large two-storey building, its frontage painted a warm shade of blue. The door was dark stained and made of heavy wood, in the middle of which was an old-fashioned brass knocker. A pleasant faced rotund woman opened the door. Her hair was tied back, and she was wearing a green cardigan and tweed skirt.

'Mr McCarthy? You're very welcome, come in. Would you like a cup of tea? I'm sure you must be tired after your long drive from Dublin.'

Mick was dying for a cup of tea, and it was a most welcome invitation. He followed the elderly lady into the hall, and she indicated a sitting room just to the right. The room contained a large, heavy mahogany table. An unopened copy of The Cavan Celt laid spread along its length. On the mantelpiece was a stuffed bird in a glass case, a clock in a recess ticked softly. The curtains were heavy and had sheen to them. What appeared to be holiday souvenirs adorned the mantelpiece. Mick chose one of the two armchairs and sank into it; the fireplace was once functional but now housed an electric fire.

'I'm Mrs Fitzpatrick, but everyone knows me as Mrs Thom, so you may as well call me that as well.'

As she entered the room carrying a tray with a pot of tea and some ham sandwiches, Mick rose to help her, and slid the tray onto the low coffee table to his right.

'I'll leave you in peace for a while, when you're ready just come through and I'll show you up to your room.'

Mick had the strong feeling he was going to like it here, Mrs Thom had an easy manner, and spoke to him more like a houseguest rather than a paying one. He finished his tea and sandwiches, picked up the tray and gently nudged the door across the hallway. A muffled voice invited him in, turning slightly he managed to push down the door handle and he entered the room.

'Now Mr McCarthy, are you rested? I'll show you upstairs.'

His room was at the top of the stairs and to the right; it looked over the rear of Dwyer's, but beyond that he could see green fields and the lake. Placing his bags on the floor next to the bed, he looked around him. 'This is grand Mrs Thom.'

'Anything you want Mr McCarthy, just let me know. Here's your room key and one for the front door.'

'Would you call me Mick, I'd prefer it to Mr McCarthy?'

She nodded and made to go. She turned at the door. 'There are a lot of people in from your part of the country this week. Isn't it Yorkshire you're from?'

Mrs Thom pronounced Yorkshire as if two distinct words. Mick nodded. Her next pronouncement took him by surprise.

'I suppose you'll need a good rest before you start filming.' Mrs Thom gazed at him expectantly. At first he didn't quite know what to say.

'Filming, what filming?' he said with an air of slight panic.

Mrs Thom smiled at him indulgently, and stood with folded arms, 'For the T.V. programme. Now don't get yourself all worked up. I am the soul of discretion.'

It took him a couple of minutes to work out what she was talking about, and then the penny dropped. He had clearly been booked in as working for the non-existent T.V. Company. He knew only too well what small town Ireland was like. The chances were that the whole of Duncarrick, and surrounding townlands, knew his name, where he was staying, what time he arrived, and why he was supposedly in the village to start with.

He remembered the time he was staying at his mother's village of Aughaveanes and used to go over to Keogh's every day to buy the paper. The day he was due to fly out, Mrs Keogh had wished him a safe journey home and asked him how he'd enjoyed his week with Kathleen. She had then glanced at the clock and told him to watch the time as the flight left Dublin at two thirty. The most he had said to her each day was just The Indo and Irish Times as he'd handed her some money. Keogh's was ten kilometres away from Aughaveanes in a different town altogether, so if Duncarrick was anything like his mother's place, word had already got around.

'What time would you like your evening meal?' she asked Mick.

He thought about it for a moment, 'Well whatever time suits you, I don't mind particularly. I thought I might just have a lie down for an hour or so. Would 6.30 be O.K. with you?'

Mrs Thom nodded and made her way downstairs.

Setting his alarm clock for 6.15, Mick lay down and covered himself with the duvet.

At 6.20 he made his way down to the dining room and was surprised when a man of slight build, a mop of ginger hair and moustache join him at the table some 5 minutes later. The stranger nodded at Mick, and produced a newspaper. Mrs Thom arrived spot on at six thirty carrying two large plates of boiled bacon and jacket potatoes.

'Well now, you've both met, that's grand,' with that

Mrs Thom headed back through the door.

The mystery guest didn't identify himself, so Mick thought it best to start the introductions. 'Mick McCarthy,' he said proffering his hand.

Mick's new mystery companion folded his paper, 'Des O'Mahony,' he replied and shook Mick's hand. They both began to eat. He occasionally glanced over at Mick, and finally he spoke. 'How's the auld fishing around here these days?'

Mick knew next to nothing about fishing, the closest he normally came to fish was when it was wrapped in newspaper next to some chips. 'Up to its usual standard I expect.' The conversation seemed to stall as his dinner partner took this in.

'So you've been fishing then?'

'No,' replied Mick, another long pause punctuated the dialogue.

'So you'll be going fishing tomorrow?'

'No.'

Des seemed slightly agitated, even perplexed by these replies. 'So if you've not been fishing, and don't intend to go fishing, what in God's name are you doing in this place?'

'It's to do with work, and yourself?'

'The same', replied Des, 'I'm a relief bank manager for the Royal Meath; they've sent me down to look after the branch in Pottlebawn, I only got here an hour ago. It took me hours to find this place.' He looked at Mick hopefully.

'Do you fancy a pint later?'

Mick couldn't think there was probably much else to do. As they were next door to Dwyers, they'd hardly be putting themselves out. Anyway, might as well find out if the natives were friendly, and you never know, he might meet some of the Yorkshire crowd Mrs Thom mentioned were about.

'You must be a mind reader, I was thinking the very same thing, we could go over at about eight for an hour or two if that's suits?' The rest of the meal was amicable enough, fortunately Des liked the sound of his own voice, and so he didn't delve into finding out about Mick's line of work.

Dwyer's may not have appeared much from the outside, but inside was totally different. The lounge looked like it had been refurbished comparatively recently. The woodwork was pristine and there was a deep burgundy red carpet on the floor. Along the side of the room were slightly recessed seats, and there was a large, ornamental fireplace along the back wall. To the right of this was a T.V. To the rear of the lounge could be seen the public bar. There were a few of what Mick took to be locals sitting on stools along the length of the bar, a more likely collection of corner boys he had yet to see.

Mick got the drinks in and they picked a seat near the door. Des was a nice guy once you got to know him. Mick came to the conclusion that rather than being egocentric, the tendency to talk was almost an occupational hazard. As he seemed to wander the country filling in for people, he spent a lot of time away from home in strange towns with people he didn't know. Mick concluded that the tendency to monopolise the conversation came from being basically lonely. He discovered Des was from Galway, they spent a pleasant hour or so discussing the city, the Aran Islands and Connemara. It was now getting on towards 11.00, Mick decided to get the last round in. The area around the bar had filled up, no empty stools now, and he had to nudge his way through to get served. A small dark haired individual with a slightly torn pullover, large muddy boots and a ruddy complexion turned to face him, 'So you're the Englishman. Fierce warm day.' It wasn't a question, more of a surreal statement, which eluded Mick entirely. What did he mean by saying you're the Englishman? Couldn't he just be an Englishman?

'Desperate all together,' replied Mick

'I'm John Joe Reilly,' he said, proffering his hand.

Mick shook hands, 'Mick Mc Carthy,' he replied.

The other three sat along the bar shifted slightly, and made as if to clear a space for him to join them. The woman behind the bar suddenly appeared. She was an individual of few words, but she managed to imbue them with great meaning. She initially addressed John Joe and the others occupying the bar stools.

'Howayas boys? Wasn't it a grand day for washing?' She picked up a glass and studied it carefully as if looking for minute cracks.

Boys, thought Mick to himself, was a very generous turn of phrase as far as these four were concerned. She completed the examination and turned her attention to Mick.

'Now?' she asked. He ordered a pint of Guinness and a Smethwicks. Mick handed over the money for the drinks.

'Now,' replied the barmaid in acknowledgement of being given the money. She turned to put the cash in the till. The pint of Guinness was left to stand, and settle ready to be topped up. She turned back to the bar, topped up the pint, and handed him the two glasses. 'Now', came the ubiquitous statement.

Mick turned back to the table. Seated with Des was a thin man. As Mick approached the man motioned at Mick to sit down. The thin man turned to face him.

'Are you all right there. Will you have a drink?'

Mick half raised his pint to indicate he had one.

'No, I mean a real drink'. Mick assumed the new arrival was someone Des knew, so it wouldn't be polite to turn him down; anyway a small one at the end of the night wouldn't hurt. He nodded and was trying to decide on a Paddy or a Bushmills when the thin man shouted over to the woman behind the bar.

'Be a good girl and fetch three glasses will you Siobhán.'

Mick was waiting for her to say now, but it never came.

'Is it,' Siobhán nodded down at a shelf near the cash register; 'You want Liam? I think it's all gone.'

'O.K. so, I'll go and fetch another bottle.'

With that the thin man stood and disappeared in to the darkness of the public bar.

'Is he a friend of yours?' Mick asked Des.

'God Bless us, he's the man owns this place. He's Liam Dwyer. He seems to be a nice sociable sort.' Liam returned within a few minutes carrying a tray with three glasses and a jug. He sat down, filled the three glasses and handed one to Des and another to Mick.

'Good luck,' said Liam as he tipped the contents of his glass down his throat in one gulp. Des followed suit and they both looked at Mick expectantly.

'Sláinte', said Mick as he drank it all in one slurp.

It was as he had suspected, Poitín. He normally only drank it for medicinal purposes, it was a sure fire guaranteed cold cure. Despite a limited acquaintance with Poitín, Mick knew enough to be aware that this was the real stuff, smooth and potent. He first felt a long warm glow develop outwards from the pit of his stomach, and travel outwards along his arms and legs. The lights in the lounge suddenly became brighter, conversations seemed louder. Liam refilled their glasses. It was after his second glass that Mick suddenly became conscious of the fact that he could hear the T.V. but hadn't the slightest idea what anyone on it was saying. The room became a kaleidoscope of colour, and that lucky leprechaun figure on the windowsill suddenly jumped onto the middle of the table where Mick was sitting. Mick looked at his glass, then at the Poitín bottle, and back to the glass. This stuff was total rocket fuel he thought to himself, through all the years he'd never got to the stage of seeing things. He smiled unsteadily at the diminutive figure. The leprechaun gazed steadily at Mick and said in a low deliberate tone, 'I'm watching you boyo.'

'Wher'sh yer crack of golg?' It was the last thing Mick said before a red mist descended.

The alarm clock went off at seven thirty, and initially he hadn't the slightest idea where he was, or why he was in this place. The room was moving, he felt sick and someone seemed to be tap dancing on his head. He stumbled out of bed. At least he didn't need to get dressed; his clothes were still on him. Mick looked in the dressing table mirror, a grey-faced man with eyes like pinholes looked back. He grabbed the electric kettle and made a strong cup of coffee, then another, then one more. With difficulty he focused on the clock; it was now eight fifteen and he felt able to attempt making his way to the bathroom, even if the support of the landing wall was likely to be needed. He soaked his face in a washbasin of cold water, and at long last began to feel slightly better.

Steadying himself, he made his way out of the bathroom and gingerly walked downstairs to the front room for breakfast. Des was already seated when Mick entered, busy demolishing a plate of egg, bacon and white pudding. Mick eased himself down onto his seat, and then reached for the teapot and some soda bread. Des looked across the table at him.

'The craic was mighty last night, and aren't you the dark horse,' Mick smiled weakly, Des obviously took this to be some kind of gesture of modesty, not realising the delicate state he was in.

'I suppose you have to be multi-talented in your line of work. I know a felleh works for R.T.É. He reads the early evening news on the telly after the six o'clock Angelus but you'd never guess to look at him that he was known as Mary Bridget until he had the operation. Last year he won the Leinster bare knuckle fist fighter championship, but keep that to yourself.'

Mick took deep breaths, focusing on trying to keep the soda bread down. 'I mean, fair play to you, offering Liam and the crowd of lads in the bar a piece of the action in the drama. And the way you played that tea tray as a bodhrán singing Molly Malone whilst standing on that table brought tears to me eyes.'

Des looked at his watch, 'I have to go, want to be on time for my first day. I'll see you tonight, we can drop into Dwyer's again.'

Mick doubted he'd still be in the land of the living by then. He forced his breakfast down on the basis that if he was going to be sick, he may as well have something to use as ammunition. Despite his expectations, it stayed down. Mick decided that attempting to drive a car was probably not a wise option. If this had been a normal work-day at the office he'd have called in sick. As he wasn't at the office and he could hardly stay in Mrs Thom's all day, he decided to sample the delights of Duncarrick and its environs by walking the district. He looked at his watch, ten o'clock, time to make a move.

Father Peter Antheney had just finished saying nine thirty Mass and hurried into the Sacristy, keen to escape the attentions of Murtagh's nun. He had spotted her moving up the church as he had genuflected and turned down the altar steps. He wasn't quiet fast enough however, a few seconds later she arrived to congratulate him on his short homily. Peter looked at his watch, ten o'clock, time to escape.

'Well that was just grand Father, a real thought for the day, a theological conundrum to ponder on. I had never really considered life on other planets, treating aliens as our dear brothers and sisters in Christ adds another dimension all together. Sure they could be atheists, do you think Father they would be Catholic atheists or Protestant atheists?'

'Well now sister, think of the parable of the lost sheep. I'm sure I don't need to say more to someone of your faith.' It had the desired effect, she felt she had been given an explanation and at the same time had been flattered, his ability to utter totally meaningless platitudes with deeply profound overtones, was an art form. It was not the first time Father Peter had met her. He had arrived on his supply holiday the day before, and Father John Horan had alluded to Sister Murtagh whilst showing him around the

Presbytery.

'The Parish more or less runs itself, if there's any problems Murtagh's nun will sort them out for you, but watch her or she'll take over given half a chance.'

'Who is Murtagh's nun?' Peter had asked.

'Well it's a long story, but basically it's like this. Sister Maria Murtagh went away and joined the contemplative order of The Little Flower of Lough Ramor. She used to come down from Virginia every weekend to help out. Then about a year ago she came down for good. She told us she was on some kind of leave from the convent. I've never got to the bottom of it, but she still insists she's part of the order, and dresses appropriately. You'll meet her, no doubt about that. She's harmless enough poor crathur.'

Peter did indeed get to meet her, no sooner had Father Horan's car departed the Parochial House than there was a knock at the door. The resulting hour had been more like an intensive job interview than a welcome to the Parish.

'Mass is at nine prompt tomorrow morning at Duncarrick Father. Tis a special day, The Feast of the Assumption see you then,' had been her parting words.

'It's a date so,' he had said smiling and with a wink.

'Oh Father!' she had giggled hysterically.

He glanced at the clock, five past ten, 'I must be going Sister, an urgent appointment, a poor distressed soul is in need of spiritual guidance...' his voice trailed off in what he hoped was a can't say any more tone. She had offered to show him around the Parish, but Father Peter wasn't sure that was a good idea, he was of the opinion that once she had staked her claim on him there wouldn't be a minute's peace. He edged towards the sacristy door leading to the parochial house. Father Peter wanted a smoke, and a cup of tea before he made any definite plans for the day. He shuffled into the living room and took a seat. Stuck down the side of the chair he found a copy of The Longford Leader, he glanced at the date, it was that week's edition. Turning the pages he came to news from the local area, scanning down, his eyes came to rest at the News from Garryowen section, this would give him an idea of the parish if nothing else. It was very much the usual, whist drives – Fianna Fáil Cumann meetings – Macra Na Feirme. However there was one item that caught his attention. He read the paragraph with care, there is great excitement in the district at the news an English T.V.company is to start filming for a series about fishing in the area. A visitor from the company is expected next week to look about him and report back.

Father Peter's hair stood on end, now he knew what Brian Ború had been talking about when he said, 'You mind yourself now. There's a fishy thing afoot in Brefnie, and I don't mean the quare crathurs with the tails.' Whatever it was all about, there was some link between this motorway business and the man from England. The trouble was that the place was crawling with Englishmen, so it would be a matter of trying to find out which one he was, where he was, and what he was up to. Anyway why get excited about that today? It was sunny and warm, just the morning for a drive out somewhere and a stroll. He considered his options whilst making the tea. If he stayed around Garryowen the danger was that trouble would come and find him. If Murtagh's nun found out he was still about the place he'd never get a moment's peace. He brought his tea back into the living room, lit a cigarette and studied the map. If he went for a drive around the Lough, he could also visit the chapel at the north end of the Parish, that way he'd have a day out and do something useful. His eyesight wasn't quite what it used to be, but from the map it seemed straightforward enough to get to Duncarrick from Garryowen. Just beyond Duncarrick on the map, he could see the town of Ballykillmichael, where his nephew was stationed as a Guard; if he had time he'd call over and see him.

A Long Way From Being Clear

Martin Adams watched Niamh Comiskey make her way to the escalator and slowly disappear from view. If she thought she could pull a fast one over this, she was sadly mistaken. This was his big chance to be famous, and he wouldn't let any spin doctors get in the way of that. He could see it now, the chat show circuit, T.V. documentaries and exclusive interviews. 'There he is', they'd be all saying, 'Martin Adams, the man who exposed Roman Ireland'. That'd show them, especially that eejit on the paper who was the Sports Editor, he'd once found the remains of a cheese sandwich in his desk drawer, 'Hey brain box,' he had shouted at Martin. 'Come over here and tell me how old this is.'

He reached for his mobile, Brian Kelly owed him a big favour and it was payback time. It was a while before Brian answered, and to begin with he was less than cooperative. The initial response of 'Mick who? never heard of him,' only confirmed Martin's suspicions.

'Look, I know you know who I'm talking about, and you know that I know you know.' There was a pause whilst Brian both tried to make sense of this statement, and considered his response.

'Well there could be someone of that name working here. I can't be expected to know everyone in this department.'

'As of this morning he did work for you, but now he's

been transferred to The Department of The Taoiseach. I need to talk to him; he knows something about the cover up, about the Romans in Ireland.'

Brian was baffled, a cover up about *Ronans* ? There were lots of people called Ronan in Ireland, sure his own brother boasted the name. Brian was also loath to be forthcoming, not only had Niamh Comiskey issued a threat to Mick McCarthy, she had also made it clear what the consequences would be if he said the wrong thing to the wrong person. He liked to travel, but volunteering to join the E.U. Heritage Taskforce studying Inuit culture in the frozen wastes of northern Canada, didn't appeal to him. Living in a tent listening to gales blowing straight from the Arctic, with three intense Germans, two Poles and a Russian who thought rolling around in the snow naked in sub-zero temperatures did wonders for your skin tone, made him shudder. As Brian wasn't going to play ball, Martin decided it was time to try a direct approach.

'Listen bollock brain, either you come clean, or the truth will be out. Everyone wondered what happened to Shergar, well we know don't we? If the Chinese find out that peat bog preserved Irish elk, now on display in Beijing in a temperature controlled box, is really Europe's most famous missing racehorse, there'll be hell to pay. I'm telling you boy, saying you did it for the craic is hardly going to enhance Irish - Chinese relations.'

Brian was now between a rock and a hard place. He paused to consider the best option, 'Just give me a minute

Martin will you?' The Irish elk would finish him, no doubt about that. If he gave Martin some clues, he wouldn't actually be telling him.

'O.K., he's gone to look at a dyke and take some measurements.'

'Are you winding me up?'

'Not that sort of dyke you eejit, the earthwork sort.' Brian sometimes wondered if Martin was as stupid as he first appeared, he still wasn't certain.

'O.K. McGuiness, here it is, and you never got it from me, Duncarrick.' With that Brian put the phone down.

Martin closed the flip top of his phone, pushed his chair back and headed for the escalator down which he'd seen Niamh disappear some ten minutes previously. He'd hold fire on the photographs until he got a bit more detail on what was going on. It was even more obvious there was far more to all of this than met the eye. Brian had been nervous and very reticent. Martin was dead sure there was a big story behind all of this, and he was even more determined to get to the bottom of it. He raced out of the Stephen's Green Centre, desperate to get to the office and logged on. Once he was safely seated in front of his computer he got to work. A clear picture began to appear, this is better than a detective novel he thought to himself. He had narrowed down his search area; it was the Cavan - Longford border! There were still unanswered questions, where exactly was Mick McCarthy staying, which part of this dyke had he gone to look at? Martin ran out of the office and headed for the nearest bookshop, he needed an Ordnance Survey map.

What exactly Niamh Comiskey had in mind when she talked about Duncarrick being an interpretation centre, was a long, long way from being clear to Mick. As he stepped out of the door of Mrs Thom's house, still feeling decidedly ill, he decided he might as well look into that until he began to feel on the mend. Mick had got an overall impression of the village when he drove in the day before, but he was sure there were still things to see and places to go around the place. Just below Mrs Thom's and on the others side of the road, was the old National School, now seemingly converted into some kind of accommodation.

To his left and over the cross roads he could see the Post Office and newish looking National School. As he didn't really have a clue, Mick thought it would probably make little difference which way he went first. He walked past Dwyer's; ahead of him he could just make out the shape of a church over to his right, may as well pay that a visit he thought to himself. As he crossed over he heard a car behind him, the driver seemed familiar, but how on earth could he come across anyone he knew down here? The Volkswagen passed him, and turned into a driveway just beyond the church. A smallish figure got out of the car, looked at Mick for about ten seconds in a searching kind of way, and vanished into the large house adjacent to the church. Peter Antheney was puzzled, the felleh across the road had looked familiar, but how on earth could he know anyone in Duncarrick?

Mick glanced at the house as he passed; it was a large two storey grey stone building, with fold back window shutters on the outside walls. From the look of it, there were at least four rooms on each floor. In front of the house was a neat semi-circle of grass, in the middle of which was some kind of large bush. Whoever owns that place has a grand view, Mick thought to himself. The house looked out across the road towards Lough Duncarrick, an undulating landscape of drumlins nestling beside lakes. Mick was unsure whether to continue his rambles along this particular road, beyond the large house was a graveyard, but apart from scattered houses there appeared to be little else. He paused and looked over the ditch at Lough Duncarrick, whichever direction he looked, right, left or straight ahead, was Co Longford. Mick wandered a little further, somewhere to his right, so the information board in the village had told him, was a Mass rock, but there was no obvious sign from the road. He retraced his steps and returned to the crossroads bisecting the village. Mick turned right at the sign pointing towards Granard. The sun was now out and there was a slight breeze, it certainly was a lovely day, no doubt about that. Mick's work often brought him out into the country, but that tended to be just quick visits, it was nice to have the chance to appreciate and savour the countryside for a change. Mick glanced up at the sky; large fluffy cumulus clouds ambled from one horizon to another, apart from the occasional car, there was little to disturb the idyllic scene around him. The engine note of some far off tractor could be heard as he trudged down the road. He consulted the map, if he continued on down this way he'd come to somewhere called White Walls, turn left at that and you'd hit part of The Black Pig's Dyke. The one thing Mick had concluded was that no matter which road you took around Duncarrick, sooner or later it invariably gave you a view of the Lough.

He wandered on past the neatly kept and maintained Church of Ireland church. It was a mystery to Mick how Catholic church buildings always seemed to exude a slightly scruffy air, yet Protestant ones were invariably well presented and pristine in appearance, he sometimes wondered if it was to do with their level of usage, or a cultural thing. With the Calf Lake to his left and a string of new bungalow style houses to his right, he continued on. Just beyond the crest in the road, and slightly set back, Mick suddenly came across a whitewashed thatched cabin. It was a substantial building, and from the look of it, it had wattle and daub mud walls. There were three windows, and in contrast to the rest of the house the windowsills were painted red. Immediately in front of the house was a yard. For some reason he couldn't work out, there was a rusting van parked there. Along the edge of the yard area, fronting the road were two large whitewashed walls, set into the middle of this wall were two large green wrought iron gates. At each end of the house, but entirely separate from it, were two smaller buildings facing it at right angles. Wispy smoke was making its way out of a brick chimney, so this was no museum piece he thought to himself. The top part of the red half door was open, and a large white dresser was just visible along the back wall of the main room. The bottom part of the half door swung open and an elderly white haired lady emerged accompanied by a small Jack Russell terrier. She was talking to the dog, and had an old metal teapot in her hand. The lady walked slightly stooped and with a swaying motion. At first she didn't see Mick, but became aware of him as she got close to the gates.

'Are you alright there?' she asked Mick; it was as much a greeting as a question. She was wearing green wellington boots, a brown skirt, and a well-worn zipper jacket with a hood. The dog trembled slightly and whined.

'I was just looking at your house; you don't see many like this today.' Mick was certain he wasn't the first to have said this to her, and he was sure he wouldn't be the last.

'Would you like to come in for a sup of tae, and have a look?'

'I would, thanks a million.'

He opened the gate, and followed her in to the house. Mick had to stoop slightly to enter the low doorway; surprisingly the floor was slightly sunken below the door level. The inside was slightly dark and gloomy, and it took him a minute to get used to it. The elderly lady stood facing him with her back to the fire, and gestured to a seat below a small window.

'Now sit down and rest yourself whilst I fix us some tae.'

Mick sat down and looked around him. To his right were a large fireplace and a crook crane, an enormous black kettle hung from one of the hooks, steaming quietly, the flames from the logs and peat briquettes occasionally licking its base. The fire occasionally gave an angry crackle and snap, the smoke blowing back into the room and hovering hesitatingly, before an unheard intake of breath sucked it back up the chimney. Opposite was another room, the door was slightly ajar, its edges uneven and worn. Just to the left of this door was a large wooden chest, perched on top of which was a metre high statue of Our Lady. Mick peered at the statue closely; from where he was sitting it seemed to be concrete. The door of the room to the right of the chest was slightly ajar, and he could see his host wandering around with a teapot in her hand, the dog trotting after her. She emerged in a few minutes with a battered souvenir tray from Lourdes, on which were two cups and saucers, sugar, milk and some iced buns on a plate.

'NOW,' she said in an emphatic but warm tone of voice. 'You rest yourself and we'll céilidh.' Mick noted she had removed her wellington boots and just above the shin had a bandage, attached to which there was a miraculous medal. The dog forced its way into the cushion cover on the chair next to him and vanished from sight. The elderly lady spoke to it indulgently.

'Now Sheila White, don't be bold.' She looked at Mick expectantly, 'You're from England by the sound of you. I have a sister, a niece and nephews in England.'

Mick nodded, 'Yes, I come from Wykeford, but my mother and father, God rest them, were born in this country. I may be from England, but being born in a stable doesn't make you a horse'. He smiled and she smiled back. Mick picked up his cup and tasted the tea, good and strong. It was one of the things he liked about Ireland, when you asked for tea you got something worth drinking, not the anaemic brew most people in England presented you with. He looked around him, it was hard to tell, but he guessed the house must be over a hundred years old.

'I'm Mick McCarthy', he said introducing himself. 'I'm here for a few days on business. Have you lived here all your life?' She nodded and lowered her cup close to the floor, the dog shuffled out from below the table in front of Mick and noisily lapped at the tea, then turned and headed for the yard.

'Don't be footering about on the street now,' she called after the dog.

The old lady introduced herself; she was called Bridget Brady, and she patiently waited for his questions. She must have done this so many times thought Mick to himself. Her great, great grandfather had built the cabin; he had been a blacksmith and had set up a forge in one of the outbuildings

Mick had spotted as he came in. In fact the outline of the entrance for horses and carts could still be seen in the gable end of that building. Her great, great grandmother had been a teacher, and Bridget guessed the marriage had been a match. As she talked Mick did some quick mental calculations, if he was about right, then this cabin had been built somewhere between 1840 –1850. To have had great, great grandparents, one of whom had been a teacher and the other a blacksmith in 19th century Ireland was something impressive. It was no wonder the cabin was so big then; the family must have been comparatively very well off when it was built.

She talked of how her great grandmother had gone to America, worked in New York for some years and then came back to Cavan. Mick was fascinated; to go over to the U.S and come back again was virtually unheard of in 19th century and early twentieth century Ireland. Bridget told him of her brothers and sisters, how she herself had gone to America and returned and of the Blueshirt dances of the 1930s. Mick had read about the Blueshirts, the nearest thing Ireland ever had to a Fascist movement. Her grandfather had apparently been no fan of the Blueshirts, in fact he often misdirected anyone trying to find their dances. She told him of the Grady's who had lived near the Lough, and how when their only daughter got married, she and her new husband moved in with her father. She told him of the rows the daughter and father had had, and how eventually the father moved out, taking his home made coffin with him. People like Bridget were like gold dust; she was describing not just another era, it was another place altogether. There was more than time separating Bridget's Ireland from the Ireland they now saw around them. Mick told Bridget of his family, of his job in Dublin, about the Wykeford Irish Centre and about Clare. He found it so easy to talk to Bridget, probably because she reminded him so much of the Irish he knew so well in Wykeford. Mick glanced at his watch and got a shock, he'd been there for three hours.

'Bridget I have to go, work calls. Thanks so much for the tea. How long would it take me to walk to the White Walls from here? '

'Sure you can do it in about half an hour, just turn right out of the street and follow the road. After you cross Ballyduff bridge keep a look out for a small cross roads, the white walls will be plain enough.'

'Come on, answer,' said Clare to herself. She moved forward in the queue towards the departure gate. Out on the airport apron stood the Boeing 737 that was to take her to Dublin, a last minute whim made her decide to cross over to see Niamh and Mick. Mick's phone went onto voicemail and she left a message.

'I don't know what you're up to now, you dirty skite, but I'm on a plane heading your way. Speak to you when I'm landed.'

Mick got his directions from Bridget and headed off. It

was now three o'clock and he reckoned he could at least locate White Walls before it was time to return to Duncarrick. He got there after a brisk fifty-minute walk, consulted the map and turned left. Walking towards him was a lone figure carrying two heavily laden shopping bags. As Mick appeared to be in the middle of nowhere, he wondered where this mirage had come from, and where there could possibly be a shop. As they passed they exchanged polite greetings.

'Grand day.'

'It is thanks be to God.' The thought occurred to Mick that perhaps this solitary shopper could be of assistance. The tarmac road, such as it was, was becoming increasingly broken up and patchy, he didn't want to trudge endlessly down what seemed to be a boreen, if there was any chance of spotting the Black Pig's Dyke earlier than the map seemed to indicate.

'Excuse me,' shouted Mick after the trenchcoated figure, the man paused, looked over his shoulder at Mick and put his bags down.

He surveyed Mick quizzically. 'You a fisherman? There's no water round here boyo, going in the wrong direction all together for that type of craic.'

'No I'm not, I'm a tourist on a walking holiday,' replied Mick. No need to needlessly complicate things with tales of T.V documentaries. The man smiled at him.

'Are you a header? No one in the right mind comes around here for a holiday unless it's the fish they're after, and who the hell would walk around here for enjoyment?' Mick smirked and shifted uncomfortably from one foot to the other. His newfound friend continued to smile at Mick, which was very disconcerting. Was he continuing to smile because he thought Mick was a head case, so humour him, or was he smiling because he was a header? They eyed each other warily for a minute or two, the silence could be felt.

'Where did you start this walking holiday from anyway?' enquired the solitary shopper.

'I'm staying in Duncarrick, and set out from there.' The solitary shopper reacted as if Mick had just announced he had crawled out of a bog and liked eating pig shit.

'Glory be to God boy, what are you doing amongst the likes of them? You want to be careful with Cavan people, they're not like us at all.'

Based upon his experience of the trenchcoated shopper so far, Mick was under no illusions that Duncarrick people were anything like the character that stood before him.

'Is that right? But Cavan is only the other side of the lake,' replied Mick somewhat taken aback.

The trenchcoated shopper took Mick by the arm. 'There's more than a stretch of water between Cavan and Longford. Ulster people you see, half of them came over here with Cromwell's chancers, and the rest are just bog savages, different crowd all together to Leinster and the sweet County Longford! Did you see all them sheep in the fields coming down here?' Mick had indeed noticed fields full of sheep, but had thought nothing of it.

'Where do ye think they came from? I'll tell ye, from across the border, just come down to Cavan for a day trip, a bit of a rest. You mark my words boy, them sheep will be long gone by tomorrow morning. The Cavan men pocketing bags full of euro's for moving them woolly moneymakers from one jurisdiction to another. Take them to Fermanagh, get a subsidy, and move them back to Cavan, another subsidy. I'm surprised them poor crathurs don't get dizzy with all this travelling.'

Mick was beginning to regret having started this conversation. Whilst trenchcoat delivered his summary on inter-county variations in character, he looked closely at his newfound friend. If anyone resembled a bog savage, it was this vision in front of him. Trenchcoat had a thin covering of hair parted in the middle, his face was a ruddy red colour and he had clearly not shaved for at least two days. In fashionable circles he'd have been described as having designer stubble. Emerging from his V-neck pullover was a tatty check shirt, minus top button, but with a loosely knotted, faded blue tie. The trousers were a type of camouflage Mick had never seen before; closer inspection brought the realisation that this unique colour pattern had probably been acquired in a farmyard, from the look of trenchcoat, he had more than a nodding acquaintance with slurry pits. Mick suddenly noticed movement in one of the shopping bags, it bulged and squirmed, and then a small black and white whiskered head appeared, looked at Mick, yawned, blinked, and then vanished again. Why someone was taking a kitten for a walk was somewhere Mick didn't want to go. Where he did want to go was anywhere apart from here.

'Now, what can I do for ye,' enquired trenchcoat.

Mick thought it might not do any harm to ask for directions anyway, the man was obviously local, even if he was barking mad.

'Well if you look at this map, you'll see I'm here, and I want to be there.'

'So, you want to go and stand in the middle of a field? What's wrong with the one over there? Isn't that one good enough for ye?' Trenchcoat pointed at a stretch of bumpy ground scattered with whin bushes just over to his left. There were half a dozen cows ambling around grazing on tufts of tough looking marshy grass.

'Sure this one is far superior to the other yoke, there's cows in this one.'

'Well I'm not bothered about cows; it's not the cows I'm interested in.'

'So, cows are optional, is that it? Or do ye have one of them phobias? Sure cows are harmless, just look at them, not a bit of harm on the one of them.'

His mobile saved Mick, he had been fumbling in his pocket in an attempt to turn it on, and he couldn't believe his good fortune when it rang. He looked at trenchcoat with a this could be important look and stuck the phone to his ear. Pretending there was actually someone at the other end of the phone, rather than a voice mail message from Clare, he had a one sided conversation.

'Hello Clare …I'm grand thanks, yeh, yeh, I know.' Trench coat had lost interest and proceeded to pick up his bags.

'Good Luck to ye, and don't forget what I told you, them Cavan bastards are cute hoors.'

Trench coat turned on his heel and headed off in the direction from which Mick had just come. Mick looked at his watch. Clare would most probably be off the plane and be in Dublin airport by now, however he decided to ring her later.

Clare left the terminal building and headed for the metro north station, the bus was too slow, the taxi too expensive and she fancied the novelty of travelling by underground. Arriving in central Dublin she got off at Parnell Square, rather than Stephen's Green. She had some time to kill before heading out to meet Niamh, and fancied a wander down O'Connell Street. She emerged from the station and surveyed the Spire dominating the whole vista. Whoever had come up with this twentieth century monstrosity was surely trying to compensate for a huge inferiority complex. Size doesn't count? It wasn't the message Clare got. If she'd had time she'd love to go shopping, but perhaps a visit to a couple of bookshops could be fitted in. She headed towards the Liffey and Ormonde Quay.

As she approached the corner of Abbey Street, her mind

wandered back to her childhood. As a child she had spent a lot of time in central Dublin, in those days the Liverpool catamaran had docked at the North Wall, no budget airlines for them. The whole family had formed an orderly line on the quayside, and boarded the shuttle bus to Busáras where the luggage was left, then proceeded to kill time in central Dublin before catching the midday Donegal Express. One of her abiding memories was of her dad at the front of the line with a suitcase on his shoulder leading the way. She looked around her as she stood on the corner of Easons preparing to cross Abbey Street. The Dublin she was enveloped in was so different from that of her childhood. The affluence and self-confidence were so tangible you could nearly touch them. The Eastern European accents and languages she could hear all around her now as much part of Dublin as Nelson's Pillar had once been. Turning right at the corner of O'Connell Bridge she headed towards Ormonde Quay.

Mick continued his perambulation. According to the map, there was a track to his left, which would lead to The Black Pig's Dyke. According to his background brief he was looking for something fairly substantial. The object of his quest was some five to six metres high and in the region of seven to eight metre wide. In the light of his recent encounter, he thought it ironic that the dyke was thought to have been built to keep the Leinster men out. He came to a large iron farm gate, loosely attached to its gatepost with a length of string. Mick gingerly lifted it clear of the gravel scattered around the entrance to the track; the gate squealed and groaned in protest at having its rest disturbed. Mick looked at his watch, it was now a little after four o'clock, so he had time for a cursory look before setting back to Duncarrick. Ahead of him, and parallel to the road he had just left, was a line of bushes, which snaked away to his right and then vanished behind some trees. Mick plodded on. He thought to himself that perhaps he should take some photos with the department digital, it would help in his final report, and add authenticity to his supposed location shots quest for the non-existent T.V. programme. The track he was on was fairly substantial and slightly higher than the surrounding fields, but then he assumed it would have to be. The adjacent land was poorly drained and low lying and Mick could imagine that the surrounding fields became an extension of Lough Duncarrick during the winter months. The end of the track dipped downwards, diverged to his left and right. Ahead of him lay a large earth bank. To Mick's eye it didn't appear anything special, but in its time it must have been a major piece of constructional engineering. Considering what he was looking at was getting on for about two thousand years old, it was in remarkably good condition. He scrambled up the bank to see a marshy area between him and the shore of the Lough. Looking to his left and right he tried to imagine what the landscape had looked like when building was in progress all those years ago.

Clare checked her watch, it was getting close to four thirty, it would soon be time to head off and meet Niamh, but she had to collect her bag first. Making her way back to Busáras, she got her luggage and then walked to Pearse Station. The rush hour had begun and the streets were more crowded, the volume of traffic far heavier. Westland Row was one solid line of cars. Clare bought a copy of The Evening Herald and stood at the entrance to the station trying not to look too conspicuous. After about ten minutes she felt a light touch on her arm and saw a stressed out looking Niamh standing next to her, a strained smile on her face.

'Howaya Clare, had a good flight? Hope you haven't been waiting too long.'

'No, no, I'm grand thanks. Only been here about ten minutes.'

They headed up the station steps towards the platform for the Dun Laoghaire bound DART They were lucky enough to find seats, and as Niamh wasn't in talking mood, Clare looked out the window as south suburban Dublin shot past.

'Had a heavy day at work?' asked Clare.

Her cousin was looking slightly more relaxed, even if a little distant. Niamh gave her a short sharp one-word answer, 'brutal'. If her day at work was anything to go by, then the next few months would probably be worse. Donal had decided to put the Government and party on a war footing for the planned General Election. As the representative of the Department of The Taoiseach Media Relations Secretariat, she had attended a fiscal revue meeting held at The Department of Finance. The Department had brought in a Norwegian economist as a consultant, and he had presented his findings in a three-hour presentation. Olaf Erickson spoke American English and his jargon was as impenetrable as a Scandinavian forest. He may have come all the way from the land of the midnight sun, but Niamh was in the dark as to what he'd been talking about; she fumbled in her attaché case and handed a piece of paper to Clare.

'I asked him for a summary of the afternoon, and do you know he produced this, all pre-prepared. Smug is hardly the word for the likes of him. Imagine, I'm the woman behind you with her head stuck in In Dublin, tell me what you think that says.'

Clare took the sheet of A4 paper, unfolded it and started to read. In the last fiscal period, taxation interface expenditure pathways have seen a binary orbital progression. This trend, combined with the lateral integration of Socio economic nodal points have converged in alliance with retrograde transnational outsourcing. Self-actualising needs have produced zero deficits. However, on the optimistic flip side, collaborative and incremental cluster income flows have reached target attainment. Externality has been further empowered. Product differentiation is in zero deficit. Have a nice day!!

Clare folded the paper, and handed it back to Niamh. 'How the hell am I supposed to know what it all means?'

'I had to sit through three hours of this kind of thing, complete with an interactive whiteboard presentation. It might as well have been in Norwegian. I asked someone in the room how much he was getting paid. Do you know what they said? Four thousand euro a day, and they thought he was worth every cent!'

Clare looked out of the train window as the wide sweep of the bay came into view as they approached Booterstown station. Clare tried to be comforting.

'Ah well Niamh, it's a long road that has no turn in it.'

'Don't talk shite.'

The train pulled into Dun Laoghaire station and they moved towards the doors. In the harbour a high-speed ferry could be seen heading for its berth as they exited the station.

'It's only a five minute walk,' said Niamh to Clare as they crossed over Queens Road, and headed up Marine Road.

'You know,' said Clare, struggling to keep up with Niamh, 'There's this guy I know at the Wykeford Irish Centre, and his granddad worked for An Post in the late 1940's. Every time he came across a letter addressed to someone in Kingstown, he used to write on it, no such place in Ireland, forward to Jamaica, and stick it back into the postal system.'

For the first time since meeting up with Niamh, Clare

saw her smile. Smirking she glanced over to Clare.

'The way the postal system is in this country, those letters are probably still in circulation somewhere.'

They arrived at Niamh's apartment building, which was new in appearance and had the obligatory security code lock on the outside door. Sitting just inside at the reception desk was a uniformed guard, a badge proclaiming Scrabby Security affixed to his light blue shirt. He nodded at the two of them when they entered. The outside door closed with an almost imperceptible whoosh, and the street traffic became a muffled hum. The reception area was lined with a green coloured marble, and set into the wall were mailboxes and individual buzzers for each apartment. Niamh pressed the button for the lift, and they rose four floors to the sound of The Town I loved So Well, by Phil Coulter. Stepping out of the lift, they turned left down a thickly carpeted corridor, the floor illuminated by discreetly hidden sunken ceiling lights, until they came to the apartment. Niamh punched the numbers into the keypad and swung open the door.

'Thank God, home sweet home. You can have the spare room to the right. Just dump your stuff and I'll make us a cup of tea or coffee, or would you like something stronger?,' asked Niamh.

'No, tea would be terrific thanks.'

The apartment was bigger than it first appeared. There was a bathroom to the left in what amounted to a hallway and two bedrooms on the right. Ahead of them was a large open sitting – dining room and to the left of this was a kitchen. The sitting room had a small balcony, large enough for two chairs and a small table, Dun Laoghaire marina was just visible in the distance.

Clare sat down and looked around her. The dining table was glass topped with shining steel legs, a pot pouri rested in the middle of it. She was sitting on a sofa, which from the look of the design was probably Swedish, and there was a low coffee table in front of her. On the walls were photos of Niamh and Donal, formal ones, obviously taken at official functions, and some more natural ones with just the two of them. Just to the right of the photographs were three book shelves. Niamh came in with tea and put the tray down on the coffee table so interrupted her cousin's visual inspection of the room.

'Here you are now, tea and biscuits. We'll get something more substantial later. I could do with a sit down and relax a bit more.'

Clare nodded towards one of the photos of Niamh and Donal. 'Still going strong then?'

Niamh sighed, 'Yes, God love him. We just came back from Italy last Friday. I suppose you won't have heard about Donal's meeting with one of the plain people of Ireland?'

'Oh, but I have. Mick McCarthy was back over at the weekend and had last Friday's Evening Herald with him.'

Niamh appeared to have some kind of seizure. The tea spurted from her mouth and she looked at Clare with a glazed far away grimace.

'Sorry about that, this tea can be just a bit too hot. Here, give me yours and I'll cool them both down, can't have you burning your mouth and I'll get something to mop this up.'

Niamh grabbed the cup from Clare, jumped to her feet and ran for the kitchen. She leaned over the sink and took some deep breaths, it was just coincidence she told herself, there must be hundreds of people called Mick McCarthy, no thousands. Yes that's it, just coincidence. Don't panic, just get a grip Niamh told herself. But what if it was him? No it couldn't be! Niamh composed herself and came back into Clare.

'There you are now, cool tea.'

'I thought you were going to get something to mop this up?'

'Oh yes, silly eejit that I am, forgot.'

Niamh ran back into the kitchen, grabbed some absorbent paper towels and came back to attack the tea.

'Good job this is a real wood floor; I used to have a sheepskin rug down here. T'would have been hard to get tea stains out of that.'

'Anyway, how is Donal these days, or should I say An Taoiseach?'

'Oh, he's grand. Pressing the flesh today. He went to open a new community centre for Estonians in Port Laoise. He's all for the new Irish, thinks it's a real gas. He might even put in an appearance later. If he does, try not to comment on the nose. Some of them gutter snipes in the

Dáil have nicknamed him Pinocchio since it happened, and I'm not talking about the opposition either. He's a bit sensitive about it.'

Niamh looked at her watch; it was now close to six fifteen.

'Look, why don't we go out for something to eat, have a few drinks and come back about nine? I can't go on the tear, I'm not on holiday and it's work again tomorrow morning.'

Clare nodded in assent, then asked expectantly, 'O.K., but where are we going?'

'There's a New Irish place just around the corner, does that suit?'

'That sounds grand, I'll just finish the tea, have a wash and get changed, and we'll be off, I won't be more than ten minutes.'

Saturday Night Fever

Mick arrived back at Mrs Thom's at about six twenty. He had been desperate to think of a good reason not to go out with Des again, but everything he rehearsed in his head sounded unconvincing. He made his way upstairs, had a wash and changed, then crept downstairs for his evening meal. The table was only set for one, so where was Des? Mrs Thom came in looking a little agitated.

'I can't give you a feed tonight Mick, there's been a bit of a crisis. The cooker is totally banjaxed. I thought it was the gas, and Dervla went to Longford for another cylinder, but that doesn't work either. Anyway, my cousin from Butler's Bridge is coming down to have a look, but that won't be for another hour. I could do you some salad if you like?'

'No, don't worry, I can fend for myself, it's not the end of the world.' Mick suddenly had a horrible thought, Des was out there somewhere, better find out where and avoid it.

'So where has Des gone for food?'

'Oh he's away to Cavan, turns out the deputy manager at the bank is someone he knows. I'm not sure if he won't move out of here and over to Cavan itself, anyway what harm?'

Right, thought Mick to himself, eating in Cavan was definitely a non-starter.

'I suppose there's nowhere in Duncarrick does food?'

asked Mick.

'The pubs do bar meals, and there's always the chipper around the corner. The Famished Fisherman, belongs to Dwyer's, does burgers and the like.'

Mick didn't feel like another trip to Dwyer's, and thought perhaps he'd go further afield.

'Anywhere else I could try?'

'You could go down To Granard or Longford town if you liked, there's a rake of places there. Wait a minute now, there's a place in Ballykillmichael, I forget the name, but they do good food, steak and that kind of thing. If you go to the top of the town and park you'll find it on the Cavan road.' And so it was that Mick went for his evening out to Ballykillmichael.

The New Irish place was, assumed Clare, the name of the restaurant they were going to. When they got there, it turned out to be a non-descript brick building on a street corner. A tatty sign above the door featured a sheep with Bah – Bar coming out of its mouth. Niamh saw the slightly bemused look on Clare's face. 'That's what it used to be called; it's now under new management.'

They entered and went down some steps to a cellar, resembling something Clare thought would not have been out of place in post war Berlin. On the wall above the bar was a mosaic making up the words Na Zdrowie and a large eagle surmounted by a crown. To the left were bare brick columns supporting some rickety looking tables and the ceiling. At the back of the dining area was a pay phone, attached to this was a clearly exasperated man of about twenty five. Even if Clare couldn't understand the language, she could still pick up the general tone of the conversation, he wasn't happy.

'Co? tak, tak... przepraszam!' There was a pause as he realised Clare was looking at him; he dropped his voice, turned his back and cupped the receiver in his hand. Clare was surprised, this didn't seem like Niamh's kind of place at all, she had imagined some expensive up-market, nouveau riche place. The barman, or what she assumed to be the barman, was leaning on the counter, one hand supporting his chin, whilst he slowly turned the pages of a newspaper with his other hand.

'Do you come here often?' Clare asked Niamh.

'Yeh, it's got a lot going for it. The food is good and it's cheap, plus no one knows or cares who Donal or I are. They do think it a bit odd when we turn up with two cops though.'

'You come here with a police escort!'

'It's O.K., Frank and Phil aren't in uniform. Anyway, let's get a couple of drinks and sort out the food.' Niamh turned to the bar man who closed his newspaper and looked at them expectantly. 'Dobry wieczor, er.'

She held up two fingers and nodded at Clare.

'Wodka prosze'

The barman turned to the optics behind him, filled two glasses and silently put them down. Niamh fumbled in her handbag and handed him a twenty Euro note. He turned, opened the till and placed the change in front of Niamh.

'Dziekuje,' said Niamh smiling.

Picking up their drinks they headed for a table at the back of the room.

'My God, but he's miserable,' said Niamh.

'That was impressive, you talking Polish like that,' said Clare.

Niamh was highly flattered, and tried to make as if it were no big deal.

'Oh, one has to make the effort you know, it's nothing really. I could with some ice with this.'

Clare stood up and turned towards the bar, 'There's an ice bucket up there, I'll get you some.' The barman had now stopped his perusal of the newspaper, he had his back turned and seemed to be checking on the crisps. Clare tipped the ice bucket towards her, empty. What to do now? Clare rattled the ice bucket, no response from the bending figure, 'Excuse me.' He still seemed engrossed in the box of Tayto cheese and onion.

'Hey!' she said more urgently; the bent figure straightened up and stretched. Clare was momentarily taken aback by the response, it was pure Dublinese For Can I Be Of Assistance Madame?

''Wha do you wan loike?'

'You're not Polish,' said Clare taken aback.

'Polish, me? Jaysus!, bleedin hope not. Not loike herself.' He waved in the direction of Niamh who, under the impression he was being friendly, waved back. 'Your wan, she's doing well for herself from the look of her.' He said to Clare. 'Just the two of yus is there, no boyfriends tonight?'

'What do you mean boyfriends?' Clare was intrigued.

'Her and the lanky felleh, he's the spit of that fecker Brady he is, and them other two thickset fellehs they always have with them, are they dope dealers or wha?' Clare decided to leave him in suspense over that one.

'Have you any ice?' she asked. He produced a bucket from below the bar counter, and plonked it in front of her. Clare got a couple of cubes and headed back over to Niamh, who was by now looking at the menu.

'Well what do you recommend?' enquired Clare.

'Depends what you like,' was the reply.

'Well let's put it this way, what are you having?' Niamh passed the menu over to Clare. Fortunately there was a brief description in English for each dish. Clare grinned and pointed at where it said Chlopski Possilek.

'I'll have one of those.'

'You come to a Polish restaurant, and you order bacon and cabbage?'

Niamh was amazed, but if that's what she wanted, that's what she wanted.

'I'm having the pierogi, I can't stand bacon and cabbage, my mother used to shovel it down us on a Saturday when I was a girl,' said Niamh.

A large and very friendly woman had silently appeared

next to them whilst they selected from the menu. They ordered the meals and four bottles of Lezajsk pils lager to go with it. Niamh decided to be circumspect about Mick McCarthy, no need to get alarmed and she definitely did not intend to spook Clare. She decided to take things in a roundabout way, so she chatted about Donal and their Tuscan holiday. Clare thought it was a real gas when she heard about the incident at the cafe and this prompted her to air some of her holiday disasters.

Clare told Niamh about Bridie Kelly and her attempts at self-improvement, and this time it was Niamh's turn to laugh. They both moaned about work, and how overworked, underpaid and undervalued they both were. Clare was dying to know about Donal, what was he really like? This was a really useful opener for Niamh, after all she was desperate to know more about Mick McCarthy. Without giving too much away, Niamh proceeded to paint a fairly balanced picture of Donal. He had a good sense of humour, even if it was bit weird and off the wall at times. Donal was also loyal to those loyal to him, and he couldn't abide yes men. His hobby, if you could call it that, was reading history books, he had dabbled with Stalinist Russia, but Germany under Hitler was his main interest. Donal was totally hopeless when it came to anything practical like D.I.Y. If he hadn't been a politician, Niamh could imagine him being a doctor or a vet.

'When did you two meet anyway?' asked Clare.

'Oh a long time ago, I can't remember exactly when it

was, but Donal knows.'

'Unusual, a man remembering something like that.'

Niamh laughed, 'The only reason he knows is because that French guy knocked us out of the 2010 world cup the same day.'

Donal seemed quite a character, thought Clare; it certainly would be a novelty having a doctor or vet who was an amateur expert on Nazi Germany, the two bracketed together seemed a bit incongruous. Niamh looked pensively at Clare, it was time to steer the conversation on to safer ground Niamh thought to herself.

'So is this felleh McCarthy your friend, or is it a bit more?'

'Well at the present it's just good friends, he's a bit slow if you know what I mean,' replied Clare.

'He most certainly is,' said Niamh in a very affirmative tone, nodding her head. Clare looked intrigued.

'You seem very definite about that, have you met him?'

'What! Oh no, no. It's just that he must be slow on the uptake if he's not made a move yet.' That was a bit close thought Niamh, must be more careful.

'Anyway, tell me about him. What's he like?'

It soon became abundantly clear that the Mick McCarthy in question was one and the same person sent down to Cavan. Mick, Clare informed Niamh, was a case of what you saw was what you got. Unlike most other men he was not totally egocentric, and actually listened to what you said to him, you could have a conversation with him.

His dress sense left a lot to be desired, but that was part of the charm, Mick didn't feel the need to try and impress someone just so it looked good; he was straightforward and could show real care and consideration. Whilst Clare talked, Niamh pondered how to deal with the situation. It might be best to see what Donal thought about the way forward, the Clare - Mick liaison could add a complication. Give Donal credit, he was pretty good on strategy and tactics.

Clare looked at the clock on the wall. 'I think we'd better go soon, it's 7.30 already and you have work tomorrow. I'd better give Mick a ring, I said I would.'

'You can phone him from my apartment, it'll be cheaper,' said Niamh silkily. It might be as well to have a word with him herself thought Niamh; it wouldn't do any harm to put the fear of God into him, especially if Clare was intending to pay him a visit.

'Let's have a coffee and another drink, then we'll hit the road,' suggested Clare. They eventually left at 8.45, after a two more vodkas and a bottle of beer each.

When they got back to the apartment building, there was a four wheel drive with darkened windows parked outside. As they approached the car, the nearside window silently slid down and a man eating a burger looked at the two of them.

'Evening Frank, how's the craic?' asked Niamh as she peered inside the darkened car.

'What have you done with Phil?'

Frank nodded in the general direction of the back of the car. 'He's gone to get a packet of fags. Anyway I'd better not delay you, himself is up there waiting for you to come back. We dropped him off about ten minutes ago.'

'How was the day with the Estonians?' asked Niamh.

'Oh they were O.K. not sure I can say the same about the rest of the crowd down in Port Laoise though. They're not my sort of people at all.'

'Who's he?' asked Clare as they made their way to the apartment entrance.

'Frank? He's one of Donal's minders, so's Phil., they're O.K.' The two women made their way up to the apartment and opened the door.

'It's a bit quiet,' said Clare, heading towards the main room; they could hear someone singing badly and out of tune. Clare could just make out the words staying alive, staying alive, floating out towards them. The last staying alive being slightly more drawn out than the others. From what Frank in the car had said, Clare guessed the crooner had to be Donal. Sitting on the sofa with his eyes closed and feet up on the low coffee table, was a thinnish man wearing round-rimmed spectacles and an immaculately dark blue tailored suit. He had a lighter blue shirt and burgundy coloured tie, complementing the jacket and trousers. He had taken his shoes off, placing them under the coffee table. An Ipod rested on his knee and tiny earphone wires snaked up the side of his head. Seeing the state of his nose, Clare could see where Pinocchio had come from.

Niamh put her finger up to her mouth and made a 'shush' with her lips. Suddenly she leaned over and smacked Donal on his thigh.

'Mother of God!' exclaimed Donal as he suddenly gave a jump and began massaging his leg. 'What the hell did you do that for?'

'Time to come back to the real world a stór mo chroí. What are you listening to this time, Adolph Hitler the musical is it?'

Donal gave her a withering look and continued to rub his leg, 'It's The Bee Gees.' He suddenly became aware of Clare and tried to look more dignified.

'How did your day out go?' asked Niamh.

'It wasn't a day out as you put it; its work, the way you go on you'd think I had a full time nixer.' Donal attempted to change the subject and insert some decorum into proceedings 'You must be Clare, Niamh said you were coming over. A pleasure to meet you.'

Niamh interjected, 'So lots of brotherly love back smacking down in Kildare was there?'

'No, it was business and lots of speeches, most of them in Estonian.'

'So, it was lots of brotherly love speeches in Estonian?'

'I don't know what was said exactly. I told you, it was in Estonian, all Greek to me.'

Clare wasn't too sure what to make of the exchange, and decided that perhaps it would be diplomatic if she left them alone.

'Can I use the phone Niamh?'

Niamh's tone changed to charming and accommodating, 'Yes of course, take it into your room, it'll be more private.'

Clare picked up the handset and made her way out, Niamh hissed to Donal, 'That gobshite we sent to Cavan is a big friend of hers. She's gone to phone him, and intends going to see him.' Donal looked puzzled. In his line of work gobshite could apply to any number of people.

'Which gobshite in particular?'

Niamh looked exasperated, 'The one we selected for the special project, you know, Ruairí and his friends.'

A look of recognition crossed Donal's face; he had left the selection process to Niamh, and he vaguely remembered her having drawn up a short list. He hadn't paid a great deal of attention, as he was trying to watch Fair City at the time.

'So find out what she says to him,' said Donal tersely.

'You mean ask her?'

'Not exactly,' he replied as he handed her the other telephone hand set.

'You mean listen in?' Niamh was scandalised.

He nodded, 'It's a sure fire method and leaves no doubts as to what they both say.'

'Well, O.K. then, but I'm not that happy about it.' She took the handset and put it to her ear; as she pressed the green button she suddenly heard a voice behind her.

'How are you missus?' Niamh turned to see Ruairí

sitting on the edge of the bookshelf. He was wearing a flat cap, a yellow silk shirt and lime green plus fours, on his feet were spats.

'Jamie Mac! Isn't that better yet?' said the leprechaun pointing at Donal's nose. Ruairí began to slowly swing his legs, and stared towards the floor, deliberating about something.

'What are you up to in Cavan?' he asked Donal with a slow and forceful tone.

'Me, nothing of any concern,' was the answer.

Ruairí looked closely at Niamh as he heard the reply, looking for any kind of reaction.

'There's some funny business afoot, that Englishman you sent down there is up to no good.'

Donal and Niamh exchanged meaningful glances, the same thought in each mind, what did Ruairí know, and how much did he know?

'Look Ruairí, I don't want bad relation between us, I guessed you were all a bit unhappy, so I've arranged for someone to come down to Sligo to see you tomorrow; any misunderstandings will be cleared up then.'

Ruairí pondered the news; from his expression he was still not completely convinced. 'You try and pull any strokes and you know well what'll happen. Remember them that went before you. That one who decided to put that motorway past Tara, he wouldn't listen. We thought he'd get the message when he had to keep turning up at Dublin Castle to explain all that cash he was so fond of having around the place.' Here Ruairí paused for dramatic effect, and then said in a very loaded way, 'But we all know what eventually happened to him. He was a nice fellah though, said he'd invite me out to his yacht, if he had one, for a cup of tea. He had a funny dress sense when he was younger, used to wear a Parka.'

The thought of Ruairí criticising anyone's dress sense amused Niamh. Donal looked a little rattled but didn't lose his composure.

'By this time tomorrow,' he said, 'all our worries will be over, just listen to what Eoghan Dempsey has to say to you Ruairí.'

The leprechaun pondered this; he seemed to be concentrating on nothing in particular.

'O.K, until tomorrow so, but if he's spouting ráiméis be it on your own head.'

The last part was said with an air of menace, then he was gone. The door of Clare's room could be heard closing and she came back in to join them. She looked around surprised.

'Oh, I thought Phil or Frank were here, I could have sworn I heard someone else talking, or was it the T.V.?' Niamh ran her fingers through her hair and gave Donal a sideways look.

'It was just the radio Clare, I was hoping to hear something about Donal's day out with our Baltic friends in Port Loaise.'

Clare looked around the room puzzled, radio, what

radio? Settling herself down on the settee she folded her legs under her, 'Mick's in grand form. I got hold of him in Ballykillmichael, I'm going down to see him late tomorrow afternoon.'

Niamh was a little perplexed; what the hell was he doing in Ballykillmichael? Once she got the chance she'd phone him and give him some friendly advice.

Clare turned to face Donal, 'I didn't know you were a Bee Gees fan.'

Niamh put her head back and laughed, 'He likes all sort of things, Enya, Brian Eno, Westlife. The Bee Gees are his favourite though. You know that one who was Prime Minister in the U.K. some years ago, Tony Blur or something like that?'

Clare nodded, a bit before her time but she had heard the name. 'Well, Tony what's his name', said Niamh, 'got himself an invite to stay at the home of one of the Bee Gees in America. Whereas the best An Taoiseach here could manage, was to win us a weekend away with Daniel O'Donnell. I wouldn't mind, but Daniel O'Donnell! Jesus Christ of all the people and then he won it under an assumed name, Paddy Murphy or something wasn't it?'

It was Donal's turn to get annoyed. 'Well I could hardly enter the competition under my own name, what with who I am, anyway you said you liked Daniel O'Donnel.'

Niamh leaned forward 'We've been here before, I said my mother liked him – not me you half brained eejit.'

'I think it's about time I made tracks,' said Donal. 'I've

had a long day.'

Niamh was disappointed at the news; she had assumed he'd was staying. 'Are you going so soon. Can't you stay over until tomorrow?' she asked.

He shook his head. 'It would hardly be fair on Frank and Phil if I did.'

Clare yawned and stretched her arms. 'I think it's about time I went to bed as well. It's been really nice to meet you Donal, hopefully we'll meet again.'

He put on his shoes and jacket, 'Good night, God bless Clare,' he said, as they both watched her head towards her room and heard the door close.

Niamh opened her attaché case and produced a leather bound diary; she leafed through it, picked up the phone and dialled. She waved at Donal to sit down, a computer generated voice announced the mobile you have phoned is switched off, please redial later. It seems that she was fated not to get in contact with Mr McCarthy.

'I've just phoned gobshite, no luck though. I'll try again in the morning.'

Donal stood up and moved towards the door of the living room.

'I really must go, it's nine thirty. I have to see yer man who's going down to talk to the sídhe in the morning, and work on this speech I'm giving north of the border. I'll catch up with you around lunch time.' He moved towards her, put his arm around her waist and brushed her hair to the side.

Niamh looked at him quizzically. 'So, who's this felleh you've got lined up for this trip to see Ruairí and his friends then?' she asked.

Donal scratched his head, and tried to think. 'Eoghan Dempsey, he's one of us, a staunch party man, someone we can trust. His family has the gift.'

Donal looked adoringly at Niamh, 'You know I'm crazy about you, don't you? God knows you drive me mad at times.'

She looked straight into his eyes, 'I know Donal. I had a heavy day, and you just got in the firing line.'

He kissed her softly, lingering for a while, drawing her closer. They stood, arms around each other, cheek to cheek. And then the phone rang.

'Jesus, this had better be important,' said Niamh. Donal made as if to head for the door, but she waved at him to sit down. She listened intently, and then put her hand over the mouthpiece. 'Seems our boy Mick McCarthy has only gone and got himself arrested, two head case Gardaí in Ballykillmichael have taken him in for questioning. You'd better stay around just in case of complications.'

Mick left Pearson's steak bar and checked for traffic, to his right was the road to Killashandra, ahead of him the town's main street and just behind the steak bar was the old main road to Cavan. Crossing the road ahead of him with caution, Mick walked down the main street. Apart from a few parked cars, there was little sign of life. Mick walked downhill towards where the car was parked. He could see that the two supermarkets were both still open, shafts of light illuminated the pavements as customers came and went ahead of him, just above Centra was a parked Garda squad car, its lights off, with two officers sitting in the front. A third policeman was examining a bicycle, minus lights, propped against a stack of butane cylinders outside Centra. Mick bristled, he was wary of these guys after the last time he had dealings with them. He could either just walk straight past them, or cross the road to avoid them, but crossing over could be construed as suspicious. He glanced across the road at the general store and souvenir shop, a large lucky leprechaun doll stood in the window, it was wearing plus fours, smiled at him, and appeared to make an obscene gesture. He did a double take, must have been a trick of the light, he thought to himself, nothing there now at all. He pressed on, deliberately ignoring the boys in blue and their squad car as he passed.

'I'm sure I know him,' said officer Murphy to his companion, pointing at Mick through the windscreen. Sergeant O'Connor closed his novel, balancing his cup of coffee on the dashboard and peered out at the rapidly retreating figure.

'So, what makes you think you know him then?' Murphy looked at his sergeant and grinned, 'Policeman's instinct.'

O'Connor seemed sceptical, 'The last time you said something like that, was when you stopped the Archbishop of Santiago in a hire car on the M3 for having defective break lights. Only your instinct told you he was a shaggin Columbian dope dealer so you arrested him. Sheer stroke of brilliance that was, if I remember right, the diplomatic incident that provoked rumbled on for weeks.'

'Ah but this is different.'

'How is this different?'

'I recognised him from the back. That man there is the gurrier responsible for writing off the Granard squad car.'

Sergeant O'Connor now began to take an interest; he had heard all about the famous Granard road affair. 'Is he now, are you absolutely certain?'

Mick had at this stage got into the car and was fumbling with the ignition key.

'Shall we pull him in?' enquired Murphy.

The sergeant was about to say yes, then stopped. 'He hasn't done anything, so what do we pull him up for?' he asked. As he was speaking, officer Murphy was already opening the car door. 'You leave that to me sergeant.'

Mick was adjusting his seat belt strap, when he glanced in the rear view mirror to see first one, then the other policeman, get out of their patrol car and head towards him. Can't be anything I've done, he thought to himself, I haven't even started the engine yet. The sergeant came and tapped on Mick's window, indicating to him to wind it down. Officer Murphy meanwhile slowly circled the vehicle, writing things down in a notebook, he then turned and spoke into his radio.

'Good evening Garda, lovely night,' said Mick to the crouching figure to his right. Murphy eyed him steadily as he circled the car.

'Good evening sir, is this your vehicle?' asked sergeant O'Connor politely, a fairly standard enquiry, harmless enough in itself. Strictly speaking of course, it wasn't his vehicle. It belonged to Teach agus Talamh, but as a government department, did that mean the government? Mick hesitated, a fatal mistake with a policeman, duly noted by sergeant O'Connor.

'Well, er... not exactly.'

Murphy looked hard at Mick, and tried to contain his excitement, it was him, that gouger from the incident with the squad car on the Granard road!'

'Can you tell me the registration number of this vehicle sir?' asked officer Murphy. Mick looked blankly at him; he didn't have a clue and had just recognised Murphy as the homicidal cop from their last meeting. Murphy beckoned to his superior officer and they had a whispered conversation.

The sergeant returned to Mick, 'I must ask you to accompany us to the Ballkillmichael Garda station sir, just a matter of some minor irregularities to clear up.'

Mick was wary of going anywhere with these guys. 'So what's the problem officer?'

A check on the car had revealed it was actually registered in the name of one Niamh Comiskey, and Mick was obviously not Niamh Comiskey.

Officer Murphy now joined in, 'We have a suspicion

that you have been driving with intent, and need to clarify some details. Please leave your vehicle here and accompany me to the patrol car.'

Mick decided it would be wise to show willing, in case things took a turn for the worst. 'Am I under arrest?' he asked incredulously as he locked up his own car.

The sergeant looked at him gravely, ''Tis a serious matter sir.'

Officer Murphy was in the driving seat, both sergeant O'Connor and Mick got in the back.

'Hey O'Brien,' shouted the sergeant to his colleague across at Centra. 'See you back at the station.'

The third policeman nodded and began checking the spokes of the bicycle. The police car did a U-turn, drove up the street about twenty metres and parked outside the Garda station. What the point of driving there was, Mick failed to understand.

Officer Murphy turned around, 'Nice to see you again sir, I thought I never would.'

Mick sunk down in his seat; he guessed that this could turn out to be a long night.

Mick had not been in many police stations, but no matter which country they are in, the layout and procedure is basically the same. Ballykillmichael Garda station was not large, but then Mick hardly thought it would be. The reception area only had room for about three or four people. Along the back wall, which was festooned with crime prevention notices, was a wooden bench, officer

Murphy pointed at it and Mick sat down. In front of him was a counter, the top of which was virtually at chest height. Behind the counter and set back, he could see two desks, on one was a computer. To the right of the counter was a keypad security door. This gave access to the interview rooms, cells and office area. Sergeant O'Connor, punched the door keypad, and the two police officers vanished through it. When the sergeant reappeared he was in shirtsleeves and had a large form attached to a clipboard.

'Now sir, if you will follow me, just one or two questions.'

Mick stood and followed him through the door. He was led into a small room containing two chairs and a desk.

'Could you tell me your name, address, date of birth and occupation sir.' The way he said sir was as if Mick was some kind of simpleton. The sergeant filled in the details on the form.

'Proof of identity?' asked officer O'Connor.

Mick searched his wallet and produced his driving licence.

'This is an English driving license,' said O'Connor somewhat surprised; he examined it and checked the details. The sergeant stood up, pushed open the door with his foot and shouted, 'Seamus, run this through the computer while I get our friend some tea.'

Mick looked at his watch, it was 8.30. He gazed around the walls; there were four large posters to entertain him, some general notices and graffiti, nothing much to look at here. There was one poster he imagined could well be a collector's item, it was years old and produced for the time speeds on Irish roads went metric. Apart from that were ones on zero tolerance for drink driving, and Community Alert. Mick stood up to stretch his legs. The results from the computer check revealed information beyond the wildest dreams of either officer Murphy or sergeant O'Connor. Not only was Mick McCarthy not what he appeared to be, it seems he wasn't who he claimed to be. The address he gave in Lucan belonged not to a Michael James McCarthy, but to a Gabriel Patrick McLaughlin. It appeared that Gabriel was wanted in Ireland, and other European police forces were evincing interest in him.

'Hey John Joe, come and look at this, we've won the Lotto!'

Sergeant O'Connor put down the polystyrene cup of tea he was about to bring to Mick and joined Seamus at the computer. He scanned the page in front of him.

'So yer man is really a wanted criminal. What about the woman who owns the car?' Seamus Murphy spoke quickly, his words almost tripping over each other.

'She lives in Dun Laoghaire. Very clever, he comes in by ferry, and she's his contact here; he uses her place as a safe house and borrows her car. No wonder she vanished into the night when he wrecked the Range Rover.' Sergeant O'Connor was indeed impressed; he could see glory, fame and promotion beckoning.

John Joe examined the face on the computer monitor,

'But it looks nothing like him, he has hair for a start.'

'Plastic surgery, he's had plastic surgery,' replied officer Murphy. 'You can't expect him to stay looking the same now he's in the big league; that would make our job too easy. He's obviously had electrocution lessons as well.' This latter piece of detective work alarmed John Joe. Was Murphy saying he was some kind of mass murderer?

Murphy continued, 'By having electrocution lessons, it makes him sound like an Englishman, and he has an English driving license, forgery if you ask me, or stolen.' A link up with the U.K police computer systems confirmed their suspicions. Gabriel McLaughlin had clearly stolen the identity of one Michael James McCarthy who lived in West Yorkshire, not Lucan. It was now a matter of interviewing this dangerous criminal, confronting him with the evidence, and getting him to confess.

Mick knew the two policemen were up to something. Officer Murphy was obviously out to get revenge for the Garda car incident at Granard, and he guessed the sergeant would go along with whatever was cooked up. He was at a loss to what they could come up with, but doubtless he would find out soon enough.

The door was opened to reveal officer Murphy carrying a polystyrene cup of tea; he smiled and sat down opposite Mick. 'How long have you been in this country Mr McCarthy?' The way he said Mr McCarthy was loaded with meaning.

'Oh, not long, a few months,' replied Mick. 'Why do

you ask?'

Seamus Murphy leaned forward slightly, an expression on his face like the cat that had the cream. 'Would I be right in assuming you came into this country from Holyhead by ferry and landed at Dun Laoghaire?'

Mick was tempted to say, no he'd walked across The Irish Sea. What kind of a dumb question was that, how else were you supposed to arrive at Dun Laoghaire?

'Well I have used the ferry in the past, but the last time I came and went was by plane. Could you tell me what all of this is about? You can't still be annoyed about that accident can you?' asked Mick.

Seamus Murphy stood up, 'We have bigger fish to fry now, don't we Mr McLaughlin'.

McLaughlin, why the hell is he calling me McLaughlin? Mick was bemused.

'Wait here whilst I fetch the sergeant,' said officer Murphy. After about five minutes he was joined by both policemen. They both sat down opposite Mick and had a large folder in front of them.

'It would be best for all of us if you cooperate fully,' said the sergeant gravely. 'First there is the issue of the car.' Mick knew the squad car was behind all of this. 'Next we have the aspect of identity theft, selling government property, consorting with known and wanted criminals, and illegal entry into this country.'

Mick looked at them in disbelieve totally stunned. 'Are you two out of your tiny minds?' The two policemen just sat there, expressionless. 'Just because me and my friend had a bump with a Garda Range Rover, you now make up ridiculous charges to get your own back.'

Officer Murphy shot him a glance. 'Oh the car in question isn't the Range Rover, in all the excitement we'd forgotten about that, we'll add destruction of government property to the list. That car was a total write off, and we never did get the fecker who was with you, last seen running towards Longford town, are they running still?'

Mick thought it was now time to send for the cavalry; he needed the contact Niamh had given him.

'I want to make a phone call, and refuse to say anything until my representative is present.'

'O.K, make your call and we'll wait outside.'

Mick opened his wallet and fished out the piece of paper he had been given; he just prayed there would be an answer. He dialled the number and waited; at long last it was answered. In the background he could hear loud music and cheering.

A distant voice asked what he wanted. 'I need to talk to Gerry Forde urgently, it's an emergency.' A distant woman's voice said they'd go and get him.

Mick heard someone asking her, 'Who is it?' There was a muffled exchange then he heard a man's voice. Mick explained his predicament and made it clear his instruction to phone came from Niamh.

'What the hell did ye go to Ballykillmichael for at all boy? I'll be there in 45 minutes.' The voice sounded familiar, but Mick couldn't place it. Meanwhile the two policemen were deliberating. They came to the conclusion they definitely had Mick rattled if he wanted representation.

'You go and sit in with him Seamus,' said sergeant O'Connor. 'We don't want him to feel lonely.'

Mick was staring at the walls, trying to make sense of it all, when officer Murphy came back into the room. The policeman sat down opposite Mick and unfolded a newspaper.

'Can't have you beating yourself up and claiming Garda brutality, can we?' Time dragged, Mick looked at his watch; he hoped Gerry Forde would turn up soon. He assumed him to be a trained solicitor and was sure Gerry would soon get him out of this nightmare.

Sooner than expected, the door of the interview room swung open and the sergeant appeared followed by trenchcoat! Only this time his friend with the shopping bags was wearing flared trousers, a jacket, with lapels, which could have doubled as airplane wings, and platform shoes.

Sergeant O'Connor guffawed, 'Your representative,' he announced as he ushered trenchcoat into the room. Mick looked at him, and for a few minutes was lost for words.

'Gerry Forde?' asked Mick hesitantly. Mick looked at the clock on the wall, 9.25.

'So me boyo, came for a walk up this way did ye? O.K. so, what's the craic?' asked Gerry. Mick described the turn of events since meeting up with the policemen in the street. Gerry listened and nodded occasionally by way of encouragement. At the end of Mick's explanation, he produced a mobile phone and dialled. Mick could only hear one side of the conversation.

'Yeh it's Gerry... Grand thanks... and yourself? Listen, I have this English felleh here with me... Mick McCarthy he says he is, do you know him? Where are we? In a Garda station...' Every now and again Gerry looked over at Mick and smiled encouragingly. Gerry described the night's events. The person at the other end of the line was clearly giving instructions to Gerry; every now and again he nodded and gave assent to whatever was being said.

'O.K, I'll do me best to get your boy out of here; these two gobshites need to be aware of the score.' With that he went out to where the two policemen were.

After about five minutes Mick was joined by Gerry, and officers Murphy and O'Connor; they both looked like two schoolboys who had just been given a good telling off.

'These boys,' said Gerry, pointing at the two policemen, 'have been messin.' Officers Murphy and O'Connor both began to intently examine their shoes.

'Yous two are a right pair of bollix,' said Gerry to the two policemen.

'Come on boyo, let's get out of here,' he said addressing Mick. They both left the room and headed towards the security door.

Officer Murphy came running after them, 'Mr

McCarthy, sorry about the misunderstanding.' He stood holding the door open and smiled at them nervously as they departed.

Out on the street Gerry Forde headed as if to go. 'Hey, hold on a minute, aren't you going to tell me what happened?' Mick was desperate to know how he'd been sprung. Gerry paused, his car door partly open.

'Did ye see those two beyond?' he said indicating the Garda station. 'Did you notice how they both had squinty eyes and a real look of each other?'

As far as Mick could see, the only links between the two of them were the uniform and insanity.

Gerry continued, 'Inbreeding, the pair of them is probably brothers, has a bad effect on the auld brain box. Cavan policeman ye sees.'

Mick paused to digest this diagnosis of two of Ireland's finest. 'But one's called Murphy and the other one's O'Connor,' exclaimed Mick.

Gerry looked at him, 'Sure them two probably live together in some shack in the Cuilge mountains and play the banjo in their spare time,' he smiled, leaning his arm along the car roof. 'Well me young bucko, it's like this, ye have friends in high places. I couldn't follow it all, but the Archbishop of Santiago had a hand in getting ye out, the two poor old crathurs went quite pale at the sound of his name. He's not your daddy is he? Never can be too sure after the Bishop of Galway.'

Mick was stunned; what the hell had a South American

cleric got to do with it? He had been suspicious that whatever Niamh had sent him to do in Cavan wasn't as straightforward as it seemed; this piece of news only confirmed it.

'Anyways, I have to get back to the lads at the John Travolta Tribute night,' announced Gerry. 'I can't stay here blathering to the likes of you.' That pronouncement at least explained the outfit Gerry had turned up in. Mick had never seen a solicitor rigged out like Gerry before.

'It must be grand having a relaxing night once in a while,' said Mick to him. 'Must make a pleasant change from all that legal work.'

Gerry looked highly amused. 'Do ye think I'm one of them blood sucking solicitors. The sort that charges a hundred euro to tell ye something you knew already?' Gerry could tell from the look on Mick's face that he did indeed believe him to be a solicitor. 'Jesus, Mary and Joseph!' exclaimed Gerry as he fumbled on the front seat of his car and handed Mick a lurid flyer, Saturday Night Fever – John Travolta Tribute Night was emblazoned along the top of it. In the body of the piece of paper were a list of venues and dates. Along the bottom were the words Gerry Forde, yer only man for rocking and rolling country and western. First Communion parties a speciality! Gerry left Mick in the street staring at the flyer transfixed, got into his car and gave a parting wave.

Jesus Mary and Joseph indeed thought Mick as he started his own car; he was now a free man thanks to a Co

Longford rock and roller, The Archbishop of Santiago and mystery friends in high places.

Sergeant O'Connor gave a huge sigh of relief and looked at his subordinate as he closed the door and came up to the reception counter. 'You know, for a minute there John Joe I thought we were in trouble,' announced officer Seamus Murphy to his superior.

The sergeant pulled himself up to his full height, a strange gleam in his eye, 'Are you mad?' he asked, his hands reaching for Seamus's neck.

Sídhe Who Must Be Obeyed

Clare woke up at eight, to the sound of voices in the area just outside her room. She had been under the impression that Donal had gone home the previous night, but unless Niamh was talking to herself, this had not been the case. Whilst Clare couldn't hear everything, she was able to make out most of what was being said. Much of what was being discussed was just mundane, she heard Niamh asking Donal what he wanted for breakfast, and the sound of a kettle boiling. The conversation was now coming from the kitchen and took a decidedly more interesting turn; Mick McCarthy and her own name suddenly come up. Slowly and carefully she moved the duvet back and crept to the door to listen more clearly. What she heard next both puzzled and disturbed her. It was clear that both Donal and Niamh were better acquainted with Mick than she had been led to believe. From what she could hear coming from the other side of her door, Niamh had actually met and spoken with him. This begged the question as to why Niamh had pretended she hadn't met him. Having sorted out who was having toast and cereal, the conversation in the kitchen resumed its subject matter. Clare couldn't follow what came next, but some character called Ruairí had a bearing on why Mick was in Cavan. Was Ruairí a friend of Donal and Niamh? It also seemed from what they were saying that Mick had had a run in with the Gardaí the night before, but had been released without charge; how did Donal and

Niamh know about that, and what did it all mean? Time to get up, get dressed and see what she could find out. .

Mick finished his breakfast and glanced at his watch, 8.30, plenty of time for 9.00 Mass. As it was the Feast of the Assumption, Mick had checked with Mrs Thom about Mass times; he had a choice, either morning Mass or in the evening. As Clare was due to arrive later that day, he decided to go for the morning option.

The church in Duncarrick was reasonably full when Mick got there; he could tell from the number of cars parked outside the church. As he strolled up towards the church he could see the last few stragglers making their way in. Mick followed them, wandering up the semi-circular gravel path to the church entrance. To the right of the church was a well-kept area of graves. The large heavy wooden door was ajar revealing a small vestibule area, with entrance to the church itself through side entrances. Mick chose the right hand entrance and stepped into the main body of the church, walking about halfway up. He genuflected and then looked around him. Facing him was a small Scared Heart altar with electric votive candles; to the left of the sanctuary area was a small Our Ladies altar. Looking up towards the roof of the church, he could see large areas where the paintwork was clearly suffering from rain damage, the light blue paint showing large ugly blisters. Mick knelt down and said some prayers. An altar boy appeared, rang the sanctuary bell and the congregation all stood for the start of Mass. Accompanied by this solitary altar boy, the celebrant appeared from the sacristy to the left; facing the congregation he kissed the altar and began the opening prayers. Mick recognised him from his walk the day before. He was the mysterious character with the Volkswagen who had reacted as if he knew him. What happened next, and for the entire duration of Mass, could only be described as a liturgical Mexican wave.

Due to his speed and inaudibility, only the front benches could actually hear what the Priest was saying; those in the following benches took their cue from those in front and were about fifteen seconds behind. The responses rippled down the church like an incoming tide; by the time those at the back had said the response, the front benches had started on the next one. Mick wondered if he was trying to beat the Mass in 15 minutes record set by a Galway Priest. He examined the celebrant closely during the Gospel and bidding prayers, but still was at a loss as to who he was. The congregation all sat down for the homily, so Mick put his deliberations on hold.

The sermon began on safe enough ground, by initially focusing on what was meant by the Immaculate Conception and its significance. It was only to be expected that reference be made to the appearance of Our Lady at Knock in County Mayo in 1879; it was at this point that things began to take an interesting turn. Apparently the celebrant saw the apparition as some kind of heavenly seal of approval of the foundation of the Land League by Michael

Davit, behind Mick and slightly to his left was a bout of uncontrolled coughing. The fact that both the apparition and the foundation of the organisation took place in the same year, and occurred in the same county, was clearly something the priest thought was more than just coincidence. Exactly why Our Lady thought an organisation fighting for Irish tenants rights was worthy of her support was not explained. There was a slight ripple amongst the congregation as this line of thinking began to sink in. Unfortunately, at this point, the celebrant began to get somewhat carried away. It seemed that Our Lady had not stopped at endorsing the Land League: the G.A.A. and the demise of Parnell had also received her approval. Somewhere in the diatribe the moral dangers of holidays featured, apparently two weeks in Iberia was virtually guaranteed as a one-way ticket to an eternity spent in hell. The only reason that Our Lady had put in an appearance at Fatima and Lourdes was because neither location was in Spain; it appears the moral standards of the latter would make your hair stand on end and even the Mother of God couldn't stomach it. People around him began to shuffle on the wooden benches, whether from a feeling of guilt or due to sitting too long in the same position was an open question.

At the end of Mass the celebrant was standing by the door shaking hands with the congregation as they left. Mick heard the odd comment from the elderly contingent of the congregation as he made his way out. 'Powerful

sermon Father... Howaya Father...Grand day Father...'
One of the oldest and most decrepit of the congregation
paused by Father Peter, 'Them Eyetalians were always a
bad influence Father, fair play to ye for giving out to them,'
said he, clearly having missed the content and point all
together. The younger generation just kept their heads
down and tried to make a quick exit. There was also the
odd comment in lowered voices, 'Do you think he's right in
the head?'

Mick tried to edge his way past the logjam at the door,
but found himself facing an outstretched hand. Mick
viewed the priest warily, but was not that rude that he
wouldn't shake hands with him. 'Morning Father and how
are you today?'

Father Antheney looked back at Mick; he didn't look
like a typical tourist, and he definitely wasn't local. 'I'm
grand thanks, and yourself?' Mick smiled in a conciliatory
way.

'I'm fine.' Father Antheney had a deaths grip of Mick's
hand and eyed him steadily.

'Here on holiday are you? You're definitely not local,
any more than myself,' said the Priest.

'No I'm from the city of Wykeford in England Father.
I'm here on businesses.'

'Ah Wykeford, I know it well. Sure I was a young
curate there some years ago.'

'That must be why you seem familiar Father. I must
have bumped into you at the Irish Centre. I thought I'd seen

you before.'

What Mick had failed to pick up was that Father Peter was a consummate liar and had no qualms about dissembling where the means justified the ends. Father Antheney had no more been near Wykeford than he had been bungee jumping. After what Brian Ború had said, and what The Longford leader article had pointed towards, Peter Antheney was on the lookout for some Englishman up to no good; this shifty article in front of him seemed to fit the bill perfectly.

'You say you're here on business, what kind of business would that be?'

Mick prevaricated; he didn't want to add to his present woes by direct lies. 'Well it's linked into bringing the beauties of Duncarrick to the wider world.' That was not in the strict sense of the word a lie; in a manner of speaking it could describe his real job and cover story.

'Are you now?' Father Antheney replied in a tone of voice, which clearly intimated he'd like to know more. He could tell from Mick's demeanour that he was not coming clean, and this only added to his feeling that this was the man he was looking for.

'I didn't catch the name,' said Father Antheney.

'Mick McCarthy, Father.'

'Perhaps we could have a meet up whilst you're in the district. I can catch up with what's new in Wykeford. Are you staying somewhere locally?' asked Father Antheney hopefully. 'Yes, I'm staying here in Duncarrick, at Mrs

Thom's.' Peter Antheney made a mental note to find out where that was. He didn't want to ask Mick too many questions, it might seem suspicious.

'I'll give you a ring so and we can arrange something.'

Mick nodded and headed down the gravel path. As Clare was due to arrive later that day, Mick thought perhaps they could all meet up. It suddenly occurred to Mick that he didn't know the priest's name, but he could sort that one out with Mrs Thom.

Turning left out of the gate at the end of the path, Mick headed back towards the village proper. He passed the National School and Post Office and came to the crossroads. As he made his way over towards Mrs Thom's, he passed a man getting out of a four-wheel drive outside of Casey's Bar and Lounge. He was struggling with a large suitcase and had a lap top computer over his shoulder. Mick detoured onto the road.

Having sorted himself out with his luggage, Martin Adams went in to the pub to book in.

The phone on Donal's desk buzzed, glancing away from the computer screen, he sighed. He had been reading a draft speech for his forthcoming visit to the North of Ireland Legislative Assembly, but wasn't making a lot of headway. Donal wasn't particularly looking forward to the occasion; some of them up north made creationists look positively progressive in their thinking, as for the shinners... he shuddered. The intercom light on his desk flashed, 'What is it Máire?'

'Your 9.30 appointment is here Taoiseach.'

'O.K., show him in, and Máire, will you bring in some tea and coffee please.' As the door opened Donal rose from his desk, pushed back his chair and made his way towards his visitor with an outstretched hand.

Eoghan Dempsey was overawed to be in what he considered the holy of holies. Initially he just stood there awkwardly, like a naughty schoolboy called in to explain himself to the school principal, he shuffled forward taking in his surroundings. Donal Brady was standing behind an imposing Irish oak desk to Eoghan's right. The floor was carpeted with a rich blue pile and three of the walls had oak panelling along their length. To his left was an ornate fireplace, above which hung a painting of Eamon De Valera, on the wall behind the Taoiseach's desk hung a side profile picture of Patrick Pearse. In front of the desk, three upright chairs were arranged in a semicircle. The full-length curtains were a rich burgundy colour, and along the low-slung window frame were small pictures and sculptures. To the left, near the fireplace and windows were a low coffee table and comfortable chairs. Donal came from behind his desk and strode towards Eoghan Dempsey. 'Delighted to meet you Mr Dempsey. I have heard a lot about you and you come with the highest recommendation.'

Eoghan Dempsey made his way towards Donal, a big smile on his face and he bowed. 'Taoiseach, tis an honour and privilege to meet yourself, the greatest yet in an august pantheon of Taoisígh. I offer my humble self in the service of the nation. I have heard Ireland's call, and here I am.'

Donal didn't react. Years of experience of dealing with fawning underlings, and the more recalcitrant members of his administration, now stood him in good stead. Eoghan Dempsey managed to make previous instances of sycophantic adulation seem tepid by comparison. Donal indicated a clustering of soft upholstered chairs around the low glass topped table near the window and they both sat down. Above the fireplace to Eoghan's left, the imposing portrait of Eamon De Valera, surveying the room with a firm and steady gaze. Eoghan beamed at Donal with the look of a born again Christian who had finally met his saviour. There was a hesitant knock at the door and Máire appeared with a silver tray laden with tea, coffee and biscuits.

'Now Mr Dempsey.'

'No Taoiseach, call me Eoghan.'

'O.K, Eoghan. Do you know why you have been specially selected for a mission vital to the interests of the state?'

He clearly had no idea at all, but wasn't going to let a simple matter of detail get in the way of that. 'All I know Taoiseach is that it's in the national interest, this is my country's hour of need and here I am.'

Donal guessed that Eoghan would gladly stick his head down the toilet and pull the chain, if he was told it was in the national interest. Donal decided to boost his ego; it had worked before to win friends and influence people, no reason why it shouldn't work now. Donal had a reputation of being all things to all men; his ability to connect with the man or woman in the street was the envy of many. He gently leaned over towards his visitor and spoke in hushed conspiratorial tones.

'Eoghan, I know you are a man I can trust with the affairs of the nation. There are powerful forces working to frustrate, and even destroy if possible, the future we are trying to build. What I have to tell you must not leave this room.' At this point Donal stood up and closed the curtains; this totally meaningless and ineffectual gesture always had the desired psychological effect. To add to the dramatic impact, Donal glanced around him as if checking there was no one who could eves drop. Eoghan looked at him wide eyed, as if he was to be told the secret of everlasting life. 'Do you know what this country needs to bring us fully into the 21st century? We need freedom of action, to be the arbiters of our own destiny. There are those actively working to frustrate our programme of government,' said Donal.

'Is it those gob shites on the opposition benches, or that shower of shites up Ben Bulben? It must be them little feckers in Sligo if you need my services. I've had dealings with them before, when I was but a young felleh. I won't let that collection of Halloween freaks get in the way.'

Donal knew that Eoghan's family had the gift; their

services had been called on when there were problems over building Knock airport. What he didn't know was that Eoghan was convinced Donal was a reincarnation of Eamon De Valera. The only trouble as far as Eoghan was concerned, was that Donal himself wasn't aware of his previous incarnation. The portrait over the fireplace was a potent omen as far as Eoghan was concerned and explained his devotional rapture. Donal adopted a serious demeanour and gave a big sigh. 'Indeed it is the sídhe that are the problem, Eoghan. God knows I have been as accommodating as I can be, but they just throw it back in my face. I'm not one to seek confrontation; I want conciliation, harmony and peace. I seek to further the welfare of all who inhabit our island.'

'Leave it to me Dev, er.. Taoiseach. If the like of them are giving you grief, I'll tear them to pieces, I'll … I'll murder the little feckers, so I will. They tried to break me you know, make me back down over Knock airport, bean sídhes wailing all night long, Púcas running round and round the house, leprechauns hammering shoes all day long. I didn't sleep for five days. Do you know there wasn't the bit of harm on me at the end of it.' Eoghan turned a deep shade of thrombosis purple as he spat this out and concluded by banging his fist on the table. It was then Donal noticed the twitch. There was a loud, urgent and fortuitously timed knock at the door, it opened and Máire appeared.

'Taoiseach…' she began in a rather distressed tone.

'Máire, I told you we were not to be disturbed under any circumstances, there are no exceptions, whatever it is will have to wait. Do I make myself clear?' Donal's voice had a determined tone, and betrayed a strong feeling of anger and irritation. It was clear from the expression on his face that he meant it. Máire was perturbed, she closed the door hesitatingly and with great reluctance, what should she do? Donal hadn't remembered to switch off his end of the intercom, she could hear every word.

'I don't think homicide will be necessary Eoghan. We don't want to do anything silly now, although I am most impressed by your enthusiasm and clear aptitude for the task in hand. The sídhe need reining in, that's what I want you to help me with. I'd like to have them where I can see them, if you know what I mean, so I'm going to move them into County Cavan.'

'Do you not think Cavan is too good for them? Did you ever see the film? Escape From New York Taoiseach, it was on R.T.E. 4 the other night?'

No Donal hadn't and he couldn't care less. 'Unfortunately not Eoghan and particularly so as I'm a great fan of... oh what's his name?' Donal had never heard of the film, but this strategy had worked before.

'Kurt Russell or Donald Pleasance is it Taoiseach,' replied Eoghan

'That's him, he's just a gas. So you're suggesting America are you?'

'Not at all, Limerick city Taoiseach. It's just that I was

reminded of it watching the film.'

'No, Cavan it is, and I want you to go down to Ben Bulben and arrange the move. I have a man down in Cavan now looking for a suitable place for them; only he doesn't know that's what he's about. He's an Englishman who's looking at the Black Pig's Dyke.'

'Did you ever hear tell of The Book of Invasions Taoiseach?' asked Eoghan.

Donal nodded, of course he had, it was a classic Horslips album from the 1970's, Niamh had bought him it for his birthday.

'Well you'll know them below on Ben Bulben are more slippery than a bag of eels. The Milesians had to do a dirty on them to win the battle of Tailtiu, had to find out their weak point and go for the kill. So what's the secret weapon you have up your sleeve to banjax the lot of them?'

Donal shifted in his seat and stared hard at Eoghan; he was in a quandary as to how much to tell him, even if he was a trusted party man. Like all the previous Taoisígh of Ireland he was custodian of a secret, one that had so far kept the sídhe under control.

'What do you think the sídhe would like, Eoghan, what would they sell their souls for, metaphorically speaking?'

'Well there you have me. Thinking off the top of my head, I'd have to say they'd want...' Eoghan's eyes bulged and his mouth hung open. An Taoiseach couldn't be implying what he seemed to be implying could he? 'You don't mean... you can't mean...'

Donal Brady leaned forward and delicately picked up a biscuit from the tray in front of him, as he slipped it into his mouth there was an imperceptible nod of the head.

'That's the deal if they move to Cavan, I tell them where it is.'

Eoghan was both disturbed and animated at this piece of news; he couldn't have been more surprised if he'd just been told Mary Magdalene was buried under the Gresham hotel.

'Jesus, Mary and Joseph, you can't do that Eamon, er... Donal.., I mean An Taoiseach. Are you serious? Give them that and you're opening Pandora's box.'

Donal looked at him perplexed, why on earth had he called me Eamon? Anyway back to the matter in hand, he had not actually said that he would give them it, but he wanted Eoghan and the sídhe to think that was what was on offer.

'Now Eoghan, don't go getting yourself all excited, tell them that the Department of Defence wants to turn Ben Bulben into an air – sea rescue base for Western Command. The constant clattering of helicopter rotor blades 24/7 isn't something that I'd think appeal to them, sure it would keep them awake.'

Donal paused, a pensive look on his face, 'Apart from the crowd who roam around after night fall of course.' He continued, 'Tell them it's time to move on, to become an integral part of the new Ireland, butter them up. We have transport arranged for you down to Sligo. You are to meet your contact on the slopes of Ben Bulben, and you will be escorted to your rendezvous with the sídhe. I have total faith in you Eoghan.' With a dramatic flourish Donal concluded, 'I would trust no one else with this sacred duty. The destiny of the nation rests in your hands, don't let the people of Ireland down!' With that Donal stood up and proffered his hand, Eoghan too rose and they shook firmly.

'Who is it I'm meeting Taoiseach?'

'It's a leprechaun called Ruairí. He's a bit taciturn and can be difficult at times, so take care.'

'Ah sure, I know him well, at least I know of him. Me great great grand da had dealings with him, they fell out over Parnell. Sure poor old Charles Stuart wouldn't play ball with them.' Donal looked startled. 'You look surprised Taioseach. Who do you think stirred up the Kitty O'Shea bag of tricks? These fellehs on Ben Bulben go way back with their messin.'

'Just see Máire on the way out. Your appointment with destiny awaits you at 1.30.'

Clare stared out of the window of the Bus Éireann coach as the countryside flashed past. She was in a pensive mood, Niamh and Donal definitely had something to hide, that was clear enough, but what exactly it was raised more questions than answers. When she had emerged from her bedroom, there had been a pregnant pause in their conversation. Both Niamh and Donal suddenly developed an obsessive interest in washing up the breakfast dishes, and tried to make non-committal small talk. Clare got her breakfast whilst thinking of how best to deal with the situation; she decided to try and spook the two of them, and watch for reactions. She said how much she was looking forward to seeing Mick again, and intimated that Mick knew Ruairí. The effect of this piece of information was electrifying. Donal and Niamh were both momentarily flummoxed, but rapidly regained their composure. An attempt to be nonchalant by Niamh didn't fool Clare. 'So is this Ruairí a work colleague of his then?'

'I don't know really, he mentions him now and again in relation to work, but I lose track of who everyone is.'

'What work would that be, exactly?' interjected Donal

'Something to do with the Black Pig's Dyke in Cavan I think,' replied Clare in a deliberately unsure tone.

The two of them looked at Clare with fixed smiles and said nothing.

'Ah, Cavan. A beautiful part of the country, so scenic. All those lakes and rolling hills,' said Donal after a few seconds.

'So I believe, replied Clare. 'Well I'll be able to judge that for myself soon enough. Mick is such a drama queen in some ways, he always dresses things up, God knows why!'

The smiles on the faces of Niamh and Donal now looked like an advert for botox. Clare knew she was on to something, but what?

'Well be sure to phone when you're in Cavan, to let us know you're alright, and how Mick is getting on,' said

Niamh with a tone which now tried to sound disinterested. 'Where are you staying?'

'I don't know yet. I thought I might be able to stay wherever Mick is.'

'The Crannóg,' Niamh murmured softly to Donal.

Clare was lost in her own thought as the coach came to a stop, and came back to the real world with a jolt. Retrieving her bag from the luggage compartment, she first of all phoned Mick to let him know she had arrived.

'Howaya Mick, I've landed in Cavan... No, just arrived. I'll go for something to drink and have a look around. See you in about an hour, is that O.K.? Look, how about I meet you at the bus station that should be easy enough to find. What? O.K. so...' Clare looked around her and began to wander along Farnham Street away from the bus station. Her first impressions of Cavan were favourable. Farnham Street had what appeared to be elegant Georgian houses on one side, most of which now appeared to be offices. Further down and to her left could be seen the towering spire of St Patrick's and Felim's Cathedral. On the opposite side of the road was a car showroom, and further along was a tourist information office. Crossing the road she walked up Thomas Ashe Street and stopped at the corner when she reached Dunnes. She had now obviously reached the heart of the town. Turning right she headed towards the Post Office. Clare picked a pub at random and went in for coffee and sandwiches. The White Star was on a corner, and the bar area consisted of sunken wooden floored lounge area with alcoves. The seating was in fairly good condition, and each partition had framed stained glass separating it from its adjacent seating. From the look of the clientele, it was a lunch break venue for local shop and office workers. Clare chose a high stool by the bar and examined the menu; she settled on the soup of the day and small pot of coffee. Piped music came from unseen loudspeakers hidden in the ceiling. The food arrived after about 10 minutes; she ate her soup and had nearly finished her coffee when the man next to her at the bar struck up innocuous conversation. He had, it soon became apparent, latched onto her due to the accent, and moved onto the wind up the tourist game. Unfortunately for him he had picked the wrong victim. Looking around him and nodding at nothing in particular he asked,

'Do ye hear that?'

'Hear what?' asked Clare

'The music, its U2,' he announced.

'Sounds like Westlife to me,' replied Clare.

'No, its U2, they're in the basement. They come here for a session, seem to think no one outside Dublin will recognise them. I might go down to watch them later. Are you going for the craic?' he asked.

'No, I'm going to the bus station,' replied Clare looking at her watch and waving over the bar staff so she could pay her bill. Her newfound friend turned away and stared down at the bar counter as he sipped his Magners. Clare slipped off her bar stool and headed for the door.

She took a circuitous route back to the bus station; the town wasn't that big and she doubted she'd get lost in it. Turning right from Abbey Street the bus station came into view, just beyond it was a Dublin registered Opel with its hazard warning light flashing and engine running. Even from the back she recognised the driver. Clare paused, got her mobile out and phoned Mick's number. As Mick's phone rang, she saw the driver fumble and put a phone to his ear. 'Hello sexy, big sister is watching you,' Clare enunciated in what she hoped sounded like a husky and alluring voice. She saw Mick smile and begin to look around him. Crossing just beyond the mini roundabout, she waved to let him know she was there. Mick had seen her in the rear view mirror and had already opened the passenger door 'This is a bit swish,' she said easing herself into the seat. 'You must be doing alright for yourself to be driving one of these.'

'It's not mine,' he said as he indicated and pulled away down Farnham Street.

'So is that why you were pulled by the Gardaí then, driving stolen cars?'

Mick very nearly lost control with surprise and shock.

'How the hell do you know about that?'

'Let's go for a drive and I'll tell you all about it my dear.'

'Strange you should say that. I thought as it was a nice afternoon we could go up to Killykeen Forest Park for a walk.'

They drove in silence, but neither really registered this fact, both had too much on their minds. Mick drove into the nearly deserted car park and parked. 'Come on then, let's go for a wander,' he said.

Over to their right was a lake, the surrounding area being heavily wooded. They could see a solitary fisherman in a boat several hundred metres away; his lack of movement and evident concentration conveyed the impression this vision was some kind of permanent fixture. The occasional swoosh as he recast his line was the only sound breaking the silence. Mick and Clare found a bench and sat down. 'Well come on then, tell me about the boys in blue,' said Clare in anticipation.

'How about you start as you seem to know all about it,' was the retort.

Clare told her part of the tale, how Niamh and Donal knew of Mick but were pretending they hadn't, that there was something funny going on in connection with his work project, and that someone called Ruairí was caught up in it somehow. She also recounted that Niamh and Donal knew of the run in with the cops. All the time she was talking, Mick listened intently and impassively; he only showed any kind of emotion when it was mentioned about Niamh not knowing him, he then shook his head slowly and smiled. Clare looked at him with an air of finality. 'So there you have it, what does all that add up to?' she asked.

Mick stretched and gazed across the lake, putting his

head in his hands as he did so. 'Well it's like this' he began. Mick told her his side of events, from the meeting with Niamh and Brian Kelly, down to the events of the night before.

'Jesus, the Guards didn't mention me did they?' asked Clare alarmed.

'Ah no, they don't even know you were driving; you're in the clear. It's a queer state of affairs all together as me father would have said. As for this Ruairí character, never heard of him,' replied Mick. Maybe things weren't as suspicious as they appeared he thought, maybe they were all just getting paranoid, neither the Taoiseach nor Niamh could afford to be involved in underhand conspiracies, especially if there was the risk of leaks. As for the Guards, well the car wasn't his, but then they hadn't really been interested in that in the first place. Ruairí was a puzzle though, who was he? A slight breeze got up, breaking the surface of the lake, making the sunlight reflected in the water dance and shimmer. Clouds rushed across the sky, their edges a billowing dark grey. Mick stood up, yawned and looked at Clare. 'Come on; let's have our walk before the weather changes.'

Eoghan had made good time on his journey; he was past Sligo town and heading north on the N 15 by 2.00 o'clock. He was looking for the road to Castletown once he was through Drumcliffe. Ahead of him he could make out the brooding shape of Ben Bulben, its summit making fleeting appearances through the low cloud. A vast grey blanket filled the sky, racing in across Drumcliffe Bay from the Atlantic. It was predictably starting to drizzle. Eoghan reached an unmarked cross road and pulled over, Carney was to his left, so the turning to his right had to be his, he indicated and pulled out, the spray from a passing wagon splattering the windscreen. The land began to rise gently as he approached Castletown, a village of about ten buildings strung out along the road. After about half a kilometre he reached a fork, he could turn left or right. He surveyed the scene through the rain-speckled windscreen whilst deliberating, the surrounding land was boggy, and with small whin bushes dotted here and there, the fields littered with large boulders. Interspersed amongst all of this were grazing sheep, oblivious to the increasing intensity of the rain. He turned left and along the road leading to Cartronwilliamoge, the gradient becoming steeper. The road, such as it was, petered out ahead of him, and became a track. From the look of things this was as far as he could get by car, the rest of the way would have to be on foot.

Eoghan double checked the car was locked, zipped up his cagoule, slipped on his boots and put his shoes in his back pack. Ruairí would find him, of that he was sure, but how long would he have to be out in this before they rendezvoused?

He was finding the going hard; the lower slopes of Ben Bulben were lumpy areas of tough grass, but with increasing amounts of scree. Looking over to his right he could see the town of Sligo in the distance, an oasis of civilisation compared to his present predicament. The wind was whipping his face and driving the increasingly heavy drizzle into every pore of his skin. Ahead of him was a track zigzagging up the mountain slope, the plateau summit shrouded in low cloud. Keeping his head down, in an attempt to minimise the effects of the now near horizontal rain, he concentrated on maintaining his footing on the unstable rock surface below his feet. In front of him the pathway disappeared behind some large boulders, on one of which someone had apparently left a toy doll. As he got closer, he saw that the doll was in fact a diminutive human figure; it was swinging its legs and watching his progress up the mountain. Pausing to catch his breath, he leaned against the clump of rocks next to him; Drumcliffe Bay and Coney Island made fleeting appearances through the mist below. Eoghan adjusted the hood on his cagoule and checked the time, 3.15. He plodded on upwards. As he approached the boulders with the watching figure, he saw it get off the rocks, smooth itself down, and stand expectantly in the middle of the path. The welcome committee was wearing a top hat, white gloves, a long frock coat, riding breeches and highly polished black boots, which reached the knees. Eoghan paused when he reached this surreal vision, which despite the torrential rain, was perfectly dry. The small figure bowed and extended its right hand. 'I am Ruairí, your host, guide and the emissary of the sídhe. And you are?'

'Eoghan Dempsey, representing An Taoiseach Donal Brady.'

Ruairí gave him a sharp look. 'Dempsey you say. I had a run in with some one of that name once, over Parnell it was. Charles Stewart Parnell, he was a nice felleh, a real gentleman. I got on great with him. That man Dempsey though, a total gobshite.'

Eoghan considered discretion was the better part of valour and said nothing. The leprechaun turned and headed up the path at a fast pace, beckoning Eoghan to follow. Ruairí suddenly turned off the path and towards a large solitary rock.

'Come on, no time to lose, people to see, places to go, things to be done.' And then he was gone.

Eoghan stood and stared perplexed, where was Ruairí, was it some kind of trick, had he been lured here to be left to die of exposure? Suddenly two disembodied arms appeared out of the ground and grabbed his legs pulling him downwards. 'Will ye ever come on now,' he heard Ruairí say. The next thing Eoghan knew he was falling into a vortex of half-light, strange shapes swooped out of the gloom, peered into his face and rapidly vanished again. He could hear high-pitched whistles and what seemed like the sound of thousands of flies, a hollow booming was somewhere below. He could see a rapidly moving disk of light rising towards him, it squirmed and bubbled, and the pulsing mass seemed intent on collision, a black dot appeared in the centre of the kaleidoscope of light, and he realised it was some kind of opening. The colours were migrating to the rim of the disk, and began rotating around a pure black heart. As the ring of light approached, a whooshing sound was heard; it momentarily encircled him, and then accelerated away. For a second he was blinded, and heard the whispered conversation of thousands of voices. All was silence again as the ring picked up speed and vanished into the void above him, the colours snaking inwards, coalescing to reform a disk. Below him was the tiny moving speck of Ruairí, silhouetted against a green square, which appeared to be gently waving and undulating. Eoghan bumped into something unseen which lashed out at him and sent him spinning, its voice of displeasure like that of an Atlantic storm wave breaking on a strand of pebbles. Eoghan felt himself slowing down, the green square below him growing larger by the second. He hit solid ground and found himself rolling down a grassy bank, when he looked up he could see Ruarí's face close up to his own. 'Close your eyes until I count to three, you took a hard knock there,' said Ruairí in a concerned tone.

Eoghan did as he was told; he was feeling dizzy, disorientated and his head thumped.

'Aon, dó, trí. Now what do you see?' he was asked. Eoghan leaned forwards, supporting himself on his elbows. Next to him was a tree, and ahead of him was a lush green grassy bank. In the distance he could see a village of thatched houses grouped around a cross roads, blue wispy smoke lazily made its way out of neat brick chimneys, dissipating in the still air, a smell of burning peat just discernable. The sun sparkled and danced on the waters of a lake, which meandered its way across the landscape behind the cluster of houses. He looked immediately to his left, at the tree; up the length of its trunk he could see names, letters and years carved after them. Eoghan described the scene in front of him and Ruairí motioned at the tree.

'You'll have to sign the visitor's book,' replied Ruairí handing him a large sharp knife.

Eoghan found himself a small free area below *C.J.H. 1971* 'What were those things I saw and heard on the way down?' he asked Ruairí

'Those are the creatures, or at least some of them, which we found here in Ireland when we arrived. There is a deeper and darker magic than ours, but few of your kind know of their existence. Anyways, you rest yourself awhile,' replied Ruairí. Eoghan lay back and gazed up at the clear blue sky above him, the tranquillity was soporific. Ruairí's solicitous attitude had an alterior motive. Over all the millennia that he had brought visitors from the other side to the world of the sídhe, he had always asked that same question what do you see? What the visitors never knew, and never would know, was that their deepest subconscious created the scene before them. It was the perfect smoke screen, for no two visitors ever agreed on what they saw and what they found, so who would believe they had been to the land of the sídhe? The little people

147

would never risk allowing visitors from the other side to see their world as it really was. Ruairí turned on his heel and gave Eoghan a beckoning look.

They walked down the slope and came to a wrought iron gate, beyond which was a rutted and apparently badly maintained tarmac road which had a healthy crop of grass growing along the middle. Ruairí didn't speak, but just strode onwards with a very determined air. After about half an hour he turned to face Eoghan, walking backwards as he did so.

'When we get below I'll show you where you'll be staying.'

'Staying? I've only come for a short visit,' replied Eoghan slightly alarmed.

'Ah sure you'll stay and céilidh, sample our hospitality.'

He wasn't too sure if this was an order or an invitation. He smiled and nodded. Ruairí turned around and they continued on. The countryside was good farmland, it was like County Meath writ large, the fields neatly arranged and separated from one another by well-trimmed hedges, but all were strangely empty. The tarmac road petered out and became more of a boreen with deep ditches on either side. There was something missing Eoghan thought to himself, but at first he couldn't think what. It suddenly came to him after a few minutes, birds; there were no birds, neither in the sky or squawking in the trees.

They were approaching the village now, forming a crucifix shape ahead of them. The thatched cottages he had seen from beneath the tree were more substantial than they appeared from a distance. The houses were made from white stone rather than whitewashed clay he had assumed them to be. Rather like the fields he had just left, there was little sign of any kind of life. Behind the village he could see extensive tracts of bog land fronting the lake. When they reached the middle of the village, Ruairí swung right and Eoghan followed, they stopped in front of a red brick two storey building with a porch, and what suspiciously looked like double glazed windows. There was a well looked after garden in front of the house, and a sun lounger was positioned next to a small ornamental pond. Two garden gnomes sat side by side, their fishing rods dipped in the water. Eoghan saw one of the gnomes turn his head and address Ruairí, 'Nah then cock, 'ows it goin?'

'Grand,' was the reply.

Ruairí turned to Eoghan, 'This is the guesthouse. Don't mind Ted and Harold,' he said nodding at the gnomes. 'Visitors from England, Cornwall I think they said they were from. You make yourself at home and I'll come back for ye later.'

Eoghan opened the gate and headed up the path. The two gnomes gave him a sly look, whispering and sniggering as he passed. One of them pointed at Eoghan and they both laughed.

The front door was unlocked and he walked straight in. The entrance hall was a huge oval shape, with a beautiful light oak stained parquet floor. A white marble table stood in front of a sweeping staircase. A clock chimed in the deep recesses of the house. Eoghan looked to his right and left, trying to spot doors, which had been cleverly hidden in the panelling covering the walls, fortunately each entrance was labelled.

There were three main rooms on the ground floor, a sitting or drawing room, a kitchen and large dining room, which could seat up to six. The drawing room was spacious and contained a three-piece green leather suite, the furnishings reminded him of a hotel lobby. A large, flat screen plasma T.V. was on the wall. He closed the door and turned to see his backpack making its own way up the stairs followed by a strong odour which hung in the air, trailing like an invisible fog. Whoever or whatever it was, it had apparently stolen his bag as an empty space now occupied the area by the table where he had left it. Following the smell, he pursued the thief to a large bedroom; flinging open the door he was amazed to see the contents of his backpack neatly arranged on the bed. Of the pungent one there was no sign. Somewhere on the ground floor he could hear banging and clattering, and then the sound of what seemed to be a kettle boiling. If Eoghan's intuition was right, there was a grogoch in the house; this could be a blessing in disguise, but they could be dutiful to the point of being irritating. He left the first floor, and went down to the front door for a breath of fresh air, hanging his cagoule on the door hook. The two gnomes had their backs turned, but one of them called him over. 'Hey, Paddy, come here.'

Eoghan felt his hackles rising at this invitation; these two obviously needed manners putting on the pair of them.

When Ruairí came back he found the three of them in the front garden with one gnome jumping up and down on the prone Eoghan, and trying to insert his fishing rod up his nose. The other one had attached himself to Eoghan's shin, and seemed to be trying to tear lumps out of it with his teeth. Ruairí stood and watched the scene before him with amusement. 'Will the three of you quit fooling around, the grass is being destroyed all together, it doesn't grow on trees you know.'

Eoghan's suit was now all green streaks and he had tears in the right leg of his trousers. The concentration of the two miniature assailants was broken by Ruarí's intervention; this gave Eoghan the opportunity to free himself and tip the two of them into the ornamental pond.

'You two had better learn how to speak to people more politely, next time I won't go so easy on ye,' Eoghan's breathing was laboured.

The gnomes climbed out of the pond. They were dishevelled and water dripped off them. Behind them their red pointed hats filled with water and sank. They pointed at Eoghan and in unison said, 'He started it.'

'Didn't' said Eoghan.

'Did.'

'Did not.'

Ruairí raised his hands and spoke to them like naughty children. 'Boys, boys, come on now. Them days of Anglo

Irish relations are in the past, we have to be more civilised.'

The two gnomes wrung out their wet clothes and tried to find their missing headgear, all the while muttering and giving Eoghan evil glances, he in return glared at the two of them.

'I thought you only found gurriers and gougers in Dublin, seems they have them in England too,' he said to no one in particular.

'You won't get away with this mate, come on if you think you're hard enough,' Harold shouted at Eoghan, shaking his fist. Ruairí nodded in the direction of the house and Eoghan dutifully turned and headed indoors. The leprechaun made for the side of the staircase and opened the kitchen door in the side panelling; it was then Eoghan noticed that each door had two knobs, one at normal height and another about 0.75 metres off the ground. They entered a kitchen, and fussing about was the source of the clattering he had heard earlier, there was indeed a grogoch in the house. Eoghan studied him carefully, they normally only made themselves visible to the select few, so this was a rare treat. He was about one and a half metres tall, and covered with ill kept ginger hair; his face was wizened and aged but had a kindly look about it. He was busy sweeping the floor when they came in, but what on earth he was brushing up was impossible to say, the floor was spotless. As he moved around the room, an occasional twig fell off him onto the floor.

'Annoying them two in the garden wasn't a wise move;

they're like the rest of their kind, vindictive and just biding their time for revenge. You should be thankful they are from England. We had Vladimir and Boris from Siberia here a month ago, spent all their time swilling whiskey and picking fights, belligerent would be putting it mildly,' said Ruairí in matter of fact tone.

Eoghan examined his trousers, ruined, and as for the jacket, he was none too sure if dry cleaning took out stains like that; he'd have to claim a new suit on expenses. On the table was a mound of soda bread and a pot of tea. He poured himself a cup, reached over to the bread and helped himself to a few slices. The kitchen was different from the rest of the house; this room was functional, cosy and welcoming. There was a peat briquette range exuding a warm glow that filled the room. A large pot of stew was simmering on one ring; a kettle on the other, and two large pans of boiling water fizzed and spat on the remainder. Eoghan leaned across the table to get a drop more milk, on seeing this, the grogoch dropped his brush and grabbed the jug, tipping a measured amount into Eoghan's cup. Picking up a spoon he began to lazily stir his tea, the ever-helpful ginger one again intervened. 'It's alright, don't fuss yourself, I'll do it.'

'No problem, Jimmy,' replied the grogoch in a broad Glaswegian accent.

In the ensuing tussle Eoghan won, and got sole possession of the teaspoon. He looked around the rest of the kitchen. There was a large Belfast sink, a rarity these days, and a sunken stainless steel rectangular area next to it for draining dishes. The granite work surfaces running both sides of the sink area gleamed. The fitted kitchen units were a cream colour; on the floor were grey farmhouse tiles, each one about five centimetres square. The grogoch had now opened the cupboard doors and was rearranging the contents symmetrically in height order, the larger tins and packets going to the back, the smaller towards the front. 'What's your name?' enquired Eoghan.

'Ronnie,' replied the bent figure, busy shifting tins.

'Well Ronnie, this is a grand cup of tea, and the soda bread is the best I've ever tasted.'

When he had finished with the food, Ronnie turned his attention to the cutlery draw. He took out the knives and forks one by one, started to wash and dry each one, and then buffed them until they shone. Eoghan turned from this scene of perfectionist domesticity and gave Ruairí an enquiring look. 'So when do I get to meet the lads?'

'Anytime now, when you're ready. That's what I came back for. If you're set we'll go.'

Eoghan stood up and inspected his suit, it would have to do. The grogoch was making tut tut sounds, as he mopped the pools of water around Eoghan's chair, shaking his head in disgust at the dried mud that fell like confetti from his trousers. Ronnie grabbed a bucket and mop and busily set to work.

Ruairí led the way to the front door and they set off down the garden path. Ted and Harold were both lying on the sun lounger, their arms folded across their chests and their eyes closed. He ignored them, and they ignored him. Once they had exited the gate, they both turned left and walked down to the end of the street. Set back slightly was a single storey red brick building resembling a parish hall. A couple of steps led to two full length frosted glass doors, their frames a darkish red wood colour and looking like they could do with some attention. Pushing the doors open they came to a small hallway, corridors leading away to their right and left. Ahead of them were sets of similar looking doors and Ruairí strode towards them; he opened one and beckoned him forward. Eoghan had anticipated rows of fold back chairs and some kind of podium or table on a stage at the far end. What stood before him beyond the doors was unexpected. The auditorium was semi-circular and vast. To his left and right were blue velvet upholstered benches, which followed the contours of the gently sloping floor. The seats focused in on a large glass podium resembling an altar, upon which spotlights were playing. The roof gently arched and had a milky translucent quality. The walls were made of multi-coloured crystal, which twinkled and shone; the floor was green marble. Bisecting the semi-circular seating, and leading directly to the podium, was a series of carpeted steps some seventy metres in length. The auditorium was entirely empty. Taking a deep breath, Eoghan began a measured journey down towards the podium, which was now glowing with a low intensity kaleidoscope of red and purple. He was aware of a rustling sound, which seemed to parallel his progress, and glancing to his left and right, noted that as he passed each row, it filled up. He surmised that his passing acted as some kind of trigger to make the sídhe visible. He reached the last step, went round the back of the podium, and turned to face the gathering. Ruairí stood beside him. Eoghan surveyed the gathering, most of the sídhe he recognised, but there were some that were unknown even to him. He produced a piece of paper from his breast pocket, carefully unfolded the sodden item and gently laid it out in front of him.

'A duine sídhe. I have come here today as representative of An Taoiseach Na h-Éireann, Donal Brady.' He paused for dramatic effect and looked around him. They were a fairly representative crowd, he thought to himself. The sídhe were all sitting in groups, like with like and in alphabetical order.

'For many years, we Irish have lived in brotherhood and harmony, sharing our island through the good times and the bad, wiping away Roisín Dúbh's tears, and standing up for what we held dear.' There were murmurs of agreement; he had obviously made a good start. The dullahans clapped their hands, a weird glow coming from their heads which had been carefully placed on their knees. It was always best to try and build a bond with your audience, make out that we're all in this together. 'However, times change and we must face up to that. There is nothing wrong with happy memories of the past, but it's time to move on, broaden horizons. Take the púcas for example. It's all very well tearing around the likes of Waterford and Laois, but surely even they must be tired of the same old lanes and tracks.' He looked up to see what reaction this provoked. It wasn't clear whether the snorting and shaking of their manes was agreement or dissent. 'You fear deargs and cluricauns, don't you get sick and tired of being confused with leprechauns? Isn't it about time you got the recognition you deserved? As for bean sídhes, well who'd want to hang around the O'Neill's, or Kavanaghs with never a thank you for all your laments and wailing. I knew an O'Brien once, and I can tell you I was none too keen to be in their company for very long. Why not try something new and go to County Cavan, the land of beautiful lakes and home of the O'Reilly's and Brady's, sure you'd like it there and even fit in. You could even go across the border, no one would pass any remarks; they'd just think you were locals they hadn't met before. Why should Ulster people be the ones who hardly ever see you. Why does it always have to be Leinster, Connaught and Munster?'

The bean sídhes, some bent over and wizened, stopped combing their hair and looked at Eoghan from with red-rimmed eyes, their grey cloaks wrapped tightly around them. At this point Ruairí interjected. 'So is this the best your Donal Brady has to offer? Are you in touch with the real world at all?'

'Ben Bulben may be alright now, but even that is going to change. Once the air sea rescue helicopter base is set up, you'll never have a minute's peace,' retorted Eoghan.

Ruairí shot him an incredulous look and sniggered. 'You mortals are mad altogether, who in their right mind would build an airport on top of a windswept, bog hole in the middle of nowhere?' Ruairí suddenly stared at Eoghan with a look of recognition and indignation. 'Knock airport! I knew the name Dempsey couldn't have just been coincidence. Anyway, you can't just go around wrecking and tearing up this mountain, we have agreements, you can't just ignore those, and it's just not done.'

This time it was Eoghan's turn to interject. 'Oh agreement is it, what about the deal made between the púca and Brian Ború? What happened to the deal to leave good Christian Irishmen alone and not torment them, not to wreck their property?' Eoghan looked up towards the rear of the auditorium. 'Brian Ború may not be here today, but what about yer man the púca?' he roared in a challenging voice. For some reason the assembly of púcas at the rear of the auditorium had suddenly developed a fascination for examining the floor, walls and ceiling. They looked anywhere but at Eoghan, and shuffled uncomfortably. 'Look, the bottom line is that you should leave Ben Bulben, or else.'

'Or else what?' asked Ruairí.

'Or else...' Eoghan was reluctant to announce Donal's metaphorical carrot, but he thought to himself I'm doing it for Ireland. 'The deal is this...'

The offer electrified the assembled sídhe; they all fixed

their gaze on Eoghan, the silence in the auditorium was deafening. A lone figure rose from the middle of a row to Eoghan's right, and made its way out towards the steps. It was the most beautiful woman he had ever seen. She was fixing her gaze on him; her eyes were dark and perfectly formed, her face totally symmetrical. Her dark ginger hair had a subtle sheen, and her figure was the epitome of perfection. Eoghan gazed on her transfixed, he gasped, it was a lianhan sídhe. She made her way towards him; her long well toned legs revealed by her split skirt as she deftly went from step to step. She reached the bottom of the steps and floated over to where he stood, gently stroking his cheek with her hair brushing lightly against his face.

'Tell Gráinne, tell me of your deepest desires, but first share with me your darkest deepest secret, tell me where it is.'

Her voice was low, and had a husky edge to it, her dilated pupils and full lips hinted at depths of lust and passion he could only imagine. Eoghan was in a win - win situation, if he told her what they wanted to know, then he was totally in her power, if he didn't then she would be his slave. As he didn't know, Eoghan couldn't lose.

'I have no idea, only Donal Brady knows that.'

She cocked her head and pursed her lips, a longing languid look on her face.

'Sorry, can't help you there Gráinne. The offer stands though, move to Cavan and there you are now.'

Gráinne withdrew slowly and gracefully; she gave a

resigned sigh and smiled. She slowly made her way back up the steps, her hips swinging in a sensuous calculating motion.

All eyes were now on Eoghan.

Ruairí was dancing around with excitement and was highly agitated. 'This is an offer we must discuss and seriously consider. I'll take you back to the other side.'

Leaving the rest of the sídhe discussing the bombshell announcement, Ruairí and Eoghan headed back to the house to collect his backpack. In what seemed no time at all they were back at the tree where they had both landed on arrival.

'Close your eyes,' instructed Ruairí.

Eoghan did as he was told and suddenly felt a dampness blowing in his face. When he opened his eyes he found he was back on the slopes of Ben Bulben. Ruairí was nowhere to be seen, but his voice could be heard, getting fainter by the second.

'Tell Donal Brady I'll speak to him soon and very soon.'

Eoghan looked at his watch, it was 3.18; he had been away for just three minutes. Picking himself up he headed down the slope to where the car was parked.

Ruairí watched him go and returned to the sídhe where heated debate was taking place. He listened for a while and then interjected, 'May I make a suggestion?' The assembly listened to the proposal and nodded their assent. 'So, we're all agreed on the next course of action?' A smile came over

Ruairí's face 'Sure there's more than one-way to skin a cat!'

Calm Before The Storm

'What time is it?' asked Clare pushing branches away from her face and trying not to step in the mud.

Mick paused and steadied himself against a tree. 'It's three twenty. Perhaps we should make tracks and get you to Duncarrick. You haven't booked in anywhere have you?' he asked Clare.

'No, thought I might be able to doss down in your place.'

'Better give Mrs Thom a ring and book you a room then.' Mick phoned and waited. 'Hello, Mrs Thom, it's Mick McCarthy... grand thanks. No... I'm up in Killykeen. On my own...? No, I'm with a friend who's come down from Dublin and wants to stay over for a couple of nights...ah, so you can't fit her in, never mind it can't be helped. Pardon? Well I suppose they're worth a try. What... well that's good of you. Hear from you soon then.' Mick put his phone away and turned to Clare. 'Mrs Thom is expecting a group of Germans tonight, so she's booked up. But she did say she'd call into Casey's to see how they're fixed, it's only two doors down anyway.' Just then the phone rang. 'That's terrific Mrs Thom, thanks a million.' He nodded at Clare and gave her the thumbs up sign.

'She gave them a ring and you're booked in. Come on, time to go.' They made their way back to the car park and set off as Clare fell asleep.

Máire had been in a perturbed state ever since Eoghan Dempsey had left that morning. She kept running through the conversation she had heard in her mind. A whole range of possibilities had been considered. She had dismissed the possibility that it was imaginary, there were only a couple of options left, one was that Eoghan was a dangerous lunatic and Donal Brady had simply humoured him. The other option was that they were both unhinged. Máire wondered if more than Donal's nose had received a knock in Italy. In any case she needed to talk to someone, if only for her own peace of mind, and she knew just the person. It had been about eighteen months ago, but she had never forgotten him. The retreat had been just before he was all set for Spain. She dialled the number and waited, a firm voice announced. 'Good afternoon, Dundalk Park, can I help you?'

'Yes, I'd like to speak to Father Antheney please.' Máire was put on hold and had to listen to a metallic rendition of The Fields of Athenry whilst they tried to locate him.

'I'm sorry he's not here at the moment, can I take a message?'

'No, it's urgent I speak to him, a personal matter.' The mix of panic and near hysteria in Máire's voice must have registered. A few seconds later she heard a male voice.

'Father Jim Ahern here, can I be of assistance?' Máire wasn't specific, but explained she had a friend who seemed to be quite not themselves, and could be about to get involved in something silly. She lied by telling Father Jim that Father Antheney had helped out before, and had said to phone anytime.

'Well in that case I'll give you his phone number; he's helping out in a parish in County Longford. Have you a pen handy?'

When Father Peter Antheney got back to the Parochial House there were five phone messages, four from Murtagh's nun, and the other from a woman called Máire. She was phoning from Dublin and was clearly concerned about her friend. Peter Antheney listened to Máire's message two or three times; he would never turn down anyone genuinely in need of advice or help. His humanity, irrespective of his priesthood, wouldn't let him. He phoned her back and arranged to meet her that evening in Kells.

Mick and Clare arrived back in Duncarrick an hour after leaving Killykeen. Mick parked opposite Casey's and gave Clare a nudge; she slowly stirred and looked at him with sleepy eyes. 'You go in and get settled, I'll call to see you later.'

'O.K. so.'

Clare got out and retrieved her bag from the back of the car. Mick got out and followed her across the street. When Clare first entered Casey's' she thought there had been a power cut. The pub interior was dark, and it took her a minute to get accustomed to the dim light. There was neither sight nor sound of any life, and she had to shout in an attempt to find someone who might be about the place. The sound of running feet was heard coming down a flight of stairs, and a young man who looked no more than sixteen appeared.

'Are ye alright there?' was the initial greeting.

Clare announced herself and explained Mrs Thom had booked her in.

'Ah yes, just the two nights is it?' Clare nodded.

'Right, if you follow me I'll show you up to the room.'

'See you in about half an hour,' said Mick to Clare as he turned to leave.

Her guide led her around the bar and towards the pool room; a nondescript door at the rear was opened to reveal steps leading up to the first floor. Clare's room was virtually opposite the top of the stairs, and was both airy and spacious. There was the obligatory TV and electric kettle on the chest of draws along the wall. Just inside the door was a small bathroom. Clare put her bag down and turned to her host. 'What time is the evening meal?'

'It starts at six. If you go back down into the pool room and turn left, you'll see a door marked dining room. If you need anything I'll be down in the bar.'

Clare went to the window to look at the view, it was a caged in yard area containing beer kegs. Well, I've had worse to look at Clare thought to herself. It was now five, so Clare decided to have a shower before Mick returned. As the place was so quiet, she assumed that she was the only one staying there, the sound of muffled conversation from the next room pointed to her being wrong. Following her shower, Clare made some tea, retrieved a book from her bag and sat in the armchair by the bed; she had hardly opened it when there was knock at the door and she heard Mick enquiring, 'Can I come in, are you decent?'

'No, but come in anyway' There was no movement outside.

'It's a joke you idiot, of course you can.'

Mick sat on the bed and looked around him. 'Well this isn't bad at any rate. Look, you have whatever it is they're giving you to eat and I'll see you downstairs in the bar later. I have my meal about six thirty, what time's yours?'

'About six,' replied Clare.

'Well, see you about seven thirty then.'

With that Mick stood up and left.

Clare assumed you just found a vacant space in the dining room and sat down. There was only one vacant space in any case, the two other tables being fully occupied. The man at her table appeared at first glance to be normal enough, however Clare had encountered his kind before. He was an indeterminate age, somewhere in his forties was her guess, and was wearing a three-piece suit. He was sitting back in his chair, humming to himself and with his hands clasped together. The smile he gave Clare when she sat down only confirmed her suspicions, he was an egomaniac that fancied himself and thought he could charm the ladies. Clare had had plenty experience of his sort when she had worked in the Irish Centre pulling pints; some of the losers there had fancied their chances at pulling her. If he decided to try his smarmy, knock 'em dead one-liners with her, she was well fit to deal with him. Clare smiled back, she decided she might as well be pleasant until she found out where the land lay, she could be mistaken, but smarmy charm was likely to follow. 'Is this seat taken?' she asked

'No, no, not at all.'

There was no menu on the table, but then Clare hadn't expected there to be. 'Do you know what we're having?' she asked her dining companion.

'Chicken Kiev's, I've been told. There may be no flowers on the table, but with an English rose such as yourself, I hardly need them.'

Clare decided to go with the flow rather giving him an immediate put down. She covered her mouth in mock embarrassment and looked flattered. 'Oh you are a real charmer. I bet you say that to all the girls.'

'Sure a beauty such as yours will not be seen again. I'm Martin,' announced her friend across the table.

'I'm Fran,' replied Clare.

'A beautiful name for a beautiful lady!'

Pass the sick bag time, she thought to herself, had now obviously arrived, things would only clearly go down hill if that was his opening line. 'So Martin, are you on holiday?'

'No, I'm a journalist chasing a scoop.'

Clare appeared suitably impressed. An elderly woman

in a worn apron, the pocket slightly torn, appeared with a large tray and went silently around the room distributing the main course and vegetables. Clare looked at her Kiev, normally these were crisp and dry, this one appeared to have had a bath in a bottle of cooking oil. 'So, you must get to meet all sorts of important people in your line of work.'

Having been given a green light, Martin proceeded to recount all the people he had allegedly met. Clare concentrated on the food, occasionally tuning in to the monologue flowing over her like torrent.

The silent lady appeared and removed the dishes. 'So what did the Pope think of that?' she asked interrupting him.

'Well now, Martin' says he, 'you could well be right. Mass in Esperanto could solve the problem between the Latin rite traditionalists and vernacular modernists.'

Ice cream was plonked in front of them, followed by coffee.

'So what's the scoop you're working on?' asked Clare.

'It's a conspiracy in high places, a rewriting of our country's history. Here, look at these,' Martin picked up an envelope that was on the floor beside his chair and handed it to Clare. The photographs she was looking at were the same ones he had shown her cousin, Clare was as equally puzzled as Niamh had been.

'Doesn't look much to me.'

'Appearances can be deceiving, all I am at liberty to say is that this will blow your mind. There's an Englishman involved in all of this somehow, part of a government cover up, wouldn't surprise me if this felleh was really a British spy working for M.F.I or MI 5. I know he's here in the Duncarrick district somewhere, and I intend to find him.'

'It sounds very exciting, do you have a name for this mystery Englishman then, or know what he looks like?' Clare thought she already knew the answer to this one.

'Mick McCarthy. I don't know what he looks like though.'

Right then, warn Mick. Martin retrieved his photographs and then asked in an indulgent tone, 'So why are you here Fran?' The way things were shaping up; Clare imagined he was building up to an invitation to come up to his room to see his press cuttings. It was time to go for the kill and put him off.

'I'm the chairperson of the Wykeford G.L.T.F.C. and we're thinking of coming here next year. I'm here on a fact finding tour.'

'So you've got a soccer team, F.C., football club?'

Clare tried to sound puzzled, 'The Wykeford Gay and Lesbian Transsexual Fishing Cooperative hasn't got a football team.'

The look on Martin's face was better than she hoped for. The fixed oily smile slowly evaporated, and he moved his chair back a few inches as if Clare had some virulent airborne disease.

'So, Fran is short for..?' stuttered Martin.

'Frank, but being informal is far more cosy, don't you

think so?' cooed Clare giving him a come on look.

'Well...er, good luck to you Frank, I mean Fran,' said Martin in an edgy tone. 'I have to go and...phone my editor, yes that's it. I have to phone my editor and fill him in on progress to date.' After Martin had made his rapid and circuitous exit from the dining room, Clare gave Mick a ring.

'I'll explain later, but listen very carefully. When we meet up in the bar tonight your name is Pat and you're secretary of the Wykeford Gay and Lesbian Transsexual Fishing Cooperative, that's if anyone asks.' The response was agitated and strangled.

'If anyone asks! Who the hell is going to ask?'

'A newspaper reporter who's after you, but don't get all excited now Mick.'

'*A WHAT*? 'He shrieked down the phone.

'See you soon sweetie pie.'

When Mick came into Casey's he found Clare settled in a corner. He sidled over to her and sat down. She gave him a big kiss and put her arm around him.

'Pat, delighted to see you. I thought you might not make it,' she said loudly. Over at the far end of the bar was Martin Adams; he sipped a large whiskey and was giving them surreptitious glances. Clare nuzzled up to Mick and whispered in his ear. 'The smarmy looking felleh at the end of the bar is your newspaperman. He showed me some photographs and made out you're involved in some kind of cover up. He thinks we're either gay, or AC – DC, so you're safe for the moment. The things I do for you.'

Mick was lost for words; he assumed he was meant to be grateful. 'So he thinks I'm secretary of, what is it?' asked Mick.

'The Wykeford Gay and Lesbian Transsexual Fishing Cooperative. Now be a sweetie and go to the bar for a drink.'

Mick edged his way into a space and tried to get the attention of the bar man who was in deep conversation with Martin Adams. Martin looked at Mick and said something to the barman in low tones, the two of them slowly turned their attention to him and sniggered. The barman moved up towards Mick. 'Yes sir, what can I get you?' he was asked in a loaded tone. He ordered a pint for himself and a glass of lager for Clare.

'Thanks a million,' said Mick as he placed the lager in front of Clare. 'They now think I'm some kind of freak show laid on for their entertainment.'

'Ignore them and just relax. They won't bother us.'

Martin Adams finished his drink and stood up, stretching as he did so.

'Good night ladies,' he said to the two of them in a low tone as he passed their table. Mick and Clare were indeed left alone for the rest of the evening; there were few in the bar in any case and they were mostly in their early twenties. At long last Clare consulted her watch, 'Well, I think I'll turn in, it's been a long day and I'm tired. What are you doing tomorrow Mick?'

'I thought I'd go down and do some photographic work, a bit of surveying, do some sketches of the dyke. What about you?'

'Will you need the car then? I have some important shopping to do in Cavan.'

'And what important shopping would that be?' asked Mick

'All shopping is important Mick, I am a woman after all.'

'If you take me down to the dyke after an early breakfast, then you can have the car. I can always ring you to pick me up later,' replied Mick.

'O.K., so about what time?'

'Say about eight fifteen, I'll see you outside here.' Mick didn't want to bump into Martin Adams if he could help it. Clare leaned over and gave him a kiss on the cheek.

'See you then,' and in a loud voice she added, 'Good night Pat, don't do anything I wouldn't do!' Mick smiled weakly back and headed out to Mrs Thom's.

'Happy birthday to you, happy birthday to you, happy birthday An Taoiseach, happy birthday to you!' Donal smiled self-consciously as the refrain ended. 'Thank you, thank you, now without further ado let's eat.'

Niamh had arranged to book the New Irish place for the birthday bash; she knew Donal didn't like a fuss over birthdays and it was one of the few places here he could be himself. The gathering was select, and apart from herself, Frank and Phil, there were only another half a dozen guests. Sitting next to Donal was Ciarán, a friend since their school days.

Niamh produced a carefully wrapped oblong and handed it to Donal. 'You definitely won't have one of these,' she said in a self-satisfied and expectant tone.

Donal knew it was a book from the shape. Carefully unwrapping the paper he revealed the words Mein Kampf and below it a photograph of Adolf Hitler.

'This is extra special. Not only is it signed by the author himself, it's also a very limited edition,' said Niamh. She had been uncomfortable about this gift, but knew well that Donal would really appreciate it.

'Where on earth did you get this from? It's entirely written in Irish.'

'Ah well, that would be telling,' was the reply in a conspiratorial tone.

'I have something special for you Donal, but you'll have to wait until later,' whispered Ciarán in his ear. Donal's mobile bleeped and he slipped it out of his pocket to read a message from Eoghan, 'Mission accomplished. Will see you Friday as arranged.'

'Who was that?' enquired Niamh.

'A business call, tell you more later,' replied Donal.

'Talking of business, can we just focus on tomorrow for a couple of minutes. I hate to be a party pooper, but I'd guess you'll not be able to focus on anything much come morning. That Yank is coming over for his photo opportunity, and you have to meet and greet him,' interjected Niamh.

Donal groaned, it was bad enough the last time. Why contenders for the position of President of the United States felt such a desperate need to discover their Irish roots was beyond him.

'Remind me, who is it I'm meeting?'

'Chumani Rodriguez, aged fifty eight and single.'

'What kind of feckin name is that?' asked Ciarán nearly chocking on his drink.

'It's the name his mammy gave him you ignorant gob shite. He's a Hispanic Native American. Now behave yourself and stop listening in on other people's conversations. His mammy was Sioux and his daddy was Spanish,' replied Niamh in a testy tone of voice.

'Terrible sad that, not knowing who your da was,' said Donal in a melancholy tone.

'What makes you think he doesn't know who his da was?' asked Niamh puzzled.

'He knows his mammy is called Sue, my mammy was called Sue, but his da is the man with no name Rodrigues.'

'Yeah terrible sad that Donal,' replied Niamh with a giggle.

'So which part of the auld sod do his supposed relatives come from?' asked Donal.

'He couldn't make his mind up to start with, but he finally decided on Galway. The city of the tribes, next parish America, the Spanish arch, good choice if you ask me, plenty of ruined thatched cottages about; he can take his pick as to which one is the ancestral home. You'll meet him at the airport when he makes his short stop over. All you have to do is smile; say something innocuous to the media and then he's away by helicopter to Galway.'

You do know that genetically our closest relatives are in Spain, so it's kind of come full circle.'

'What the hell are you talking about now Ciarán?' asked Donal

'Us and the Spanish, research has proved us and them are genetically linked.'

'Anyway, how did he decide on which thatched cottage to go for?' asked Donal

'Google Earth is a wonderful thing,' replied Niamh sipping her drink, there was a pause. 'I hope he likes your four legged tax breaks,' she said in a needling tone of voice looking at Donal.

'Look, don't start that again, how were we to know some sharp eyed hoor of a lawyer would spot a loophole,' replied Donal in a peeved voice.

'Are those the....' cut in Maeve

'Certainly are.' shot back Niamh. 'Breeding like rabbits they are. Bollock brain the birthday boy deserves all the credit for this one; it was his grand idea for preserving and enhancing the Gaeltacht way of life that led to the tax break mania to breed donkeys. It's a time bomb waiting to go off, there was a proposal to cull them from the air with snipers until the do gooders stepped in.'

The rest of the evening went pleasantly enough and Donal had slightly more to drink than was usual; it was his birthday and what harm was there once a year? He looked over to Frank and Phil and indicated he was going to the toilet; they both nodded and put down their coffee. Donal shook his head to indicate they could stay where they were, what harm could come to him here?

In the toilet Donal studied the graffiti on the wall out of boredom rather than interest. He always wondered who wrote these things, you never actually saw anyone doing it, so when did they do it? As he stood there finishing off he became aware of someone standing behind him.

'Look boys, I told you, no need for you two to come with me as well,' he said over his shoulder, presuming his two Gardaí minders had followed him in. There was no reply, so zipping up he turned around. The sight that met him made him take a step back. Dressed in black silk stockings, attached to a red velvet Basque by suspenders, and wearing black high heel shoes, stood the figure of the most beautiful woman he had ever seen. Her eyes were dark and deep, and she looked at him with longing and desire. Her hair had a slight ginger tinge and tumbled elegantly over her bare shoulders; she took some steps towards him, her hips swinging slightly.

'Hello Donal, happy birthday,' the voice was husky and had an inviting tone. She placed her right index finger up to her lips, stood in front of him and reached out, slowly running the same finger around the outside of his mouth.

'Mother of God,' exclaimed Donal as he looked around him nervously. The female form in front of him took a step backwards as if she had just been dealt a body blow. She smiled and leaned towards him, her right hand went around the back of his neck, her head at a slight angle as she gazed into his eyes, her face only centimetres from his own as she started to caress him.

'Tell me Donal, where do you keep the treasure, I want you tell me all about it. Tell Gráinne.'

'My treasure? You girls sure talk dirty; sure I've never heard it called that before. I know Ciarán said he had a surprise present, but I didn't expect this. You're not the stripper gram me cousin booked for my brother in law's stag night are you? You definitely have a look of her. I told you then and I'm telling you now, I'm not into this type of thing. I know Ciarán booked you but Niamh would kill me if I took advantage.'

With that Donal disentangled himself, edged his way around her and slowly backed out the door. He met Phil and Frank heading towards the toilet. 'Are you O.K. Taoiseach? We were beginning to get concerned about you.'

Donal looked flushed and a little dishevelled. 'O.K.? Why wouldn't I be O.K? Let's just go and sit down, give the little lady a chance to leave,' replied Donal as he shepherded them back to the table. The two policemen gave him a strange look.

'What lady would you be referring to?' Phil asked Donal.

Donal was a little drunk and began to giggle,'Gráinne, you know the stripper gram in the toilet, the present from Ciarán.' The two policeman exchanged glances.

'You check the gents Phil; I'll stay here with An Taoiseach.' Phil returned a couple of minutes later and consulted with Frank. Niamh was looking over at the three of them clearly a little concerned. 'Nothing and no one there. There is a small window, but she could hardly have got out of that,' reported Phil. The two policemen were baffled; Donal would hardly have made this up. 'O.K, we'd better check the C.C.T V,' said Frank.

Phil turned to face Donal, 'An Taoiseach, not a word when you sit down, just say you were feeling a little unwell.'

Donal returned to his table and the two officers went up to the bar. A mini D.V.D. was slipped across by the barman and Frank secreted it in his inside pocket.

'Are you alright Donal?' enquired Niamh

'Yeh, just feeling a little light headed, but I'm fine.'

'I think it's time we got back anyway, it's getting late,' said Niamh.

They took Donal back to Farmleigh in the Phoenix Park, he was quiet and subdued and hardly spoke at all. Frank radioed ahead to warn the two uniformed lads on duty at the gates they were on their way, and to let the night staff know they'd be there soon. As the car crunched on the gravel, Niamh could see the front door already open. The two officers helped Donal out of the car and into the house. 'Where's your present?' asked Phil. 'The book I mean.'

Donal staggered slightly, Niamh did a quick search of the car, 'It must be still in the restaurant, don't worry though, we'll get it in the morning,' she told him. Niamh walked back towards the car and then turned to face him. 'You had better have sobered up by the morning, we have that Yank flying in and he won't want any photos taken standing next to you whilst you throw up and try to focus with eyes that look like piss holes in the snow.'

Niamh was indeed right, it was exactly where Donal had left it, on the floor next to his chair. Danka picked it up. A birthday card fell out of it and onto the table; she couldn't help but notice the title of the book and contents of the card. The message from Niamh was, Breith lá sonas duit a stór mo chroí, good luck for your date with destiny, onward and upward, Una Voce, una Duce. Don't let the blue shirts get you down!' Danka stared at the book, then the card, then the book again. She was appalled; it appeared that the Taoiseach was a crypto Nazi, at best a closet fascist. What about this reference to Mussolini, he wasn't planning some kind of putsch was he? 'You will never guess what I've found,' she called out to the others, now all huddled around the D.V.D player behind the bar.

'Well I bet you it's nothing compared to what we're looking at,' replied Roman. Danka joined the others and tried to make sense of the grainy images on the small screen attached to the player. 'What on earth is all that?' she asked baffled.

'That,' replied Roman emphatically, 'is An Taoiseach Donal Brady, cavorting in the gents with some floozy. No wonder the cops wanted the mini disk.' Roman patted the top of the machine. 'Thank God for back up technology.'

Father Antheney had plenty of food for thought as he drove back from Kells. It was now all falling into place. Hadn't that discussion with St Patrick in the Parochial house before he set off now made more sense.

Father Peter had been warned by St Patrick, 'Don't think I got rid of all the snakes in the grass. The odd one or two of them managed to slink away in time. Watch that woman as well.' Sure didn't holy St Kevin have problems with the likes of them, had to row out to the middle of a lake to get away from one of them, he did.

Máire had been very nervous on first meeting, but she calmed down and recounted her tale slowly and with clarity. Father Tony trod carefully; he was dying to find out exactly what was going on, but knew that too inquisitive an approach would probably make her clam up. What he had discovered was dynamite. If Donal Brady thought he could get away with this then he had another thing coming. Interference in the supernatural order of things was just not on. Why shouldn't those in the other world have an input as to what went on, it was their country too? As for this

Eoghan, well he'd like to get his hands on him. At least Father Tony now knew that this Mick McCarthy was part of it, but not in on it. As he drove along Father Tony pondered his next move. The Englishman might be able to fill some gaps; he might have information to help complete the picture. He would ring this Mrs Thom and definitely arrange to meet Mick the following evening.

The next morning dawned bright and clear. Clare had got down for breakfast at seven thirty sharp and was the first and only one there. She hurriedly ate her cereal and fry up, slurped down some tea and went back to her room to get set for the day. As she approached her landing she encountered Martin Adams locking his door; he said nothing but she decided to be sociable even if he wasn't. 'Morning Martin, lovely day.' He grunted and fiddled with his room key, turning to the stairs he descended. When Clare came back down he was sitting at the table munching some cereal. 'Have a nice day Martin, and if you can't be good be careful,' said Clare in airy manner as she headed out to the street.

The elderly lady in the torn apron came to remove his dishes. 'What do you want for your fry up?' he was asked. Martin pondered the options.

'Is she a friend of yours?' enquired the old one watching Clare leaving

'God help us, I hope not,' replied Martin

'She was with that telly man last night; I thought you

might be here together.'

'What telly man?'

'Yer man Mick McCarthy. She couldn't keep her hands of him by all accounts.'

Martin was dumbstruck for a minute. 'That baldy felleh in the bar was Mick McCarthy, and he's something to do with T.V.?'

'Come down here to make a telly drama about fishing or the like; she's a dark horse too, a cousin to that floozy the Taoiseach hangs around with, I heard her saying. Martin shoved his seat back and rushed out onto the street, but apart from the smell of exhaust fumes and the sound of a distant car accelerating away, there was no sight or trace of Clare. Martin turned and went back to his table. One thing for sure, he'd be meeting up with Fran, or whoever she really was again. It seemed to him that there was a bigger story than he had hoped for in this sleepy backwater.

Clare dropped Mick off along the road where he had first encountered Gerry Forde. 'Do you want a hand with them?' enquired Clare as she saw the pile of poles emerging from the boot.

'No its O.K., thanks, anyway you'll just get all messy. The land over there is a bit boggy,' replied Mick indicating the line of trees at the end of the track. 'So if you can come back here for me, say about three o'clock, then we'll take a drive around the Lough to have a look at possible sites for the interpretation centre.'

Mick looked at her quizzically to see if that was acceptable. If Clare was going shopping, the chances were it would be an all day trip. He found it impossible to imagine how anyone could spend over five hours looking around the shops, but knew that was no problem for Clare. He had once gone food shopping with her to her local Asda in Wykeford, this had turned into a three-hour marathon.

Clare wrinkled her nose 'So, three o'clock it is then, fair enough.'

'For God's sake don't hit anything, that car isn't mine and the last thing I need is to try and explain to Niamh Comiskey how it got dents in it,' urged Mick.

'Moi, hit something? You make such a fuss.'

With that Clare drove off. Mick transferred his equipment in two trips and set to work.

The day was just right for a shopping trip thought Clare to herself as she headed towards Cavan, blue skies and the hint of balmy weather. She hit the N55 in no time and turned off along the by-pass just before Ballykillmichael. Ahead of her she could see a checkpoint manned by two police officers and one customs officer. A customs officer meant a red diesel check. Clare didn't know for sure, but guessed the car she was in was petrol, but she still needed to slow down and join the queue. She had always assumed a country policeman's lot was a happy one, but from the look of the two she could see that was clearly wrong. One officer, the sergeant, had a large black eye and the other one had ugly red marks all around his neck. From where she was in the line she could see the one with the red neck marks pointing and getting very agitated, whatever it was that was getting him all worked up was evidently behind her. Clare turned around in her seat, nope that wasn't it, nothing behind her, she was the last car in the line. She engaged first gear and edged forward, waved over to the side of the road by the customs man who proceeded to walk around the car. In front of her she could make out one of the policemen having a seizure of some kind and being restrained by the other one. 'Is he alright?' she hesitantly asked the customs officer who seemed oblivious to the altercation.

'There's not the bit of harm on him,' came the reply. 'Murphy and O'Connor often have banter, just differences of opinion on policing matters.' The officer who was being restrained pulled and struggled, pointing at her registration plate. She heard a strangled, 'It's that fecker's car' as she engaged second gear.

Donal's day, in contrast did not get off to a good start. Eoghan had phoned to defer the debrief from his meeting with the sídhe until the afternoon. Frank and Phil were on edge, they had told him they needed a meeting about the C.C.T.V. footage urgently. If all that wasn't bad enough, Donal was coping with a hangover and the official welcoming party from The Department of Foreign Affairs had yet to arrive; the latest update was that they were stuck somewhere in traffic. In addition to the other trials and tribulations, Niamh had gone off to deal with the fourth estate, so it looked like he'd have to officiate on his own with the support of some junior civil servants, all keen bright young things desperate to make their mark. Accompanied by his emergency entourage Donal made it to the V.I.P. lounge at Dublin airport just as their American visitor's jet was landing. Sitting down to catch his breath and talking to no one in particular, Donal asked, 'What's his name again?'

'Rodriguez, Taoiseach,' shot back one of the earnest faces before him, careerist written all over her.

'Thank you…erm…'

'Áine Murphy,' she announced loudly, smirking at her other two fresh-faced colleagues like the cat that'd got the cream.

'Thank you Áine.' Down on the airport apron security was tight. Donal could see several bullet headed individuals, with short hair and sun glasses, all with ear pieces and suspicious bulges under their dark meticulously tailored suit jackets. The supposedly innocuous bodyguards weren't so much tanned, as the colour of creosote; they reminded Donal of the strong tea his aunt used to make, 'If you can't paint with it, it isn't worth drinking,' she used to announce as she plopped a steaming cup of what looked like stewed tar in front of him.

The Irish media crew behind him in the V.I.P. lounge Donal knew, but there were those he didn't, presumably the foreign contingent.

Niamh reappeared, 'He should be up with you in about 5 minutes Donal.' She nodded towards the mob of T.V. crews and newspaper correspondents corralled behind them. 'A select few are being let loose when he gets up here. Now be nice to them Donal, we need them on our side, the voters watch the news and read papers.' Niamh's mobile phone began to ring and she moved away. 'Now behave yourself Donal whilst I take this call,' she said in a cautionary and chiding tone.

Suddenly the area in front of Donal was lit up by banks of T.V. lights simultaneously switching on. Surrounded by the creosote figurines, what Donal assumed to be Chumani Rodrigues approached him, his gleaming teeth straight out of a toothpaste advert. The bodyguards peeling off to the right and left in a clearly well-worn and rehearsed move and stood facing the press pack with studied indifference. Chumani and Donal stood sideways on to one another.

'Welcome to Ireland Mr Rodrigues, céad míle failté indeed,' Chumani whispered to his aide and Donal heard an almost imperceptible, 'Who's that guy?' followed by an inaudible response. A broad insincere smile appeared on his face as he extended his hand towards Donal.

'Gee thanks Mr Teashop, it sure is swell to be back in the old country.'

Donal grinned enthusiastically. The cameras whirred and flashed as they made small talk for the inevitable sharing of a joke shot. Thankfully for Donal, Chumani then headed towards the press pack to answer some questions. As Donal turned, a microphone was suddenly shoved under his nose and he was half blinded by a T.V camera light pointing straight at him. Holding the microphone was the epitome of the clean cut all American boy.

'Sir, as Teashirt of Ireland would you say a few words to our viewers at home about what this visit means to you and your country?'

Donal's gut instinct was I couldn't give a shite, but he didn't become a politician to say what he really thought.

'Ireland and America have a long, warm and close relationship cemented by blood ties and a shared history. We are always delighted to welcome home one of the many millions of our scattered Diaspora from across the globe, and to join in with celebrating their success.'

Donal looked at the interviewer expecting him to indicate cut at the camera man, but he just stood there.

'Tell me sir, have you ever availed of the opportunity to visit our great country?' It seemed he wanted a bit more than just a general sound bite

'Well, when I was younger I was going to go for the craic, but I thought it was better here.' The clean-cut one licked his lips and studied the evident damage to Donal's nose with interest; turning to the cameraman he grinned.

'Can you tell us a little more about the crack sir?' Donal was flattered; normally he was asked barbed loaded questions that would do justice to a Pharisee.

'Sometimes we had to make the craic ourselves, but

most times me and the lads would go down town and follow our noses.'

'So, there were a group of you looking for or making the crack?'

'Yeh, me and the lads. A Garda was a good one to ask, they always knew where the best craic was.'

'You would ask a what sir?'

'A Garda, a policeman. They'd tell you where it was going down as you Americans would say.'

'So the police would point you in the right direction for the crack?'

Donal nodded.

'And do you still like the crack sir?'

'Sure and why wouldn't I?' Donal looked at him slightly puzzled; this felleh was trembling slightly, hopping from leg to leg and trying to suppress a whimper. Donal wondered if he had a bladder problem.

'Thank you for your time sir. This is Randolph Beauregard signing off from Dublin Ireland.' The interviewer turned excitably to the cameraman, 'Are you happy with that Chuck?'

'Ecstatically, Randy,' he replied patting the camera.

Donal was disgusted; if someone told him they were ecstatically randy he'd call the Guards. 'Which T.V. station are you from anyway?'

'True Way Apostolic Tabernacle Church News sir. I used to be a Mormon, then one night the healing message of Jesus came to me thanks to my digital high definition twenty eight inch plasma screen T.V. I was on the trailer roof fixing the aerial when I fell off; lying there stunned in the hog pen I had a revelation.'

'And fair play to ye, you couldn't stay a moron all your life,' replied Donal, giving him a jocular slap on the back as he and Chuck made a hasty exit.

Niamh reappeared, 'Sorry about that Donal, got caught up with the great unwashed over there and couldn't get back. Everything go O.K. did it?'

'Yeh no problemo, everything's fine and a. O.K.! Right, back to the office whilst this circus takes off for Galway.'

Now that the security blanket was relaxed, it was easier to get out of the airport. Three Air Corps helicopters in close formation clattered overhead, two of them bristling with heavy machine guns and air to ground missiles shielding the third from any unwelcome attention.

In their wake came others, all wheeling westward. 'There he goes, God love him,' said Niamh.' As long as he doesn't fall into Galway Bay and drown, we should be O.K.'

Phil and Frank weren't sure what, if anything Niamh knew about the Gráinne episode. They had made enquiries but so far drawn a blank, whoever Gráinne was she was unknown in the escort and stripper gram world of Dublin. They thought it prudent to wait until they all returned to Government Buildings before raising it. As the car swept into the grounds Phil, trying to sound as casual as possible announced 'We have the C.C.T.V. footage and we'd like you to look at it.'

Niamh looked at Phil, then Donal, then Frank. 'What C.C.T.V. footage?" she asked as they made their way up to Donal's office.

'So you never saw her before Taoiseach?' They were all watching the grainy footage, huddled around a laptop. Niamh was amazingly composed, but Donal knew what to expect once they were alone.

'Look I told you last night, I went in for a slash and then there she was. All I know is that she's called Gráinne.'

Frank and Phil were dealing with mixed emotions; on one level they felt they had made a major slip up and placed Donal in danger, on another level they felt their professional pride dented because this woman had got to Donal and eluded them.

'Is this the only copy there is?' asked Niamh in a tense voice. 'If this gets out it'll be hard to explain it away or contain it.'

The two policemen nodded in unison at Niamh's comment. 'We don't know if there's another copy, doubt it though. We went back to Bah-Bar first thing, no one there and no sign of life. We have the forensic guys lined up, so once we get in we'll pull the place apart so to speak. The DVD's going to the technical bureau for enhancement, tests and analysis. All in all we expect results pretty quick, but that woman must be known to them, you can't get in and out that handy without collusion.'

'Could you go back and see what you can do to speed things up, we don't want this situation to spiral out of control,' instructed Niamh. 'Oh and lads, can you find out if that book was found in the restaurant by any of the staff, it's the birthday present left behind.'

Without a word Frank and Phil turned and headed out the office door. Niamh towards Donal, a steely look in her eye. 'Now me young bucko, tell all about this Gráinne and what you were doing meeting up with her in a toilet. If there's any lies I'll skewer your mickey to the office door.'

'Now you be careful with that Niamh, its old and fragile,' he said as she picked up the letter opener, this was a no win situation, he wouldn't be believed anyway. God works in mysterious ways, for just at that moment there was a knock at the door and Máire came in carrying a large and very neatly wrapped box.

'This was delivered by courier Taoiseach, it's been scanned, a birthday present from an anonymous admirer apparently.'

Donal grabbed at this interruption like a drowning man at a piece of string; normally he'd have asked her to put it in the corner, but not this time. 'O.K. Máire, could you unwrap it please and we'll see what it is.' He turned to Niamh, 'Shame you can't stay to help us, but I know duty calls. It's kind of you to volunteer to call in at The Department of Foreign Affairs personally to get a rain check on our Yank friend.'

It was clearly a get lost instruction and she decided to

take it. Máire's arrival had put the brakes on and Niamh had lost the initiative. Niamh gave him the look of a cat interrupted whilst tormenting a mouse; she would be back and pick up where they left off. 'O.K. Taoiseach, I shall call over to Iveagh House as quick as possible and return to you in no time to report personally.'

Donal smiled, highly relieved, he had expected her to stand her ground or make a scene. The best case scenario he could envisage was Niamh getting embroiled in inter departmental in -fighting at Iveagh House, hopefully he wouldn't see her again until after work by which time she'd have calmed down, if not there would be hell to pay. Máire was busy opening the box and piling up a mound of polystyrene chips on his desk.

'You seem in better form today, Máire, I thought you were going home for a nervous breakdown last night,' Donal laughed.

Máire eyed him with a smug expression, nervous breakdown is it? Jesus, he was the one to talk, after what she'd heard him and Eoghan discussing. 'I am much better Taoiseach, a problem shared is a problem halved. I have sought solace in spiritual guidance; perhaps you should give it a try sometime.' Máire flushed suddenly, and bit her lip, perhaps saying that was pushing it just too far, she peered into the box and reached down; 'Now I have it Taoiseach,' she announced producing first one, then a second figure encased in polythene. Unwrapping them both carefully she turned them to face Donal. 'Well those are queer presents, very lifelike though. Look, this little felleh has a bent fishing rod and the other one has scratches on him. Where do you want them?'

Donal pondered for a while, 'Just stick them by the fireplace for now. I'm just going for a walk and to get a sandwich from the canteen, anything comes up refer them to the Media Relations Department and stall them.'

Máire turned on her heel, 'O.K. Taoiseach, but I think they may be a little tied up at present with this Yank being over here, and with all them enquiries about your drug problem to deal with as well.' Donal gave her a bemused look, drugs, what the hell was she on about now? Better keep my eye on her he thought to himself, she was clearly cracking up.

When Donal returned, Máire nodded towards his office door, 'Herself is back from Iveagh House, I'd tread carefully Taoiseach.' Donal gingerly opened the door and looked in, Niamh was sitting at his desk, staring into space vacantly. He made his way silently towards her, kneeling down he took her hands in his tenderly.

'Is there anything wrong?' he asked. Niamh turned to face him, as she did so her mouth began to form a grin then a broad smile, then she tossed her head back and laughed.

'Jamie Mac, is there anything wrong? Where do I begin? The slut in the loo is bad enough, but things are just going from bad to worse.'

Donal put his arm around her, and gave her a nuzzle, 'Look, I know you're upset about Gráinne, but you know me Niamh, I couldn't cheat on you. You mean more to me than anything else in this world, you are my world. God knows girl, you make my life worth living.' Niamh began to sob, a mixture of relief, release and happiness. She leaned over, her cheek next to his and kissed him, her sobs subsiding. Niamh produced a paper hankie from her jacket pocket and blew her nose noisily, tear streaks spoiling the lightly applied designer makeup.

'I know you love me Donal, I love you, but sometimes I just think is it worth it? I don't mean us,' she said emphatically seeing the concern on his face, 'I mean the infighting, pulling strokes, getting one over on the cute hoors, being a cute hoor.' Donal listened; it was one of the things she liked most about him. When they had first met he had asked her how the canvassing was going. She had had a really rough day and was exhausted; she had poured her heart out to him, her frustrations and annoyances. Donal had just stood and listened, didn't interrupt, didn't try to offer solutions, he was genuinely interested. It had been a first for Niamh, a man who was not totally ego centric, just waiting for an opening to turn the conversation round to how wonderful he was.

'We've been in worse straights than this Niamh, remember when I was Minister for Health and won that award for staffing rationalisation?'

'You came second for joined up thinking in the OECD. If it hadn't been for that French guy proposing metric clock train timetables, you'd have walked away with first place.'

'I know, but the point is, did I let it get us down even after being hospitalised?'

'The only reason you ended up in hospital is because you fell into the Liffey after celebrating your award down in Temple Bar with the lads.'

'I know Niamh, but....'

'And then there were those newspaper headlines, In the Shit! Minister tries some of his own medicine and Brady fails in attempt to walk on water.'

'Anyway...'

'Not forgetting you punched the consultant and there was that nurse wanting to sue you for lewd suggestions and sexual harassment.'

'Niamh, I was delirious, even the doctors backed me up on that one in court. The point is, I thought that nurse was you. Even when I'm out of mind it's my lovely Niamh I'm thinking of. You see, every cloud has a silver lining and it's always darkest before the dawn. Now you tell me all about it.'

Niamh was by now more composed; she sat up and smoothed herself down. 'So, every cloud has a silver lining has it?'

He nodded slowly and gave her a gentle smile.

'Jesus Donal, you have no idea have you?'

'No idea about what?'

'C.N.N. Sky News, B.B.C News, R.T.É 24 /7, and probably the dogs on the street, are all talking about it now.'

'Come on woman, tell me what it is,' said Donal. Clearly Niamh had cocked something up, so it was best to be as supportive as possible. He put his arm around her 'A trouble shared is a trouble halved,' he said in a warm and comforting voice.

'So then, Donal my sweet, tell me how long you've been a smack head? All the T.V, radio and newspaper people are desperate to know, following your confession to that American interviewer at the airport.'

Donal looked at her askance, his mouth moved but no words came out. 'I'm a what?' he eventually said in a high-pitched strangled tone. 'Jesus, Mary and Joseph, I'll ... I'll ...'

'You'll do what? Mother of God Donal, I leave you for five minutes on your own and look what happens.'

The intercom on Donal's desk buzzed, looking bewildered Donal pressed the button. 'What is it Máire?'

'Eoghan Dempsey is here to see you, your two o'clock appointment.'

'O.K. send him in.'

'Should I go or stay?' asked Niamh

'Better go, I'll let you know anything relevant later. Get this nonsense with the Americans sorted out; I don't need hallucinogenic drugs.'

'Certainly don't,' muttered Niamh as she headed for the door. 'You're bad enough as it is.'

Eoghan was ushered in, bowing as soon as he saw Donal. 'An Taoiseach, yet again an honour and a privilege to meet you again.'

'The honour and privilege is all mine, take a seat and tell me how things went.'

Eoghan sat down and suddenly noticed the two small-framed photographs on Donal's desk. 'May I Taioseach?' asked Eoghan as he picked one up and gazed lovingly at it. 'Tis Bertie himself is it not? A grand man much maligned and misunderstood. Does he and the other felleh,' he said nodding at the photograph of Biffo 'give you inspiration when deciding on matters of state An Taoiseach?'

'No, I have the pair of them there whenever I feel nostalgic or have a hankering for the old days.' Donal noticed Eoghan's twitch was back.

'I met Bertie and Biffo once you know, but Bertie wouldn't remember, terrible bad at recalling things he was.' Eoghan suddenly shifted in his seat and looked uncomfortable

'Sure haven't you yourself put the Bertie and Biffo era in the shade, dazzled we all are by your...'

Donal cut him short, he wasn't in the mood for fawning, pass the sick bucket adulation after Niamh's news.

'Down to business, start from the beginning.' Donal listened intently as Eoghan recounted his tale of visiting the sídhe, showing no emotion when he described his encounter with Gráinne. So, thought Donal to himself, the mystery woman in the toilet wasn't a stripper gram. Ruairí was clearly trying to play dirty; well two could play at that game! Eoghan concluded and looked at him expectantly

'Agus anois An Taoiseach?'

'Let's just wait for Ruairí to make the next move. It's Friday afternoon, nearly three o'clock and we can pick things up on Monday.'

There was an insistent knock on his office door and Máire poked her head around it.

'Sorry to interrupt, but your two protection officers are here, desperate to speak to you. They wouldn't take no for an answer.'

Donal rose towards Eoghan, 'I'll be in touch. On behalf of the nation I thank you, Ireland is forever in your debt. When the history of our times comes to be written, the name Eoghan Dempsey will be inscribed at the top of the roll of honour.'

Eoghan responded well to the flattery and rose to meet Donal's outstretched hand with his own, choked with emotion he could hardly speak, 'Mr De Valera tis but nothing,' he replied before turning on his heel.

Why on earth does he call me De Valera thought Donal to himself?

Eoghan was doing a vital job but was clearly a few hay bales short of a full thatch.

'Thanks Máire, show them in please.' Frank and Phil entered the office carrying a small box and a manila folder.

'An Taoiseach we have the C.C.T.V. analyses. Frank produced the mini disk from the box and motioned towards the computer on the desk. 'May we?' he asked, Donal nodded as the recording was loaded. Phil opened the folder, producing a sheet of paper which he pushed in front of Donal.

'This is the technical stuff, I don't understand a word of it.' Donal scanned the sheet; it was full of graphs and meaningless jargon. 'O.K Phil, you talk me through it.'

'Well the gist of it An Taoiseach is this, strictly speaking, the woman on the film doesn't exist.' The disc was playing and Frank paused it at the point where Gráinne approached Donal. 'Now do you see here where she moves towards you, no shadow?'

Donal leaned forward towards the screen,

'What do you mean no shadow?'

'See those lights on the wall just to her left?'

'What about them?'

'There should be a shadow going over to the right, you have one but she doesn't.'

'I see,' said Donal pensively leaning back in his chair.

'There's more. A spectral analysis and other bits of jiggery pokery has produced nothing of substance. In other words science says she isn't real and isn't there. The guys at the Technical Bureau have tried everything to verify it, ran numerous checks on their equipment in case of any malfunction, taken the recording apart, metaphorically speaking, but zilch. So even though we can see her, she isn't there at all it's a total mystery. Watch the rest of it and you'll see what I mean about no shadows at all.'

They all watched in silence. Good job there's no sound thought Donal to himself. 'So that's that then.'

'Not quite Taoiseach. We got into Bah Bar's. Bad news. No sign of the owner but we did have a look at his hard drive. Phil paused and looked at Donal with a serious expression. 'He has a backup recording file so there may be another copy of this floating around. We had his equipment taken away for analysis. If the recording isn't kosher, maybe there's a ghost in the machine.' Phil produced another sheet from the manila folder

'Not more technical jargon,' said Donal slightly exasperated.

'No it's a transcript of the conversation you and Gráinne had,' the two policemen sniggered and glanced at each other.

'But there's no sound, so how can there be a transcript?' said Donal mystified.

'Lip reading.'

'What?'

'Lip reading, Taoiseach. There's a guy in the Garda Technical Bureau who's specially trained; he can even translate sign language if it's in Irish. He's a genius; he could even tell us she has a Sligo accent.'

Donal pondered these pieces of information then looked at them both with a steely expression. 'So, if she doesn't exist, the conversation never happened, did it boys?' The last three words were enunciated slowly and deliberately as Donal looked slowly from one officer to the other. 'Do you get my drift?'

'What do you mean Taoiseach?'

'Well the PSNI are looking for keen, enthusiastic members of a Garda Síochána willing to share their expertise in community policing with them. They have vacancies down the Shankill Road for liaison officers. In the spirit of good relations and to enhance cross border cooperation I think we should do our best, don't you?'

'But we don't know anything about community policing, and we're not going anywhere near them psychos,' said Phil in a tense voice.

'That is no way to talk about the good people of the Shankill; anyway we have plenty of home grown psychos. I'm sure the Garda Commissioner would have no problem fixing you two up with a familiarisation posting, Finglas is particularly nice at this time of year.'

'What makes you think the psychos we're talking about live down the Shankill?' Frank looked over at Phil, 'Do you remember that cross border sports tournament, we were both at Templemore at the time?'

'What's that got to do with it?' asked Donal

'Well Taoiseach, it was like this. We were training to be Guards and volunteered to play in the team against the P.S.N.I. It was afterwards in the bar that things got out of hand. Our P.S.N.I. friends were swilling Bushmills like there was no tomorrow, then on the telly came that old ad for the mobile phone company, the future's bright the future's orange. Our coach mad Mick from Cork got the wrong end of it all together and thought the northern cops were getting nostalgic, one thing lead to another and then the fight started. The barman shouted he'd get the police if it didn't calm down. One of their guys was totally out of it and informed the bar man he was a cop, as he head butted him. It then degenerated into something like Custer's last stand. When the ambulances arrived mad Mick was the last man standing. He then tried to take on the paramedics as he thought their flashing lights, being orange, were just provocation. Needless to say it was all hushed up and there wasn't a rematch, but them guys north of the border have long memories. Do you know what time it is in Northern Ireland now Taoiseach?'

Donal looked puzzled, 'It's 16.90' said Frank

'What was the score anyway?' asked Donal

'Eight broken legs, four fractures, a few cases of concussion, bruised ribs and about 9,000 euro of damage.'

'No, what was the score in the match?'

'That was a draw Taioseach.'

'But you have to try and appreciate, even try to understand, the crowd north of the border are different from us,' said Donal sweetly.

'You know the difference between them and an open yoghurt pot, Taoiseach?' Donal shook his head. 'Given time a yoghurt will develop a culture.'

'Anyway, back to the matter in hand. A Belfast secondment can be put on the long finger for now. I want you to find out from uniform what the staff working at that place last night think they saw and heard. I want the guy who owns that place found and I want the original D.V.D.

These stay here with me,' said Donal patting the transcript and disc in front of him. 'Was there any sign of the book?' asked Donal.

'No there wasn't,' replied Frank. 'What exactly are we looking for?'

'It's easy enough to spot, there's a picture of Hitler on the front.'

'Right...' said Frank and Phil in unison, their tone was measured.

'A History book is it?'

'Sort of, it's Mein Kampf.' The two Guards looked at him blankly. 'You know, the book Hitler wrote himself.' Still no sign of recognition. 'The one where he details his political beliefs, it was his blue print for government,' added Donal helpfully.

'O.K... so it's in German then?'

'No it's in Irish.' Frank and Phil had made jokes between themselves about Donal's idiosyncrasies, one of which was describing himself, as one of the last true socialist in Dáil Éireann, what was now clear was that he meant National Socialist, they had totally underestimated him. They retreated towards the office door looking pensive. At long last Donal had some time to himself. Opening his desk draw he produced four sheets of scribbled jottings and began to read them, making additional notes and crossing some things out. He was so engrossed that he never noticed the knock on the door and Niamh's entrance.

'What are you reading?' was the first clue he had that

she had come in.

He jumped, 'Jamie Mack, I never heard you come in, this is nothing,' he replied as she snatched a couple of pages out of his hand.

'Nothing is it, we'll see about that.' She perused the notes. 'And this is...?'

'Well I thought about your suggestion when we were on holiday, and here it is started.'

Niamh's mind raced, she had made so many suggestions, which one was this? 'Remind me.'

'Carrier Pigeons on the Eastern Front 1941-1945,' Donal indicated the remaining two sheets he had. 'You know, the book you said I should write.'

'I never told you to write a book about carrier pigeons on the eastern front,' she replied sharply. 'I suggested one on Ruairí and those other weirdoes.'

'Yeh I know you did, but you said I should write a book. Do you know how many pigeons got the Iron Cross in the second world war?'

'No, but I bet you do.'

'One hundred and ninety three, most of those were posthumous. One of them was shot down with broken wings, swam the river Vistula under shellfire, climbed the river bank, walked the remaining 20km, despite hypothermia and exhaustion and still delivered her message.' With a tone reminiscent of a proud parent he added, 'Hitler himself is believed to have decorated her.'

Niamh groaned inwardly. 'So you're going ahead with

this are you?' she asked

'Yeh, fascinating stuff isn't. So what's the news then Niamh?'

'Would you like the bad news first or the really bad news?' Niamh took a deep breath. 'O.K. well the first bit is that our Yank friend is in hospital as are two members of his security team and a Garda.'

'So?'

'Well he found his photo opportunity, a suitably ruined cottage that would fit the bill for the ancestral home. Unbeknown to him the cottage was not uninhabited, the occupants took exception to being disturbed and attacked him, and they had to be tazered.'

'I see, so the other people got injured during the arrests?'

'Not exactly, no,' said Niamh in measured tone. 'That was due to the mini riot on the drive way into the hospital. The donkeys in the cottage were the problem.'

'What donkeys?' A horrible thought went through Donal's mind. 'You don't mean they tazered donkeys?' said Donal incredulously.

'They were the cottage inhabitants, they had to do something, the donkeys were going mad biting and kicking Chumani, then the incapacitated ones fell on him,' replied Niamh.

'Shaggin donkeys.'

'They may well have been Donal; it would explain why they were so upset being disturbed.'

'Where do the other fellehs fit into this?' asked Donal

'When they got him to hospital the Animals Have Feelings Too Action Group were there, waving home-made placards and shouting howdya like your ass stunned and Garda brutality to animals. Everyone was on edge and jittery, one thing led to another and then the riot began.'

'So the really bad news is that all this was also witnessed by the media?'

'Oh they saw it alright, even recorded it.'

A stricken look came over Donal's face, 'Jesus Niamh, don't tell me the Yank's dead!'

'Ah no, nothing so dramatic. The really bad news is that we now suspect there's a copy of that recording of you and that woman in the toilet circulating Poland.'

'So outside our jurisdiction.'

'That one is, we managed to trace back to Cracow the extract that's appeared on You Tube.'

'It's appeared on what!'

'There will have to be a statement to the T.V. radio and papers. The Media Relations Unit have been inundated with requests for interviews; it's a mad house down there,' said Niamh in an assured voice.

'So what do you want me to say?' asked Donal.

Niamh thought of the scene, Donal in front of a media circus that could smell blood, she shuddered. 'I'll handle it; you just keep out of the limelight until things become clearer. One thing you can do is to phone everyone else who was at that party and tell them to say nothing until I speak to them.'

'Oh, by the way Niamh, I have some good news as well. That woman in the C.C.T.V. footage doesn't exist, she's part of Ruairí's box of dirty tricks!'

Niamh looked at him dumbstruck, 'That's alright then, I'll just tell the media boys that shall I?'

The sound of a car horn brought Mick back to reality. He picked himself up from the bank where he had apparently fallen asleep; strange he thought, don't remember lying down. The horn sounded again, this time for longer and with a sense of urgency. Scrambling up the slope of the Black Pig's Dyke, he peered through the trees towards the roadway, and then his mobile rang. 'Are you O.K.?' asked a disembodied Clare.

'Yeh, yeh, just fell asleep, I had the weirdest dream.'

'It wasn't about tunnels and snakes was it? I know your mind, a total sewer. Get your stuff and we'll go.'

Mick began gathering his bits and pieces and over the course of three trips back and forth, managed to get everything down to where Clare was ready and waiting. He eased himself into the front of the car and sat back, luxuriating in the comfort of a soft and welcoming seat. 'So how was Cavan?' he asked as they pulled away, 'Dunnes having to restock now are they?'

Clare shot him a withering look, 'Sarcasm is the lowest form of wit. Mr McCarthy.'

'But the highest form of intellect, Ms Comiskey. Where

are you taking us now?'

'Well, rather than just turn around I thought we could explore a bit. The Lough has to have an eastern side, so I thought we'd do a circuit and go back a different way. What was this dream then, or is it so disgusting you can't tell me?'

'It was surreal, I was working away and suddenly there was this little guy, sat on the bank in front of me. He was dressed in a dinner suit and for a moment just looked at me, then he spoke. 'You're in better shape than the last couple of times I saw ye, falling down drunk on poitín and then being arrested by the Guards.'

'Who on earth are you?' I asked,

'Who on earth is right boy?'

Then this little guy looked around him and said,

'So, we trade this for Ben Bulben do we? If Brady delivers we won't be in this place for long.'

'It was so vivid Clare, then he vanished and I heard the car horn.'

'Mmm,' was all he got by way of reply. The road seemed never ending, but they finally came to a junction. Diagonally to their left was a Post Office, a section of the Black Pig's Dyke and Lough just visible behind it, no sign of any other houses or any habitation, just this sole solitary building. 'Right, left or just straight ahead?' enquired Clare.

Mick shrugged, it didn't make any difference really if they were exploring. They chose left and skirted the Lough as they headed back to Duncarrick, if the truth be told there wasn't much to see, but it made a change. They entered the village from a different angle, this time Mrs Thom's was on the left, with the rest of the village ahead of them.

'What do we do about the newspaper guy?' asked Mick.

'Don't you worry about him, he isn't going to bother either of us after last night.'

'I'm going to meet Father Antheney later on, he's the priest on supply and was a curate in Wykeford some years ago, he wants to catch up on what the latest is, you can join us if you like.'

Clare wrinkled her nose, 'Which parish was he in? I've never heard of him.'

'What are you going to do now?' asked Mick

'I think I might just drive around some more and see what else there is.'

'Have you finished what you came here to do Mick, or do you have to stay until next week?'

'No I think the fieldwork side has probably been done, so we can take the rocky road to Dublin in the morning. I'll see you later then Clare,' Mick stood outside Mrs Thom's and waved Clare off, then fishing his key out of his pocket opened the door.

There was no sign of Mrs Thom, but she had told him to make himself at home and to get a drink and biscuits any time he wanted. He wandered into the kitchen and boiled the kettle to make himself a pot of strong tea; just as he was sitting down he heard a key in the door. Good timing, he thought to himself. Mrs Thom strolled into the kitchen with two shopping bags.

'Ah there you are Mick, the man in much demand. I have two messages for you. I wrote one of them down so I wouldn't forget it' She produced a crumpled piece of paper and handed it to him. Father Antheney, 5.15. Will call for you.

'What's he like Mrs Thom?'

'Who Mick?'

'Father Antheney.'

'I don't know really. Father Antheney is here on supply whilst the other felleh is away on holiday. Grand sermon he preached on the Assumption, we could do with more like that. The other felleh's all for guitars and hob knobbing with…' Her voice trailed off, best to stop now, for all she knew Mick could be in to trendy guitar singing ecumenical Catholicism. 'There was someone else after you today as well; he was very excitable, red in the face, well dressed and wearing glasses. He left this for you.'

Mick opened the large envelope; inside were copies of the photographs that Martin Adams had shown to both Niamh and Clare. On the back of one of them was the ominous message, I'm onto you. There was also a circular diagram made up of Mick's name, Niamh Comiskey, Donal Brady and Clare Comiskey, all joined by arrows. Mick thought quickly, 'I have to go to Dublin Mrs Thom; I think I and my friend will have to set back this evening.' Mrs Thom looked at him quizzically, 'It's err…it's a wee bit complicated to explain,' he mumbled unconvincingly. 'My producer is coming over from England, things to discuss about the programme, would you excuse me whilst I make a quick phone call.'

Mrs Thom diplomatically vanished upstairs as Mick fumbled for his mobile, fortunately for him Clare was parked when he rang. 'Get back here pronto, we have to do a runner.'

Clare could hear the panic in his voice. 'Now calm down and tell me what's going on.' On hearing of the photos and cryptic message, she tended to agree that a strategic withdrawal was perhaps best. 'How do we get out without alerting that bollocks from the paper?' she asked.

'Simple, you give me your room key when you come back, park around the corner and I'll pack up your stuff. I grab my bag and away we go.'

'You have to pay them first.'

'O.K. so I pay them and off we go. I've made my excuses to Mrs Thom already. See you soon.' Within the hour they were speeding towards Longford, and were N4/M4 bound.

Mrs Thom had settled herself down with a cup of coffee and the Cavan Celt, she looked at the headline, County Manager lashes out at bonking dogs in Killashandra,,a knock on the door interrupted her. Folding the paper she sighed, never a moment's peace she thought to herself.

On the doorstep stood Father Antheney. ' Come in

Father, it's a pleasure to see you.'

'No thanks it's alright. Is Mick McCarthy here?'

'He had to leave in a hurry Father, something to do with his T.V. company and meeting in Dublin.'

'Did he now, when was this?'

'Oh about an hour ago'. Father Antheney seemed a little agitated at the news.

'Was it important Father.'

'No it can wait.'

'Whilst you're here, could I ask you to say a Mass for a special intention. Just wait there until I write it down for you and get you my Mass offering.' He nodded. 'Be back in a minute,' added Mrs Thom.

Father Antheney was joined on the doorstep by Martin Adams who nodded and smiled at him, 'Afternoon Padre.' Mrs Thom returned with a slip of paper and a twenty euro note, passing them both to the priest. Martin Adams put two and two together and came up with five. He opened his wallet and produced a hundred euro note. 'There you are Padre, always willing to support a good cause.'

Father Antheney looked at him annoyed, 'What the feck is this?'

Martin Adams reopened his wallet, misinterpreting the tone of irritation, 'Whoops, sorry Padre, there you are, is that better?' he said, fishing out two more hundred euro notes.

Father Antheney gave him a sideways look, he hated being called Padre but as this fecker had given him money he'd overlook it. Father Antheney pocketed the three hundred euro, headed to his car and drove off.

'What was he collecting for anyway?' asked Martin Adams.

'Collecting? He wasn't collecting for anything, he came to see Mick McCarthy and I gave him a Mass offering.' Mrs Thom looked at Martin as if he wasn't right in the head. 'What can I do for you?' she asked.

'If Mick McCarthy's gone, when was this?'

Don't you start thought Mrs Thom. 'He got a message, the one you delivered about that meeting in Dublin.'

'I know,' said Martin thinking on his feet, 'the company sent me down to pick him up, has he been gone long?'

'No, just over an hour.'

'Did he say where the meeting was?'

'I thought you'd know that,' replied Mrs Thom. 'Especially if you were taking him to it.'

'Ah yes, but we base ourselves at a hotel, and it just depends where our guys from England have booked themselves in.'

'No he didn't say which hotel. Does his girlfriend work for the company as well? She took off with him?' asked Mrs Thom.

'Oh yes, they're both in this together,' concluded Martin as he turned and headed away. So the birds had flown the coop, what to do next was the big question. If there was nothing to hide, the two of them would hardly have made such a hasty exit; this story was definitely developing into a scoop. However, if they thought they had got clean away they were sadly mistaken. Martin knew the one person who could help track down the fugitives, Teach agus Talamh departmental records would contain Mick's home address in Dublin. Time to ring Brian Kelly again.

Father Peter Antheney pondered his next move. Dublin was a big city, and Mick McCarthy could literally be anywhere in it; what he needed was assistance to find him and he knew just the person for the job.

Sergeant O'Connor heard the outside door open and looked up from the Lotto slip he was completing. 'Good evening Father, can I help you?'

'Is officer Seamus Murphy available?' asked Father Tony, lighting up a cigarette.

'Have you come to hear his confession?' asked the sergeant jocularly. 'Jesus Father, you'll need a couple of days and a strong stomach if that's why you're here.'

Father Antheney had O'Connor sized up. 'I'm his uncle ye big bollix, now get him out here.'

The sergeant jumped to attention, taken aback by the tone of authoritative belligerence, turning his head sideways he bellowed, 'Seamus get out here, you have a visitor.'

A dishevelled and bemused looking officer Murphy appeared 'Uncle Tony, what are you doing here?'

'Police business sonny. I need you and your computer to help track someone down, don't give me that look, now tap that into the keyboard,' said the Priest pushing over a piece of paper with Mick's name and Dublin written on it. 'Find out where he lives and whilst you're at it I want a print out of facts on some place called Wykeford in England.' The two policemen reacted as if they had simultaneously been given an electric shock, surely not the same Mick McCarthy?

'See,' said officer Seamus Murphy to his sergeant, 'I told you he was up to no good, even the Church is after him now.'

In a whispered aside Murphy asked his uncle, 'Does he know the Archbishop of Santiago?'

'No he doesn't and how the hell do you two feckers know of Mick McCarthy anyway?'

'It's a long story Father,' replied the sergeant. 'You do know he has friends in high places,' he said, raising his eyes towards the ceiling.

'Are you trying to tell me he has some kind of hot line to God you gobshite?' Father Antheney unnerved the sergeant; he had never encountered a cigarette smoking foul-mouthed teddy boy in a dog collar.

'No Father. I mean An Taoiseach, himself Donal Brady. We had reason to interview this Mick McCarthy and then had to release him due to the personal intervention of Donal Brady, so be aware that there's more to him than first appears.'

Father Antheney was well aware there was more to Mick McCarthy than met the eye, but was not aware of his cosy relationship with the corridors of power.

'Here it is Uncle Tony, his address and place of work and there's all this from Wikipedia about Wykeford.'

Father Antheney scanned the address details.

'Right then Seamus, now get me the names and addresses of all the Catholic churches in Lucan, and find out what deanery Lucan's in.'

The sergeant looked up from his Lotto slip, 'Is there a problem?' Father Antheney asked him in a belligerent and very challenging tone.

'No, no, not at all,' replied sergeant O'Connor.

Officer Murphy returned with more sheets of paper. 'You're a good garsún Seamus, thanks a million.' Father Antheney said by way of thanks.

Sergeant O'Connor looked relieved as the Priest left, 'Have you any more like him in your family?' he asked Murphy.

'No, the rest are just cantankerous,' replied Murphy.

Out in his car Father Antheney perused his background notes on Wykeford and Lucan, a stratagem had been brewing in his mind. He would pay Mick McCarthy a visit, so needed to be prepared. It would appear odd to say the least, to just turn up on Mick McCarthy's doorstep, so he had to have a reason to be there. He had decided on the plan where he would pretend to be on supply in Lucan, got lost trying to find the church and by pure chance picked Mick McCarthy's house for help. It was a feasible scenario, even if stretching things a bit, but not totally unbelievable, time to get something to eat and then set off for Dublin.

Mick turned off the N4 at Lucan and onto the Celbridge Road. 'Soon be there,' he said to Clare. Driving on further, they then took a right into a non-descript looking street and pulled up outside a neatly kept house. Mick led the way in and they both dumped their belongings in the hallway. 'Cup of tea?' asked Mick.

Clare nodded and walked into the front room, switched the T.V. and settled down on the settee. After about ten minutes Mick joined her. The adverts were on and Clare turned to Mick, 'Have you noticed how these people advertising soft furniture can't afford shoes?'

'How do you work that one out?'

'Well just look at them, they're all barefoot, not a sock, slipper or shoe between the four of them.'

Mick was tempted to say something but thought better of it. 'I'll just check the phone, see if I have any messages,' he said. The expression on Mick's face was hard to describe, it showed a variety of emotion ranging from amazement to disbelief and dread.

'Good news then is it?' asked Clare as he put the phone down.

'You won't believe it, really you won't. Lech is due to arrive here in about half an hour. It seems that the Western European Ukrainian Church are holding some shin dig in Dublin this weekend, somehow Lech has got himself invited and he's paying us a visit.'

'You don't seem too enamoured and wasn't he taking a chance you'd be here?'

'Well he probably assumes I'd be home from work by now, as for being enamoured, let's just say I know Lech far better than you do Clare.'

There was a loud knock at the door, 'Jesus, he can't be here that quick,' said Clare in a surprised voice.

Mick went out to the hallway and opened the door, not only was it Lech, he also had someone else with him.

'Michael, delighted to see you, how's the work in the parish going?' Lech indicated at his companion. 'This is Stan, short for Stanislavski, you might have seen him at the Ukrainian club?' The two visitors walked past Mick and into the front room. Mick had indeed met him. Stan was married to a woman from Carlow and thanks to her had an amazingly wide and diverse repertoire of Irish songs. On one famous occasion both he and Mick had sung Come out Ye Black and Tans whilst both drunk, this had been to the total bafflement of the others in the Ukrainian club bar. Did Stan have a drink problem? No, drink was no problem at all, put it in front of him and it would vanish in seconds.

'We have a drink Father, to celebrate safe arrival in your homeland,' announced Stan to Mick, producing a litre bottle of Tullamore Dew. Stan hadn't noticed Clare.

'Why's he calling you Father?' she asked Mick out the corner of her mouth. Suddenly Stan spotted her.

'You too Sister, have drink to welcome Stanislavski to Ireland.'

'Great, he thinks I'm a nun,' she muttered. 'Come on Father, let's get our visitors some glasses,' she said propelling Mick into the kitchen. 'Right then will you tell me what's going on?' she asked having pinned Mick to the wall.

'Well it wasn't my fault,' began Mick. It never is thought Clare. 'The Ukrainian Parish think I'm studying for the Priesthood at Maynooth.'

'Yes? And how did they get that idea?'

'Lech told them. I kind of went along with it and it snow balled from there.'

'Why the hell would Lech want to tell them that?'

'I don't know. I turned up one Saturday night at the Ukrainian club to meet him for a drink. I was told he was in the hall, went over there and found it packed for a wedding anniversary do. These bouncers appeared and so did Lech, he said something to them in Ukrainian, they all beamed at me and that was it, I was in. It wasn't until later I found out what he'd told them. Oh come on Clare, I could hardly have gone around telling all of them he'd made it up.'

'So how long has this been going on?' she asked

'About a year.' Clare looked stunned. Mick took the opportunity to skip around her, grab some glasses and dash into the front room.

'Here you are boys,' announced Mick planting himself next to Stan on the settee and handing him a glass.

'Sláinte Sister, sláinte Father,' announced Stan. Clare noticed that her drink was miniscule by comparison with those of the boys. She took the Tullamore Dew and topped up her glass. Stan was impressed by this and clinked his glass with Clare's by way of approval. She smirked at him, threw her head back and downed her whiskey in one quick gulp. Next it was Stan's turn; if there was to be a drinking competition Mick wasn't going to play.

He turned to Lech 'How come you're over here for the weekend?' he asked.

'There's friction between the different hierarchies in Western Europe and our set up, so we're having a conference to try and see where we go from here. Dublin was chosen as there isn't problem in this country, we get on fine with the Irish Bishops.'

'Where's the conference?'

'It's tomorrow at some R.D.S. place' Mick glanced at Clare who had now upped the stakes; standing on one leg and drinking.

'Why's Stan here?'

'He's the Parish rep, he had the edge in being chosen as his wife is Irish, so it was thought he could relate better to you Paddies. Obviously they got that right,' said Lech watching the unfolding scene between Stan and Clare.

'She's not a nun, is she?' asked Lech

'Is she a nun! How many nuns do you know drink and carry on like that? She's a teacher, you know that much,' retorted Mick.

'Ah yes, but nuns can be teachers as well.'

'My da was a nun when he was young,' said Clare

slightly slurred.

'No he wasn't,' replied Mick exasperated.

'Yes he was, when he was up in court for being drunk and disorderly, the Peace Commissioner asked him his occupation none me da replied.' Clare then shook with laughter at her own joke. Stan had now produced his other purchase from the airport shop, it was a souvenir leprechaun dressed in traditional green garb; he proceeded to dance around the room with it. Mick tried to pretend that neither Clare nor Stan were there and that the grotesque, bizarre, unprecedented and unbelievable scene around him didn't exist.

'So where are you staying?' asked Mick, hoping that both Lech and his other visitor would be soon gone.

'We're booked into a bed and breakfast,' replied Lech, 'I suppose we should soon be making tracks.'

'Oh I would if I were you; the traffic across the city can be desperate,' said Mick enthusiastically. 'I'll get you a taxi if you hand me the phone.'

Stan was now offering the leprechaun to Clare.

'No ish O.K, I'll dance with the other one,' replied Clare pointing towards the table. Ruairí had been surveying the scene with both fascination and a sense of horror until this announcement by Clare. He looked at her alarmed.

'Other one where?' asked Stan staring wildly around the room.

'The one dressed up as a fireman, why's he a fireman?' asked Clare to no one in particular.

Ruairí was concerned now, 'Can you see me?' he asked incredulously.

Clare nodded, 'Me Clare, you..?' she asked in pigeon English.

'I'm Ruairí,' he replied, shocked into replying.

'Mm... nice name. Do you know my cousin and what's his name?'

'How can you see me? asked an agitated Ruairí.

Clare shrugged, 'Dunno really, just can.'

'Who you speak to?' asked Stan.

'Ruairí hish a leprechaun.' Stan was impressed, when he had been on a bender he had seen many things, but this was out of his league. Mick now began to take an interest, he was afraid she'd start taking her clothes off if things degenerated further.

'I've been to Cavan,' Clare informed Ruairí. 'ish full of lakes and bogs and things,' she said dreamily. 'Have you been to Cavan?' she asked Ruairí

'I've seen yer man there footering around, doing Brady's dirty work,' he replied indicating Mick. The doorbell rang.

'Must be the taxi,' said Mick heading for the door, 'That was quick...' his voice trailed off as he stood looking at Father Peter Antheney.

Father Peter stood on the doorstep looking down at a piece of paper and trying to look lost. 'I wonder if you could help me,' he said looking up. From the expression on Mick McCarthy's face he clearly had thrown him off balance. Father Antheney feigned astonishment, 'What are you doing here?' he asked Mick.

'I live here, more to the point what are you doing here?' was the question back.

'I've come to visit an old friend, Father Hughes, at Christ the King here in Lucan. I've finished my fill in at Garryowen.' Father Peter was taking a gamble on this one; he guessed that as Christ the King was fifteen kilometres away, Mick was most likely to go to the nearer St Bridget's, 'I was looking for the church but got lost,' he told Mick as he stepped into the house and they both made their way into the front room. Stan was missing, apparently he'd gone to the toilet and Clare was still talking to her invisible friend.

Mick heard her saying, 'So Donal wants you and the sídhe to move does he, why's that then? Oh no you can't join the party,' she announced to Father Peter, 'You'll scare Ruairí away; his kind doesn't like your kind.' Father Antheney was totally unfazed by the scene of alcohol-fuelled debauchery in front of him, it reminded him of his stint as a holiday chaplain.

'Oh he's gone!' announced Clare. 'And juhst when it was gerrink intrestink.'

Father Peter smiled indulgently at her, clearly she was off her head, 'Who's gone?' he asked her patiently.

'Ruairí the leprechaun. Whoosh!' She waved her arm to emphasise this point. 'Whoosh! Jusht as it was gerring intrestink, he was spilling the beans on wha Donal's up to.'

Stan returned and did a double take when he saw Father Antheney. 'He is Ruairí?' He asked Clare.

She shook her head unsteadily, 'Dunno who he is, who are you anyway?'

'I am Father Peter Antheney and you are..?'

'Clare Comiskey, but...' At this point she put her arm around his neck, gazed into his eyes and breathed alcohol fumes all over him, 'You can call me Clare the bear, not becaush I bare all when I've had a few, no, no, no, that's all lies put about by nashty people trying to put me down, it's becaush I'm cuddly and lovable like a teddy bear.' She then buried her head below his chin.

At this point in the proceedings Mick came in with directions for the church. 'Here you are Father, you're all set now.'

Father Antheney was a little taken aback, 'But I thought we could have our chat about Wykeford, catch up on the news.'

'Sure there's plenty of time for that, I can arrange something later with you, how long are you stopping for anyway?' This obvious flaw in his devious plan was something he had completely overlooked.

'Well I have Mass to say in the morning and anyway I'm here now,' he said with a pleading tone. Mick was being quite insistent; he had enough to contend with as it was.

'Shall I phone them at the parish centre to tell them that you're on the way?'

'I don't want to put you to any trouble.'

'No trouble at all,' replied Mick turning the pages of the phone directory and picking up the phone. Father Antheney was now becoming a little anxious, he removed the draped figure of Clare from around his neck and stood up. 'I suppose you're right, I should be going.'

'See you later so?' said Mick deliberately.

'See you later. This is nice house, have you always lived here?'

'No it's sort of on loan, it belongs to Gabriel McLaughlin, my civil service exchange partner, but he won't be needing it for a while.' Father Antheney made a mental note of the name, he already had the address, so he could get the phone number from directory enquiries. The problem he now faced was what to do next, go back to Garryowen and come back again, or..?

An idea came into Father Antheney's mind, 'I could call in during the afternoon on Sunday.' Mick grunted in agreement. Things were now sorted out, Father Antheney had little choice but head back to Longford.

Now that one visitor was gone, Mick only had two major problems left, Lech and Stan, there was still no sign of the taxi. He rejoined the group in the front room and had hardly sat down when the doorbell rang. Mick cautiously looked out of the window, halleluiah it was the taxi! Stan was at this point telling Clare about his granddad's exploits as a war hero on the eastern front between 1941 – 1945, '... and he love those pigeons Clare, just like he love his own family, how could he eat them?'

'Taxi's here!' announced Mick helping Stan to his feet.

Lech had been silent up to this point, 'Father Antheney seems a nice guy,' he said to Mick.

'He is,' said Mick shepherding his two guests to the door. 'Now be sure to give me a ring before you go back and tell me how it went.' Lech and Stan departed, three problems down, one to go thought Mick. Clare was sitting back in an armchair, a glazed look on her face. There was a half full glass of whiskey on the arm of her chair. Mick picked it up and downed it in one, after what he'd been through he needed it. Mick switched on the T.V. and turned it over to R.T.É. 24/7 for the news, he was just in time to hear the presenters announce 'And we now take you over to Government Buildings where an announcement is imminent.' In front of the entrance to the Government Buildings were banks of T.V. cameras and amongst the melee was the figure of Niamh Comiskey. Just behind Niamh stood three other individuals, probably there to provide a back drop. Niamh produced a sheet of paper and smiled confidently at the cameras. 'I have a prepared statement which will now be conveyed to you.'

'Hey Clare,' said Mick excitedly. 'Have you seen this?' but Clare was well away snoring quietly. Niamh's well-modulated and dulcet tones spoke to him.

'During the course of a private party to mark the occasion of the birthday of An Taoiseach Donal Brady, a serious security breach occurred. A woman who was not invited, nor had any reason to be there, entered the premises unseen and undetected. On being challenged, An Taioseach acted coolly and calmly, chatting to the woman who was clearly not of a sound mind, in order to defuse a potentially serious situation. The circumstances of the security breach are being actively pursued, as is the identity of the unknown woman.

It is believed there may have been collusion, which facilitated the intrusion; a number of lines of enquiry are being actively pursued by the Gardaí. Any malicious intent at damaging the position and character of An Taoiseach will be dealt with using the full rigour of the law.' Cameras flashed as she spoke; a forest of microphones thrust towards her mouth, Niamh glanced up from her brief and then continued. 'Furthermore, scurrilous allegations that An Taoiseach has at any time partaken of any illicit substances are totally without foundation. Strenuous efforts are underway to rectify the distortion of comments, which have been taken and used totally out of context. The T.V. company concerned is cooperating fully in order to resolve the matter. Should such allegations be repeated, The Department of the Taoiseach will have no option but recourse to legal action.' She folded the paper and turned to re-enter Government Buildings, a gaggle of voices shouted questions at her back.

'Who is she?... Will you give us her name?'

Suddenly in the middle of the shouted melee Niamh heard, 'Tell us about Mein Kampf.' The voice and question struck a chord that made her hesitate by the revolving door and she looked back, but where had it come from?

Martin Adams was delighted when he saw the disconcerted look on her face; it reminded him of the expression he'd seen at their meeting in Dunne's restaurant. Martin had returned to Dublin following Mick McCarthy's departure, little point in spending the weekend in Cavan if the horse had bolted the stable. Martin hadn't got Mick's address from Brian Kelly, despite his best efforts and veiled threats. It seemed Brian simply didn't have access to that information without raising suspicion. On the drive back Martin had been wondering how to explain that a week in Cavan at the paper's expense had been worth it; all he had was circumstantial evidence. If only he'd got hold of McCarthy and his girlfriend! Martin arrived back at the office to find security in reception trying to talk a pretty young woman into leaving.

'If you don't go I'll have to phone the Guards, you wouldn't want that now would you?' She was tightly clutching a book on the front of which was a photo of Adolf Hitler.

'He's a closet Nazi, something has to be done about him, why else would he have this for a birthday present?' She spoke with a Dublin accent, but there were hints of places further east in her intonation.

Martin was intrigued; she was clearly determined and showed little sign of wide-eyed fanaticism the unhinged normally displayed. 'Who's a Nazi, Adolf Hitler is it?' he asked attempting to take the book from her hand. She clutched it more tightly.

'No I don't mean Hitler, this thing here,' she said waving the book at Martin, 'is a birthday present for our glorious leader, Fuhrer of the nation Donal Brady!' The security personnel looked at Martin and mouthed header, but Martin wasn't convinced.

'How do you know it's a birthday present for Donal Brady?'

'Because I was there at the birthday party the night his... his... floozy gave it to him.' Martin Adams had hit the mother load; this woman in front of him could be his way to fame and fortune. The possibility of two press coups now loomed, Roman Ireland the untold story and An Taoiseach's birthday party exposed.

'I'm Martin Adams and you are?'

'Danka, Danka Wawensa. I work at Bah Bars where the party was.'

'Do you now?' he said with an intake of breath, he paused and hesitantly asked, 'What about the C.C.T.V. footage?'

'It's disgusting, him, and her in that toilet.' Martin's could hardly contain himself; the big time beckoned and no mistake.

'So did you see them at it Danka?'

'No but I saw the entire thing on the security film.'

'Follow me and we'll discuss things further in my office.'

Niamh made her way back up to Donal, 'Well?' she asked as she entered his office.

'Well what?' he replied

'Did you watch it?'

'Of course, that was fine.'

'It'll hold them off for a while. The stuff about you and craic is no problem, every man and his dog in this country knows what you meant by that. The foreign media are the ones we'll have problems with, they'll never get the subtleties of craic. Next on the agenda will be the staff from Bah Bars for interviews and statements. Did you get through to the other people who were at the party?' Niamh asked.

'Sure did, fully briefed that they know nothing,' he replied, feeling pleased with himself.

'But none of them know anything to start with, even I didn't know about that woman, or whatever she was. So what exactly do they know nothing at all about?' asked Niamh

'Everything, apart from who Gráinne really is,' said Donal smugly.

'You didn't tell them what it was they knew nothing at all about did you?'

'Well....'

'You did didn't you!'

'I can't have wild rumours flying around, careless talk just produces more problems.' Niamh fumed, clearly he thought he had been helpful, God knows what version of events they had all got.

'Who else knows about my birthday present to you?' she asked.

'Just the people at the party.'

'One of the media crowd down there knows something about it, any ideas how that happened?' Donal shrugged, as far as he knew it was still on the missing list.

'Someone's talked, or there are things going on we have no knowledge about, better see if our brave boys and girls in the Gardaí can enlighten us.' Niamh picked up the phone and dialled; Donal had produced the drafts of his book and was bent over them scribbling.

He heard her saying, 'So you've tracked down all of them apart from this Danka woman... she's not at home and you don't know where she is? Is it possible she's left the country?... well find out.' With that she slammed down the phone. She looked at Donal, absolutely no sign at all that he was aware of the gravity of the situation, just sitting there scribbling away at his book.

'Do you have the slightest idea how serious all of this is, or are those feckin pigeons the top priority?'

Donal put down his sheets of paper slowly and deliberately. 'Niamh, if I let everything get to me then I would hardly be in this job to start with. Don't think that because I'm not running around like a headless chicken I'm not aware of the gravity of the situation.' With that he looked at the clock, 'Jesus is that the time, we should hit the road. Shall we get a Chinese when we get back?'

'Back where?'

'Can I come to your place Niamh?' She couldn't say no.

'Yes of course, we won't let them get us down.'

Donal phoned for a car and gathered up his papers, as he did so he told her, 'I just discovered something amazing, a guy called Stanislavski in the 1st Ukrainian Front nearly got shot in 1941 for betraying the motherland, being a fascist agent and for Trotskyite sabotage, all because he barbecued his unit's carrier pigeons. A stray German shell hit the building where the court martial was being held and killed everyone inside, except Stanislavski who was blown out through the windows, miraculously surviving. No witnesses, no documentation and so no case, he got away with it.' Niamh looked at him tenderly and touched him lightly on the arm, a cheeky smile on her face

'I just love you to bits,' she said as if speaking to a small boy, closing the office door behind them.

In the alcove by the fireplace Ted and Harold had realised they could hardly hear or see anything that went on; so much for Ruairí's brilliant plan. Ted looked cautiously around him, 'O.K. Harold off we go then, to work.'

'What did paddy fairy number one say this thing looks like?'

'Dunno mate, but he reckons this Donut O'Grady bloke will have it hidden somewhere in this office. If we find this, then Ruairí owes us big time.'

On The One Road

'Jesus,' said Donal with feeling as he opened the living room curtains and looked out onto the road below him. The place was crawling with camera crews and he could see at least three white vans with satellite dishes. The radio and T.V. had been bad enough yesterday, today looked like it could only be worse. 'Do you think these fellehs,' asked Donal indicating the mob below him, 'intend staying there all of day?'

'Probably.' Niamh replied. 'It's their job Donal, you can hardly blame them for that. After all they don't know where you went to ground and they have to try and cover all the bases.'

'We have to go out some time, I'm not spending all of Sunday marooned in here,' said Donal exasperated.

'And who said they wanted to come here in the first place? Look, if you go out there they'll eat you alive. Just be thankful they don't know you're here, I'm thinking of going out in about ten minutes to give them something to get excited about. Turn the T.V. on Donal.' With great reluctance he reached for the remote control.

'I've had enough of being pulled to pieces by those gobshites, these so called political commentators, so called experts. What do they know, nothing! Anyway, knowing I have the backing of the party and Cabinet are all that count.'

'I don't see how you can say that. The Tánaiste and the

other cabinet minister the media got their hands on, were all either evasive or non-committal when asked if they'd run against you in a leadership race, hardly counts as backing,' said Niamh settling herself down next to him.

'Ah well, that's why I'm a politician and you're not Niamh, you don't give the media anything they can twist or misquote, considering your job I'm amazed you don't know that.'

Niamh looked at him and raised her eyes to heaven. 'So you telling the Yanks that you were a smack head was intentional then?' Donal scowled and said nothing to that.

'When you went to bed I phoned around the guys to thank them for their loyalty. I know Tom McNulty told me go shag yourself, but it's because he has such a good sense of humour I made him Minister of Justice.' Donal looked at her, a slow smile breaking over his face, he obviously had just had an idea, 'Your 4 X4 is still in the car park below, isn't it?'

Niamh replied in measured tone, 'It is,' she said, wondering what brilliant idea had just come to mind.

'Well if I get in the back and you cover me over we could make our escape.'

'Escape to where exactly?'

'How about going to Newgrange?'

Niamh looked pensive; she wasn't too sure about that proposal. 'Is it wise going out?' she asked.

'Look, it's a nice day and who's going to think of looking for me there?'

'O.K. we'll give it a go, I'm not staying in here all day with you, I'll just go crazy. Anyway, shall I ring the Guards to sort out that crowd on the street?' asked Niamh

'I beat you to it, they should be here any time now,' replied Donal. At that precise moment they heard the approaching sound of police car sirens.

'O.K, time we went. I'll get the Sunday papers on the way.'

They had been driving along the M50 for about forty-five minutes when Niamh suddenly said, 'It's very odd some of the cars overtaking us honk their horns, you don't think there's something wrong do you?'

'Ah no, it's the plain people of Ireland showing they're behind me,' said Donal smugly.

'So how do you work that one out?'

'You know when you went in for petrol and got the Sunday papers?'

'Yes,' said Niamh curtly, guessing that she didn't want to hear what was coming next.

'Well I stuck a sign on the spare wheel at the back, honk if you're backing Donal Brady. Niamh gripped the steering wheel tighter as the driver of the next overtaking car waved his fist and mouthed obscenities as she speeded past.

'Well that is definitely no way to behave,' muttered Niamh.

Donal unfolded the papers and looked at the front pages, he had to admit some of them made had style and were ingenious, Toilet temptress tempts Taoiseach from The Sunday World wasn't bad, but Brady and the basque beauty, from The Sunday Independent beat it. The Sunday Tribune was predictably more sedate than the rest, Donkeys lead to diplomatic disaster in Galway.

'As soon as I can stop I'm taking that thing off the back of the car,' said Niamh in a very determined tone of voice.

'Ah come on now,' replied Donal in coaxing voice.

They had now joined the M1 north and were passing through Lissenhall. Donal gazed at the countryside flashing past, over to his right lay Malahide and the expanse of the Irish sea. Within another half an hour or so they crossed the river Boyne and were approaching the outskirts of Drogheda. Niamh slowed as they reached the N51 and indicated left, switching on her hazard warning lights, she jumped out and ran around to the back of the car, returning seconds later with Donal's marker pen sign. Niamh thrust the now tattered piece of paper into Donal's lap and without a word set off again. The road twisted and turned, the river Boyne occasionally glimpsed as they travelled towards Donore.

'It'll be much better once the M5 gets built,' said Donal. They continued their journey, heading towards Newgrange.

The car park was reasonably full and Niamh chose a spot as close to the exit as possible, 'So we can make a speedy get away if needed,' she helpfully informed Donal. Turning around she saw he was wearing dark glasses and a lime green flat cap. 'Where the hell did you get them from?' she asked irritably.

'Brought them with me, it's my disguise.' She often wondered how he ever got to the top of the political heap, looking at him now just made her wonder even more.

'Do you want to visit the graves or go around the exhibits first?' she asked.

'Let's go to the passage grave whilst it's still nice, you get the tickets and I'll join the queue for the shuttle bus.' As Donal had guessed there were very few Irish amongst the visitors, mostly Japanese and German tourists with a smattering of Scandinavians. Niamh arrived at the same time as the bus and within ten minutes they got off to survey the majesty that was Brú Na Bóinne.

'I'll just check what time the next tour is,' said Niamh. 'You wait here.' At that moment Donal's mobile rang and he stepped to one side to answer it, when Niamh returned he looked glum.

'I have to go down to Galway tomorrow to visit our traumatised Yank friend and try and smooth things over. I'd better go after that photo call at the Dublin George Formby festival. The guys from the party executive want to see me as well.'

'When are you meeting them?'

'At about five o'c'lock tonight.'

'In any case,' said Niamh, 'the previous tour group are leaving so we may as well join that crowd over there, they look all set to go.' Donal and Niamh moved over to where a knot of people were standing taking photographs of each other, using Newgrange as the back drop. The tour guide appeared on the platform fronting the entrance.

'Good afternoon ladies and gentlemen. I am Liam, your guide for this afternoon.' Donal suddenly noticed Ruairí sitting on the edge of the light box behind the guide; he was gazing at Donal and Niamh with a maddening grin.

'Bienvenue, welcome, fáilte go leir ...' continued Liam.

'You little fecker,' exclaimed a very riled Donal waving his fist. 'I should come up there and wring your neck.' Liam was temporarily thrown off balance by this emotive response, but he remembered his anger management course and ignored it. Niamh grabbed Donal by the arm.

'Behave yourself,' she hissed. Ruairí didn't react; he just studied his fingernails with intense interest.

Liam continued his well-rehearsed speech. 'Newgrange, or Brú na Bóinne, is estimated to be...'

'Don't you ignore me you withering shite, I know you can hear me,' continued Donal.

'Approximately five thousand years old and is a recognised UNESCO World Heritage site.'

'Listen to me bogey brain...' Ruairí's reaction to this was studied indifference. Niamh decided action was needed.

'Stay here a minute will you,' she said to Donal as she made her way up to Liam and whispered something to him. He listened, nodded and glanced at Donal sympathetically. Niamh made her way back to Donal. 'It's all sorted,' she said softly. 'I told him you had Tourette's.'

'The stones on the outside of this passage grave are white quartz, and the semi-circular mound is approximately...'

'Tourette's, I have Tourette's?' shrieked Donal bemused.

Knowing it would add fuel to the fire, she cooed in her most condescending and maddening tone of voice, 'You're doing really well Donal, keep this up and you'll have me convinced.'

'Jesus Christ, I'm doing really well!' shouted Donal in a strangled and exasperated tone. At this stage the other members of the erstwhile tour group were also looking sympathetic.

A wizened American lady turned towards Niamh, 'Honey, my husband is just like him, only it isn't Jesus Christ he talks to, it's Moses, you see we're Jewish.'

When Mick had ventured down stairs on Sunday morning, he had expected to find Clare still dead to the world, to his surprise she was in the kitchen drinking a big mug of tea listening to the radio. 'And what time do you call this?' she enquired in a cheery tone. At first he didn't reply, too taken aback by her being none the worse for wear.

'Clock must have stopped,' was the best he could manage.

'Where are we going today then?' was the next utterance. Mick was lost on this one, he hadn't planned anything,

'I don't know really, did you have anywhere in mind?'

'This looks nice, a bit of culture,' replied Clare, indicating an article about Newgrange in a magazine she was perusing, 'Have you been?'

'Yeah, but that was years ago. It's impressive, older than the Pyramids, but I thought we might just stick around here.'

Clare mused on this proposition for a while, 'Boring! I suppose you could always show me and our two eastern European visitors the sights of Dublin though, the two of them are good craic.' Mick shuddered at the prospect of a drunken pub crawl around the capital; the response was swift and almost instantaneous. 'You'll really like Newgrange,' he said with great enthusiasm, 'it would be a shame to miss it. Sure we can do Dublin some other time.'

'So how big is it then?'

'How big is what?' asked Mick

'Newgrange you idiot.'

'Oh, I don't know really, it's ...' he made a sweeping gesture with his arms.

'Really, as big as that, certainly is impressive! Come on, let's get a move on and go.'

When Clare and Mick got off the shuttle bus at Newgrange they could see the back of Donal and Niamh's tour group ahead of them in the distance, 'What do you think is the matter with him?' said Mick to Clare, catching the odd utterance from Donal giving out to Ruairí. 'Who knows, probably just over excited at being here,' she replied in a bored tone.

'Looks like that tour group and Mr Excitable are going in, we may as well just sit down and enjoy the sunshine for a bit,' said Mick. The view was pretty impressive; the Boyne nestled in the valley below them with the southern bank of the river rising gently ahead of them.

Clare closed her eyes, 'Wake me up when it's our turn, I'm going to have a nap.'

Ruairí made himself scarce as Donal and Niamh made their way up the steps and followed Liam down the nineteen metre long tunnel leading to the middle of the grave. It was cold and dimly lit in the central chamber with little room.

Donal muttered to Niamh about perfidious Ruairí and what he'd like to do with him. 'Now ladies and gentlemen you will see, if you turn around, the light box which is aligned with the rising winter solstice sun.' Donal's mutterings were beginning to annoy Liam. 'On the morning of the winter solstice the rising dawn sun illuminates this chamber for approximately fifteen minutes and the chamber is also illuminated on mornings either side of the winter solstice.'

'I'll murder the little shite, I don't know if he's got any bollocks but he won't have by the time I've finished with him,' was audible to one and all.

Niamh smiled sweetly at their guide and elbowed

Donal. Liam suddenly realised that the homicidal Tourette's tourist was now between him, the rest of the group and the only exit. Time to defuse what was clearly an incendiary situation with some witty banter and levity, 'So you see, this is really a five thousand-year-old Dáil Éireann. It was rarely used, we don't know its exact purpose and light of day rarely shone on proceedings.'

Donal had gone quiet, which was unfortunate, as he had clearly heard this pronouncement by Liam. 'What did you say!! Do you know who I am?' he said outraged.

'No, I don't know who you are, but if you ask your nurse I'm sure she'll tell you,' replied Liam curtly.

'Nurse, nurse, she's not my nurse!'

'Poor dear,' said Niamh. Turning to Liam she said in measured tones, 'It's very sad, if it wasn't for the name and address tags on his clothes we'd have lost him all together the last time we went to Dublin, luckily the Guards found him, he was chatting up the tart with the cart

Liam now looked carefully at Donal, an expression of amazement growing on his face, 'I know who you are, you're...'

'No he isn't,' cut in Niamh, 'it's the light in here, he just looks like him. Anyway, we have to go, I think the excitement is proving too much.' She shoved Donal back down the passageway. 'Jesus I can't take you anywhere can I,' she said when they got outside.

'Don't you blame me.'

'So who do I blame?'

'Well for a start there's...' but Niamh was having none of it and flounced off. Donal followed her down the steps and around the side of the mound.

'So where are you going now you big eejit?' asked Niamh

'I'm dying for a pee, see you in few minutes.' Rather than make things obvious to any curious onlookers, Donal examined the outside of Newgrange with avid devotion as he made his way towards the rear of the mound to find a secluded spot.

'Ah relief at long last' he said to himself when he'd finished.

'You mind where you're pointing that thing, do you want me drowned?' said a familiar voice just in front of him. 'I come in peace, now put that rock down,' said Ruairí as he dodged a badly aimed missile. He produced a piece of white cloth from his pocket and waved it. Donal was now looking round for more ammunition. 'You wouldn't attack someone under the flag of truce now would you?' asked Ruairí plaintively. 'Jamie Mack you're nearly as bad as Diarmid and Peader.'

Donal scowled at him, 'Nearly as bad as who?'

'I just came to say sorry about Gráinne, a nice girl but she just gets carried away sometimes. Anyway, that's all in the past now,' he sounded remorseful and contrite. Donal appeared slightly mollified.

'All in the past! Are you totally insane? Look, the only thing I want to hear from you is when you're moving, or is the deal off?'

'No, no, no. Me and the lads just have one or two things further to discuss and we'll get back to you.' With that Ruairí was gone. Donal made his way round to where Niamh was still waiting for him, 'I just met Ruairí,' he announced airily.

'So was he having a pee too, or don't I want to know?' she asked sarcastically. The tour group they had joined now emerged, making its way down the steps. Liam sidled over to Niamh whispering something in her ear; she smirked, suddenly slapped his face and strode away.

'What on earth did he say?' asked Donal running after her.

'He asked me if I was yer wan in the You Tube video.'

'Right that's it, I'll kill him as well.'

'Just give it a rest will you, you've caused enough trouble as it is,' replied Niamh grabbing Donal by the arm. Liam was now walking up and down with his mobile glued to his ear. 'We'd better get out of here,' said Niamh earnestly. 'There'll soon be more media here than there are flies on horse shit.'

Mick nudged Clare, 'Wakey wakey time.' Clare stretched and slowly sat up, just then Donal and Niamh shot past them.

'Did you see that?' she exclaimed, watching the rapidly retreating figures.

'See what?'

'Those two, it's Donal and Niamh, or their doubles.' Clare watched them desperately bang on the doors of a departing shuttle bus. 'What do you think they're doing here?'

This time it was Mick's turn to sound bored and disinterested, 'Who knows and who cares? Are we going around this thing or not then?'

'Yeh, Yeh, just give me a minute whilst I pop to the loo, it's over there,' she said, pointing at something resembling the Tardis.

'Well don't be long or we'll end up missing this tour as well.' Mick lay on his back watching the clouds scurry across the sky. His contemplation was interrupted by the distant screech of brakes and he looked up to see an estate car with Radio Drogheda emblazoned along its side outside the perimeter fence. Two people emerged from the car, a man and woman, the two of them raced past Mick and up to where Liam was standing. The woman thrust a microphone under Liam's nose and became very animated. Mick ambled over to where the knot of people clustered around the radio people were.

'So you're certain it was An Taoiseach then Liam?' asked the Radio Drogheda woman at the centre of the group.

'Absolutely Dolores, no mistaking that.'

'And you say he was acting strange.'

'I think the events of the last few days must have unhinged him, sure he was mad all together, shouting and roaring and carrying on. He said I was a little fecker, or something like that, and that he'd cut my knackers off.'

Some of the people standing around began to snigger, suddenly a voice shouted, 'He's not all bad.' Dolores looked delighted, marvellous, brilliant, a Donal Brady fan; things could really liven up now! There was obviously someone else at Newgrange who was unhinged thought Dolores to herself. She took a step forward towards the lone voice, 'Tell me Madame, why do you say that?'

'Donal Brady has done more for the economy of Dun Laoghaire in twenty four hours than any of yous could do in a lifetime.'

Dolores looked puzzled, 'But he's not a T.D. for that area.'

'I know that, but thanks to him local businesses have made more money in a day than they usually make in a month. Them fellehs from T.V camped out in the town are high rolling spenders, sure there's bucket loads of cash now. If he carried on every weekend, we could all retire in a month, more power to you boy is all I have to say.'

'And you are..? asked Dolores.

'Maureen Canavan, Chair of the Dun Laoghaire Chamber of Commerce.'

'Right... now moving on. You sir, what do you think of the situation as it now stands?'

'Well how would you like it, splashed all over the internet just because you went into a toilet for a quick shag, and in any case....'

'Ha. Ha, ha…' laughed Dolores manically, rapidly moving the microphone away. She felt a tug and turned around.

'Who iz Donald Baby?' asked the confused Russian tourist at her elbow.

'I think we're going to have to wait a bit for the tour,' said Mick in a resigned tone when Clare came to join him.

Niamh and Donal just managed to exit the car park at Newgrange as the Radio Drogheda car swept past.

'That was a lucky escape,' said Niamh.

'I have to face them sometime Niamh, they all think I have something to hide, that photo call in the morning gives me an opportunity.'

'So you think giving interviews which explain that woman is one of the little people, so technically doesn't exist, and that a leprechaun set you up, will set everything right do you? What about that comatose and traumatised Yank in Galway?'

'I know, I know, well that will be sorted out tomorrow. Anyway I wasn't set up, Ruairí explained it all. She was just a bit keen about my offer to the sídhe and was trying to help them out.'

'I know what offer she had in mind with the clothes she had on, or should I say lack of clothes.' They headed out of the car park and made their way in the direction of Dublin. 'So where do we go from here?' asked Niamh.

'Well I have to be in the party rooms on the fifth floor

in about two hours, so we may as well go to Government buildings.'

Niamh considered the proposal, 'Yeh O.K. I could do with seeing how things are as well, I need to make sure those five handling the media angle are earning their overtime.'

'And how are you Donal?' The three of them drew up chairs opposite him.

'Grand thanks be to God, and yourselves?'

'Can't complain and it never does you any good anyway as no one listens,' said John,

'O.K. gentlemen, what can I do for you?' asked Donal nervously as they opened their attaché cases, from one emerged a laptop, grey manila folders from the others. 'There's a socket over there,' Donal pointed out, 'that's if you need to plug it in.' Michael nodded and extended the cable, the three of them leaned across the table.

'Well now, aren't you the one,' Charlie said softly whilst the other two stared hard at Donal, who felt like he was back at school.

'We assume you've seen this already,' said Michael as he inserted a disc into the laptop, 'but we'd just like to go through it with you, if that's alright?' Clearly Donal had no choice, in any case the Bah Bars footage was hardly damming in itself.

Michael turned the laptop around so they could all see the screen, 'Just wait a minute there until I adjust the volume.' Volume, what did he mean volume thought Donal? The first minute was as before, he was in the toilet and suddenly Gráinne appeared behind him.

Charlie pushed some neatly typed sheets of paper in front of Donal, 'You might want to look at these as it starts to roll, it's a transcript of your conversation.'

'No it's O.K.' said Donal. They all gazed at the unfolding scene before them.

Suddenly a female voice enquired, 'How's it hanging big boy?' followed by the reply, 'I feel an election coming on.'

Donal looked opened mouth as the conversation descended into unadulterated filth and finally reached its conclusion.

'So what have you say to that then Donal?' He was literally lost for words.

'Are those suggestions you made to her physically possible, and even if you are both consenting adults, legal?' asked Charlie.

' But... but...'

'Just thank God the You Tube version has no sound. You have to consider your position Donal and more importantly the good of the party,' said John

'Where the hell did you get this from anyway, just because it sounds like me it doesn't mean it is me.'

'We got this from our friends at the Garda Technical Bureau, and as for who's speaking, well you heard it for yourself,' interjected Michael.

'Have you seen the latest opinion polls Donal? We can't afford liabilities,' said John in a very serious tone. 'In terms of competency to run the country, the punters have you placed just ahead of Dustin the Turkey.'

'But that conversation never happened, I'm being set up, someone's out to get me,' wailed Donal. The three of them exchanged glances; he was obviously in a state of denial.

'Now let's get down to brass tacks,' said Charlie leaning back on his chair, 'We'll start with the porno movie, donkey diplomacy and what you stuff up your nose can come later. By the way, did you threaten to cut the bollocks off some knacker at Newgrange this afternoon?'

Things didn't quite go according to plan down in The Media Secretariat. Niamh arrived to find her staff run ragged. Sizing up the situation, Niamh tried to be jocular, 'How are things then boys and girls?' she enquired over the din of ringing phones.

'It's a total madhouse down here, we've never stopped Ms Comiskey, just look at this,' Mary pointed at the computer screen, 'Those are just the e-mails we've had in the past hour.'

'Well you're all doing a grand job in very difficult circumstances. I'll stick around for a bit just to see how things are going, if anyone wants me I'll be in my office.' Niamh settled herself down in front of the computer on her desk, logging on to see the latest news on R.T.É. 24/7.

'.... so the unconfirmed rumour is that a visibly distraught Taoiseach visited Newgrange this afternoon; it is believed a woman who is his nurse accompanied him. This is Miriam Bird reporting live from Brú Na Bóinne.' The scene shifted back to the studio where a panel of experts now dissected the apparent state of Donal's mental health.

'Well it could be paranoia or even some milder form of persecution mania,' said one of the talking heads.

'What about this alleged threat of violence toward the tour guide?' enquired the studio anchor-man.

'Well I think it's significant that he threatened to defenestrate this individual, this to me says that he has some serious issues with male identity, as Freud would have said...'

Niamh logged off, the phone on her desk rang, 'What is it Mary?'

'There's been a call from Martin Adams, he said he has to see you urgently.'

'Tell him to feck off.'

'He just said birthday presents and books, and said you'd know what it meant.'

'Where is he now?' asked Niamh

'He's in reception.'

'Tell him to come up.' Five minutes later there was a gentle knock on the door. 'Come in Mary.'

'Martin Adams, Miss Comiskey.'

'Martin,' said Niamh standing up and shaking his hand, 'To what do I owe this unexpected pleasure?'

Martin had a smug expression on his face, and looked around him, 'You've done well for yourself, shame if it had to come to an end.'

'Oh I doubt very much that is likely to happen, or is that some kind of veiled threat Martin?' He didn't answer, just sat there and smirked.

'So Niamh how's your boy these days, still cresting on a political wave?'

'You know how it is Martin, gobshites in the media trying to bring a good man down.'

'I suppose a man in his position doesn't get much time for relaxation, such as reading and the like, but I hear he does get out and about to view our country's heritage. How was Newgrange?'

Niamh didn't even blink. 'O.K. Martin, cut to the chase.'

'I have in my possession a book, given to me by a concerned citizen.' So Martin had contact with this Danka woman, mused Niamh. He continued, 'Which to suspicious minds could seriously compromise the Taoiseach's reputation and question his political judgement, to whit Mein Kampf by Adolph Hitler.'

'So, having a copy of that is hardly a crime.'

'True, but the birthday card message inscribed by the donor could, shall we say, be misconstrued. Were this missive to find its way into the realms of the media, well who knows what may happen.'

'So you're trying to blackmail me Martin, is that it?'

'No, not at all Niamh, you scratch my back and I'll scratch yours.'

'O.K., cards on the table, what's the deal?'

'First of all there's the funny business in Cavan. I track your English man down and find he's in cahoots with your cousin, pretending to be a gender bender soccer player. When they realise I'm onto them they do a runner and vanish into thin air. Is the Black Pig's dyke really Roman; is that it, another cover up?' Niamh was impressed, from what she had seen of Mick McCarthy he was incapable of running rings around himself, never mind Martin Adams; clearly Clare had come up with a scam to banjax Martin.

'So am right in assuming that if I come clean about this alleged conspiracy, you keep quiet about the book, is that it?'

'That'll do to start with.'

'I see,' said Niamh standing up and walking over to a filing cabinet. 'Now let me see, where's the nixers and cute hoor file? Ah here it is, and do you know, there's a section with your name on it!' Martin smiled indulgently at the joke. Niamh sat down and opened a ring binder, 'Now where shall we start?' She turned over a few pages, 'Ah this will do nicely. Here we are, exactly how much have you made?'

Martin was thrown of balance, 'I have no idea what you're talking about.'

'Well let me refresh your memory. Framed, limited edition copies of Molly Malone, does it ring any bells?

The lyrics hand written by her good friend and acquaintance Oscar Wilde, signed by Molly herself, with a certificate of authenticity endorsed by Michael Collins. For export only to the United States I believe. Isn't it some shed in Clones where these are churned out?' asked Niamh whimsically. 'Oh look!' she exclaimed pointing at the page in front of her. Martin shifted in his chair uncomfortably. 'It says here you sell the Japanese presentation cases of bottled pig slurry you claim is original 1759 vintage Guinness stout.'

'You can't prove a thing.'

'Can't I, are you a betting man Adam, do you really want to gamble on that? Would Brian Kelly be willing to go down for you? Don't look so shocked, I know, and so do you, that he's involved in this.'

Niamh tossed her hair back, 'I have to say I admire your initiative and drive, shows real imagination. Just a word of warning, friendly advice. If you're serious about messing with either myself or An Taoiseach, you've booked a one way ticket to the Joy, sharing a cell with three drug fuelled sex starved boot boys, just itching to get their hands on a new bitch. Now what other gems are hidden in these pages I wonder?'

Martin licked his lips, sweat glistened on his forehead. 'What do you have in mind Niamh?' he asked pleasantly and in an ingratiating tone of voice, 'Sure I'm open to reason.'

'Reason,' said Niamh in a steely tone of voice, 'doesn't

come into it, now this is what you're going to do…' she said handing him the phone.

'Delighted we could have this little chat Donal, we should do it more often.'

Donal smiled weakly as the three of them moved their chairs back, 'What time is it now?' asked Charlie.

'It's six thirty,' said John, 'just time to get home to watch Coronation Street on T.V.3.' They gathered their bits and pieces and snapped shut their attaché cases. 'Now you think about what we said Donal, we'll get back to you tomorrow night to hear your decision.'

They all shook hands and Donal was alone, he got out his mobile and dialled, 'It's me…what do you mean who's me, are you taking the piss? Get over here pronto! No fecking excuses. I don't care if it is Sunday and your wife's birthday' He dialled again, 'Hello… well get him will you. Listen carefully you total gobshite, you me and that other ape that passes for a member of An Garda Síochána are in deep shit… look I'm not interested, I expect to see you within the next half an hour.' Closing the flip top of his mobile, Donal stood up, stretched then went and gazed out of the window in contemplation. A sudden thought struck him, opening his phone again he dialled, 'Put Niamh Comiskey on will you… its An Taoiseach…What? She's in a meeting…well ask her to call over to my office when she's done.'

Donal sat at his desk deep in thought and surveyed his

surroundings, that's odd, I don't remember moving those two he mused, must have been Máire. He picked up the first garden gnome from the top of the filing cabinet, the second he had nearly fallen over when he went to sit down. Placing them carefully either side of the fireplace he said, 'There you are boys, back safe and sound. Jesus, listen to me, talking to garden gnomes!' Opening his desk drawer he produced his manuscript, two books and a pen. Turning the pages of Private Pigeon – The Order of Lenin, he found what he'd been looking for. 'Do you know boys,' he said addressing the two immobile figures by the fireplace. 'Those clever Russkies came out with a secret weapon, flocks of exploding carrier pigeons.' He waved the book at Ted and Harold, 'No honestly, it's true, it says so here. They force fed them on plastic explosives and trained them for suicide missions against German flak batteries.'

Frank and Phil stood on the other side of the office door, pausing before knocking. 'He's talking to someone, who do you think he's talking to?' asked Frank.

Phil shrugged his shoulders. 'Better go in and find out what it's all about, he certainly sounded pissed off mad when he phoned.'

Frank gently tapped the door. 'Come in', could be heard in muffled tones. The two officers entered to find Donal reading aloud, '... and then in 1945 during the battle for Berlin'... What do you think of it so far?'

'Sure that's grand Taoiseach, a guaranteed best seller,' said Frank enthusiastically.

'Begob and they'll be queuing up to buy that one,' added Phil.

'I'm not asking you two shites, I'm asking these two gentlemen,' replied Donal indicating Ted and Harold. 'So you like it then, good!' he said, nodding to the two garden gnomes. 'Right you pair of total bollix,' said Donal in a business like tone, 'I have just watched the most disgusting pornographic film you could imagine.' The two policemen looked suitably contrite.

'I think I've seen that one,' began Phil pensively. 'Is it the one where...?' Frank and Donal listened gob smacked at his litany of debauchery.

'Jesus Phil, when did you see that?' asked Frank shaking his head. 'That's the stuff of nightmares.'

'No it wasn't that film, it was me and that woman that doesn't exist, only there was sound with this one,' replied a seething Donal. 'Some gobshite was impersonating me on it. I want whoever is responsible for this torn limb from limb, then transferred to traffic control duty on Clare island.'

Just then Phil's phone rang, 'Excuse me Taoiseach,' he said stepping to one side... 'Yeh...yeh.. You have, that's brilliant! So have you sent someone around... you have, even better!' Phil looked at Frank, an expression of triumph on his face, 'Anonymous tip off, we have that Danka woman!'

'Never mind that woman, what are you going to do about this shagging video?'

'Er... make enquiries at the Technical Bureau?' asked Frank.

'Just leave, go. I don't want to see you two again until you have a result.'

Frank and Phil turned on their heels and consulted in low tones outside Donal's office, 'Jesus what do we do now?' wailed Phil.

'Just keep calm, it's that gouger Eugene up to his old tricks. Do you remember when he had that recording of dog fighting in Monaghan to analyse and he messed with it?'

'No.'

'It ended up sounding like a Michael O'Hehir commentary from an All Ireland.'

'So how does that help us?'

'You leave it to your uncle Frank. If we get him a copy of that book he lost at the birthday party, that'll be a step on the road to getting back in favour, then we'll deal with Eugene.' They heard footsteps behind them and turned to see Niamh approaching, 'Right, not a word about that video recording,' whispered Frank. Niamh smiled at them serenely. 'Good news Niamh, we have that Polish woman from Bah Bars,' announced Phil.

'So she was in Bray was she?' asked Niamh

'How did you know she was in Bray?' asked Frank curiously.

'Lucky guess I suppose,' she replied sweeping past them. 'If I was going to hide out I'd choose a resort, and let's face it, Bray is the last resort.' She entered Donal's office to find him sitting cross-legged in front of Ted and Harold.

'...and then there were these fecking donkeys, I didn't know there were fecking donkeys in that cottage...'

'Are you alright Donal?' He hadn't heard her come in and was a little taken aback. He straightened up and composed himself.

'Me? Fine, never been better.'

'So what happened with the guys from the party executive?'

'It's a fluid situation.'

'What does that mean?'

'I am considering all my options. How are things down in Media Relations?'

'All under control Donal, all under control. Now my sweet, I think it's time we went abhaile. You have a busy day tomorrow and I'd guess so will I.'

'I have to consult with the policy group tonight, phone the Cumann officers and talk to some other people so it's going to be a long stretch on the phone this evening Niamh.'

'I'd just love to know what those two were doing there, I really would.'

'I know Clare, so you keep saying. Maybe they just went out for the afternoon, people do you know, after all we did!'

'Keep your eyes on the road Mick,' said Clare in a

concerned tone as an articulated wagon with Northern Irish number plates thundered past them with inches to spare. 'Yeah but what was all that about Donal threatening to castrate the tour guide?'

Mick shrugged his shoulders, 'I don't know Clare,' he said with a sigh. 'Look, we'll be home soon, let's just have a quiet night in with a Chinese, the telly and a couple of beers.' Mick sifted the CD's with one hand and selected one at random,

'Who's this?' asked Clare as the music started.

'They're called Goats Don't Shave, a Manchester Irish rock band. I don't know if they're still going; they're good aren't they.'

The rest of the journey passed in silence until they got back to Lucan. Whilst Mick parked the car he handed the house key to Clare. 'Stick the kettle on when you get in will you, I need a drink.'

'So do I,' replied Clare. When Mick joined her, he found Clare sipping whiskey.

'Have you forgotten last night already, I don't want you seeing things again,' he shouted from the kitchen.

'Me? I wasn't seeing things.'

Mick decided not to argue the toss, it was bad enough having imaginary conversation partners without believing they were real and that others could see and hear these make believe people. If you can't beat them, join them!

'Would you like some tea as well Ruairí, you would, that's grand. One sugar or two?'

Clare raced out to the kitchen, 'Where is he?'

'Who?'

'Ruairí, you were just talking to him.'

'Oh he's over there by the sink with Barney the Dinosaur,' replied Mick.

'You bastard, taking the piss, he's not here at all,' she said, her eyes blazing as she swung a saucepan at him. 'So who or what is he then if he's not a leprechaun?'

'I told you Clare, I've never heard of him. He's probably someone in Niamh's department. You want to get a grip my girl, you'll be going out for a drink with the tooth fairy next.' He was saved from her wrath by the telephone. 'Would you answer that Clare, it's in the hall.' She glared at him as she went to phone.

Clare returned a few minutes later, an evil gleam in her eye, 'It was that Priest who called yesterday, Father Antheney, he wants to come around for a chat.'

'I hope you told him we were going out.'

'I told him that was marvellous, how much you were looking forward to it, and couldn't wait in fact. He should be here in about an hour.' Mick stared into his cup of tea and groaned.

'Come in Father and take off your coat, lovely to see you again,' said Mick effusively. 'Sit down and I'll make us some tea.' Clare followed Mick into the kitchen.

'You liar,' she said. 'At least he's on hand to hear your confession, bless me Father for I have sinned, I've just been telling porkie pies.'

'Just go out there and keep him entertained for a few minutes will you Clare, there's a good girl.' Clare went out and plonked herself down in an armchair. 'So how's it going Father?'

'Fine thanks Clare, and you?'

'The same, Father, Mick, won't be long he's just making the tea. So you were a curate in Wykeford were you?' Father Antheney nodded emphatically. It had turned out to be a blessing in disguise when he had been ejected so unexpectedly the previous night; he had used his time wisely to read up on Wykeford in general and the Irish Centre in particular.

'Yes, I was at St Anthony's and a regular at the Centre, great craic we had there all together.' Mick entered the room with a tray and some biscuits.

'So you used to go to the centre? Did you ever come across poor Bridie when you were there Father?'

'Oh…er, of course, poor Bridie, a sad case if ever there was one, but a harmless enough old crathur.' Father Antheney slurped his tea and looked expectantly at Clare, 'So what do you do for a living?'

'I cast pearl before swine Father.' Peter Antheney stared into space as he absorbed the implications of this novel occupation.

'Clare is a school teacher,' explained Mick helpfully. 'Help yourself to biscuits,' he added indicating the plate.

'And you Mick, what do you do?'

'Well I work for Teach agus Tallamh, or did until I was transferred to the Department of the Taoiseach.'

Father Antheney tried to contain his excitement at this news. 'That must be very interesting, so what does it involve?' Clare sipped her whiskey and noted the look of disapproval on Father Antheney's face.

'Oh I'm sorry Father, would you like one?'

'Do you know Clare that if you drop a worm into that stuff it wriggles for a minute or two and then dies. So what do you think the message is there?'

'If you have worms drink whiskey,' said Mick seeing the potential for things to escalate.

'In that case mine are doing well on it,' replied Clare as she raised her glass and took a big slurp.

'Anyway Father back to the job,' Mick said anxiously.

'Was it Teach agus Talamh work that took you to Cavan Mick?'

'In a manner of speaking Father, but it's a bit more involved than that. I shouldn't be telling you this, but I know you'll not breathe a word. You see it's like this...'

It still didn't make total sense to Father Antheney, but the bits of the jigsaw were now beginning to fit. Brian Ború had hinted at things when he said, 'Live in Cavan? If I were a bean sídhe I'd have plenty to wail about if I ended up there.' Máire's overheard conversation also fitted in, so it seems the sídhe were going to be moved to the border of Cavan and Longford. Pondering all the information at his disposal, plus the garbled bits and pieces that had tumbled from Máire's lips, Father Peter now had a more or less complete picture which was truly alarming. If what he believed to be the case were as it appeared, then what the sídhe were being offered really would put the cat among the pigeons. What was clear was that Mick McCarthy was being used; he might be part of the shenanigans, but wasn't in on it. He had now got what he'd come for; time to make his excuses and leave. The next conundrum was how to stop Donal Brady's machinations, but he had an idea about that. 'Well that is interesting Mick. I wish my job was as exciting as that.'

'So Father,' said Clare joining in the conversation, 'did you like your posting to St Anthony's?'

'It was a grand parish, they all made me very welcome.' Father Antheney looked at his watch and feigned shocked surprise, 'I must be going, I didn't realise it was this late. I have Benediction in twenty minutes.'

'Which church is that at Father?' asked Clare. Mick was puzzled; it was an odd question to ask.

'It's at St Bridget's where I've been filling in.'

'I'll show you out Father.' When Mick came back into the front room he looked at Clare, 'Well what was all that about, get a priest in the room and you're usually crawling up their arses.'

'Something didn't smell right from the moment he appeared last night and I was on sound ground there. You know he said he'd been a curate at St Anthony's? Well, they reorganised the parishes' years ago and it amalgamated with The Holy Rosary. They never had a curate at St Anthony's and there hasn't been any clergy there for ages.'

'You're right,' said Mick as realisation dawned. 'Yesterday he told me he was filling in at Christ the King, just now he said it was St Bridget's.'

'So what is he up to?' they both said in unison.

'Now all you have to do Taoiseach is pose, listen to the music, exchange a few words with them and move on, O.K.?'

'Where are the first ones going to be?' asked Donal.

'They're just up from Browne Thomas's, the next group are outside Bewley's and the rest are strung along Grafton Street. Are you all set Taoiseach?' Donal nodded. 'Be warned, the reptiles are out in force, both domestic and foreign but we have them corralled,' his minder said with an efficient air.

Donal and his entourage strode purposefully down Westmoreland Street toward The Bank of Ireland and College Green, a cordon of Gardaí escorting them. As they crossed the bottom of Dame Street and walked parallel to Trinity College the strains of massed Ukulele's could be heard. Swinging right into Grafton Street, a disorderly mob of media, resembling bargain hunters at a January sale could be seen ahead. The fourth estate surged forward when the approaching entourage came into view.

'Mr Brady, are you going to resign...? Who is she An

Taoiseach...? Will events in Galway damage Irish American relations...? What happened at Newgrange yesterday Mr Brady...?' Donal smiled serenely at the baying pack. They halted in front of the first group of musicians who launched into When I'm cleaning Windows. Passers-by were electrified.

'Sure that's all you'll be fit for soon... I bet you'd make a bollix of that too...' being amongst the politest comments shouted. Donal remained unfazed and posed for photographs.

'Time to move I think, An Taoiseach.' Donal and his group progressed up the street to be met by massed voices singing I'm Leaning On A Lamppost. The Media relations team exchanged glances and gently moved Donal on, no need to hand the press ammunition on a plate. The third and final group were innocuous and had just finished their last number.

'Just smile, say something harmless and we'll allow the cameras in whilst you're doing it,' was whispered in Donal's ear.

Donal did as he was told and shook the musician's hand. 'That was a grand little song,' he said facing the sea of lenses. 'What's that one called?'

'Frigid Air Fanny, Mr Brady', mass hysteria swept the crowd milling around him. 'Are there any questions for An Taoiseach...? Right... first please.'

'Whilst his nibs is hob knobbing with those fellehs

down Grafton Street, we need to visit some book shops.'

'Do we have to?'

'Do you really want to be teaching road safety in Belfast to a group of six-year-old skinheads with union jack tattoos and God Save the King T-shirts? No I didn't think so, well neither do I.' Frank and Phil got out of the car and headed into the Ilac centre.

'Right we'll try the bookshops in here, let's go to No Frontiers first.' Once inside the store they split up; after twenty minutes both had drawn a blank. 'We could try customer services,' suggested Phil. They joined the queue and finally reached the desk, a gum chewing disinterested young man with an ear stud and mascara asked them mechanically, 'Can I help you?' Frank studied him with interest, he had rather fixed ideas about what was and wasn't suitable attire.

'Yes Miss you can,' replied Frank provocatively. 'We're looking for a book by Adolph Hitler.'

'What's it called?' said the disinterested youth.

'Well how many do you think he wrote? He's hardly Maeve Binchy.'

'How do you spell it?

'How do you spell what?'

'How do you spell the book title?'

'Look, just punch Adolph Hitler into the fecking computer and see what comes up.'

'No need to be offensive. Right then, there are approximately twenty thousand books on the system, all with the name Adolph Hitler in the title.' The queue behind Frank and Phil was growing both in length and discontent.

'Look, we don't want a book with his name in the title, we want the one he wrote.' Nose stud raised his mascara eyes to heaven and tapped the key board again, 'Mein Kampf, is that it?'

'So have you got it or not?'

'It's showing up as in stock, two copies. Have you looked on the shelves?'

'Yes,' they said in unison.

'Must be upstairs then, just wait here.' The mutterings behind Frank and Phil rose in intensity.

'Alright, alright!' said a testy Phil as he turned to the line behind him. 'It's not our fault we've a big bollix seeing to us.'

'The big bollix has your book sir.' Frank and Phil looked at the proffered offering, and turned a few pages.

'This is no good, it's in English,' said Frank.

'Oh you two gougers can read can you?' shot back nose stud. 'What's wrong with it, words of more than a syllable beyond yous?'

'Don't get clever with me,' said Frank in a belligerent tone.

'Well I didn't think you'd want the other one, it's not in English.'

'Is it in Irish?' asked Phil hopefully.

'No, it's in Welsh.' Two burly men wearing black trousers, black polo neck pullovers and leather jackets, tapped Phil on the shoulder. 'Look, just wait your turn until we finish talking to shite for brains,' he said turning round.

'I'm sorry sir, but I must ask you and your friend to leave.'

'Leave, what the feck for?' The original pair of security men were now joined by two more, strategically moving in towards Frank and Phil as the two officers were hustled to the exit. Three more bookshops and four phone calls to antiquarian specialists left them no further on.

'Any suggestions?' asked Frank. 'We could ask Niamh Comiskey where she got it from, but that would spoil the surprise element, she'd be bound to spill the beans to Brady, or we could go and see that Polish woman that's been taken in. That Vanka woman, or whatever she's called, was working there the night of the party, maybe she's seen it.'

'Is she still in Bray?'

'No they've moved her to Store Street.'

'What have they got here under?'

'The Criminal Justice Act, that'll keep her out of circulation for a few days.'

'O.K. down to Store Street it is.'

The helicopter took off from Baldonnell and headed west. 'I never knew you were into Ukulele's and George Formby,' said Tom.

'I'm not, no more than when you implied you were into Sushi.'

'I knew you'd bring that up.'

'If I remember rightly that's exactly what you did in Tokyo.'

'How long until we get to Galway?' asked Tom.

'About twenty minutes or so Minister,' replied the Air Corp officer.

'So what are you going to do Donal, ride it out or...?'

'Wait and see Tom, wait and see.' Donal had no intention of divulging anything to the Minister For Foreign Affairs, the jockeying for position had almost certainly started and he wasn't going to be quoted or more to the point misquoted. Machievelli had said a prince should put out rumours of their impending demise to gauge their popularity; the present scenario would do nicely.

'You do know I'm right behind you Donal, don't you?'

'I know Tom, it's good to have people I know I can rely on.' If Donal's assessment was correct, Tom was probably the one behind the handing out of the knives.

'The last time I was out in the wild west it was with Sean for that Defence Forces exercise. You do know that Sean thinks Achill is Atlantis.'

'Well we all need an interest,' replied Donal, looking up from On a Wing and a Prayer - Panzer Pigeons on the Elbe. Galway brought back happy memories for Donal; it was the location of choice for his first holiday with Niamh. They hadn't been going out that long and both had thought, even if they hadn't said it at the time, that it was make or break. If the two of them could get along together for a week or two, then there was a future for them both. It hadn't all gone quite to plan, and for once Donal was entirely blameless. Niamh had been keen to go to Inis Mór and suggested they hire bicycles in Cill Ronan, so far so good. It was when she fell off the bike, buckled the wheel and banged her face that things got interesting. The bruised area had been all around her right eye, which made it look as if Donal had thumped her. In fact when they got to back to Galway, they encountered a woman who told Niamh about a battered woman's refuge run by The Western Health Board.

Niamh's protestations that she had fallen off a bicycle sounded reminiscent of Roddy Doyle's The Woman Who Walked Into Doors. The rest of the holiday had seen Donal being the recipient of dirty looks by complete strangers who assumed Niamh's injury was down to him. To give Niamh credit, she had tried dark glasses to hide her bruises, but this then meant she couldn't see anything in shops and appeared registered blind.

'We will be arriving at Galway airport in about five minutes,' announced the pilot.

'Is there a welcoming party?' asked Tom

'Nothing official, it was thought the best option was to play this one down. It took the Garda Commissioner the best part of the last two days to talk the Yanks out of suing,' replied Donal.

Disembarking from the aircraft they strolled over to a couple of waiting limousines. 'You and I will go in this one

Tom, your people can go in the other one.' The cars exited the airport and headed west along the Ballybrit road towards the city.

'So do we just hold his hand, so to speak, and ooze sympathy, is that it?' asked Tom

'More or less, I think there might be some people from the U.S. Embassy or the like there as well, so behave yourself.'

'When do I do anything but?'

'St Patrick's Day at the White House, remember that? You told the President that American footballers were nancy boys because they wore all that body armour stuff and that baseball was known as rounders in Ireland but played by schoolgirls.'

'But they are and it is,' said Tom earnestly.

'You can't just go to another country and insult their national sports,' said an exasperated Donal.

'There's worse things than American football and baseball, have you seen cricket? Jesus, watching paint dry is more exciting than that. Anyway I hope this doesn't take too long, I want to get back to see our boys in action against the French in the European Championship match, revenge for the South Africa World cup qualifyer match!'

'Is it live on the telly?' asked Donal

'Sure is.' Tom looked out as the car stopped at the Garda checkpoint at the entrance to the driveway; they were nodded on and swept up a broad avenue to a large mansion. Donal led the way in, ignoring the rather obvious security personnel lurking in the bushes. 'Good afternoon,' he announced breezily, 'I am An Taoiseach Donal Brady and this is The Minister For Foreign Affairs. We're here to see Mr Rodriguez, you know the Chief.' Tom's two undersecretaries stood deferentially behind them.

'You want to see the Chef?' asked the puzzled man behind the reception desk.

'No the Chief, you know Hail to the Chief - well it will be if he's elected. I don't mean chief just because he's partly Indian.' Donal's voice trailed off as the receptionist looked at him as he was the one needing treatment.

'Just wait here will you.' A minute or two later the receptionist was joined by two men wearing ear pieces, dark glasses and charcoal grey suits.

'Follow them,' indicated the receptionist. Donal and his party walked down a pale blue antiseptic corridor until they came to a white door, seated either side of the entrance were clones of their escorts. The two bullet heads outside the door examined Donal's party with care, rising to open the door and ushering them in. The blinds in the room were drawn and an immobile figure lay prone on the bed.

Standing over Chumani was a well-dressed individual in a three-piece suit.

'You have fifteen minutes,' said three-piece suit.

'And you are?' asked Tom

'George Johnson the third, U.S. State Department.' Chumani beckoned Tom over, he stared wild-eyed and began to paw the sleeve of the Minister's jacket, 'los burros, los burros Simpático' he said in a whimpering tone.

'Yes indeed Mr Rodriguez and fair play to ye,' replied Tom in a jocular fashion as he gently punched Chumani's arm.

'Jesus Tom, don't do that,' said Donal in a concerned voice. 'Do you want yer man from the State Department to come back in here and find him with a broken arm?'

'For fecks sake Donal it was only a tap, look there's nothing wrong with him.' said Tom raising Chumani's elbow.

They were all at a bit of a loss as to what to do next; there was an uncomfortable silence.

'Did you ever see the film One Flew Over the Cuckoos Nest, Minister?' asked one of Tom's underlings.

'Do you think I have time to watch films about fecking birds?'

'It's not about birds Minister,' corrected the other underling, 'It's got Jack Nicholson in it, he pretends he's not right in the head so he won't be sent to jail.'

'Didn't he play The Joker in one of the Batman films years ago?' asked Tom

'He did Minister.' The first underling was clearly thinking. 'Who do you think was the best Batman Minister?' he added.

'Mother of God!' exclaimed Donal, 'We came here to see him,' he said pointing at the comatose figure on the bed, 'not to discuss someone's fecking film career.'

'Sorry Taoiseach,' the two juniors from the Department

of Foreign Affairs chorused. There was another long pause.

'Was that film you're talking about where they all went out on a boat for the day and the nurse was pally with the mother of one of the patients?' queried Tom, looking down at Chumani.

'It was Minister.'

'I have seen it so. Did either of you two see Jack Nicholson in The Shining? Scare the shite out of you that would.'

'Look can we focus on the matter in hand.'

'O.K., O.K. Stay calm Donal No need to get excited!' said Tom in a what's the matter with him tone of voice.

'So did you have a nice time in Galway Mr Rodriguez? I always enjoy it when I come here,' said Donal.

'Nice time, did ye have a nice time? Do you think Donal that he's suffering from nervous exhaustion due to excitement?' said Tom.

'Just trying to make conversation, cheer him up a bit.' They all looked at each other, another pause. 'Did I tell you he doesn't know who his da was?' Donal asked no one in particular.

'No, how do you know that?' replied Tom

'Niamh told me at my birthday party, terrible sad isn't it?'

'My da was a real character,' said underling number one with great enthusiasm. 'He once marched in the Sligo St Patrick's Day parade wearing just a pair of tricolour jockey shorts and wellies. They had to take him to the hospital at the end of it.'

'Exposure was it?' asked underling number two.

'No he got run over by one of the floats.' There was a knock at the door and George Johnson the third entered accompanied by a two-man T.V. crew.

'These are from C.N.N., so let's all gather round the bed and get this over with.' Donal and his party dutifully arranged themselves around the room. 'When this is over,' muttered George Johnson to Donal, 'I want to speak to you in private.'

The alarm went at seven thirty and Mick fumbled to find the off switch, he turned on the radio by the bed, Morning Ireland had tracked down someone from Donal's childhood and was probing his early days. He turned off the radio, he'd had enough of Donal Brady, he was everywhere you looked and listened on T.V. and radio, in any case he was beginning to feel sorry for him. Having a quick shower he went down stairs and got breakfast. Stirrings could be heard above him. Clare must be up. He turned on the T.V. '… and now other news. The centre of Dublin will come alive to the sound of the 1930s and 1940s when the ninth Dublin George Formby festival is launched this morning. Musicians will be busking in and around Grafton Street, so if you fancy a nostalgic trip down your grandparent's memory lane, come along from nine o'clock onwards.' The camera switched from the pleasant looking, smiling woman to her co-presenter, 'It is said that the U.S.Presidential candidate Mr Chumani Rodriguez is progressing well. Mr Rodriguez sustained minor injuries whilst visiting his ancestral home last week. An official from the American State Department is expected in Galway this afternoon to assess how soon Mr Chumani can be repatriated. The official, Mr George Johnson the third will also pay a courtesy call on An Taoiseach who is also visiting Mr Chumani.' Mick studied the man on the screen with interest, it was the same one who read the six o'clock news; he could see what Des O'Mahony had been getting at now. A map of Ireland appeared, accompanied by the Met Eireann logo.

'An aimsir,' announced a disembodied voice. 'Tá sé…' began the invisible weatherman.

'What time are you setting off?' asked Clare as she came into the living room. Mick looked at the clock, he was late.

'About five minutes ago,' he announced, emptying his teacup. He grabbed the car keys, the folder containing his notes and photos from his Cavan trip. 'The spare door key is on the table by the front door, see you about five thirty,' he shouted as the front door slammed shut.

Après Moi La Deluge

The Pro cathedral contained an interesting mix of people, devout elderly women lit candles in front of garish statues, people down on their luck were cadging the odd euro here and there and in the main body of the church was a scattering of Mass goers. Eilís looked for the confessionals and entered the third on the right, she knelt down, there was a strong smell of cigarettes from the other side of the grill... 'Bless me father for I have sinned,' she began.

'And what is your name my dear?'

'Eilís, Father.'

'And have you travelled far this morning Eilís?'

'Just from 44 Lower Baggot Street, Father.'

It was the cue he had been waiting for, 'Now listen carefully, Donal Brady and that hoor in the toilet isn't the half of it.'

Eilís listened transfixed; to say Donal Brady was not of a sound mind was an understatement.

'Exactly who is this Eoghan Dempsey he was talking to?'

'I don't know, my confidante didn't say.'

'And this confidante is a source close to the Taoiseach?'

'I can categorically say that is the case.'

'Would this source be willing to corroborate what you have just told me?'

'It's doubtful they would go on the record as that would compromise them, but I'm sure you have the resources to trace this Eoghan Dempsey.'

'Can I know your name?' asked Eilís, but the only reply was the sound of the mystery contact rising off the kneeler. She jumped to her feet and rushed out, but she was too late, he had vanished. Eilís looked around at the congregation; he was out there in front of her somewhere, he had to be, but which one was he? 'Oh I'm sorry Father,' she said as a Priest with a teddy boy hairstyle edged past her to join the Holy Communion line. Once outside the church she scrambled to extricate her mobile from her handbag. 'Have I got news for you...Brady is barking mad...Yeh, yeh, wait till I get back to the office and I'll tell you all.'

Mick parked the car and walked around the corner to the office. He assumed that he'd better report to Brian Kelly first as a gesture of protocol. He knocked on Brian's door.

'Come in'. As Mick entered Brian was watching the T.V and leaning back in his chair holding the remote by the side of his head.

'Isn't it great craic all together? Our Prime Minister's human after all.'

He switched off the T.V. 'Now what I can do for you?'

'I thought you might want a debrief about my Cavan trip.' Just then the phone rang.

'Just wait while I take this call.' The relaxed look on Brian's face changed to anxiety then anger then despair. 'Look Martin you fecker, I don't care what she knows...

don't you try and blame all this on me... Does she know about the rest? Are there things I should know about? What about the Titanic..? Brian looked up, suddenly remembering that Mick was sitting opposite him. 'Well that's sounds gas,' he said slamming the phone down.

'Problem?' asked Mick.

'Ah no, just a misunderstanding,' replied Brian vacantly. 'Now where were we?'

'Cavan debrief.'

'Oh yes, Cavan...' Brian was definitely preoccupied. 'Look Mick, why don't you write up your report and then we'll go through it.'

'What about Niamh Comiskey?'

'What about her?' Brian's reaction to her name was that of a vampire being presented with garlic.

'Well strictly speaking I work for the Department of the Taoiseach, so who gets the report first?' enquired Mick.

Brian looked at him with lowered eyes, 'I couldn't give a shite,' he said in a low tone, Mick smiled encouragingly and left.

'What's wrong with him today?' Mick asked his work colleagues.

'PMT probably,' said Helen pleasantly.

Mick got out his laptop, briefing notes and the rest of his Cavan material. He had been working on his report for about two hours when his mobile rang.

'Hiya Mick, just wondered what you might be doing for lunch? I'm in your neck of the woods; I'm going to pop over and see Niamh.' Oh shit! It suddenly occurred to him that perhaps he'd better go and see Niamh Comiskey.

'Funny you should say that, I'm going to see her as well,' he said fumbling with the interdepartmental phone directory.

'Well maybe I could meet you there then, I should be with her about two.'

'O.K, see you soon,' he replied grabbing the phone on his desk and dialling,

'Media Relations, Department of the Taoiseach, can I help you?'

'Yes, is Ms Comiskey available?'

'I'll just put you on hold for a second.'

'Hello, Niamh Comiskey here.'

'Ms Comiskey, its Mick McCarthy, I wondered if I could just pop over to see you this afternoon, say about two o'clock, I thought you might want a preliminary report on the Black Pig's Dyke project.'

'Just a minute and I'll check the diary... yeh that should be O.K, see you then.'

'Come in Clare, nice to see you again. How was Cavan? I heard you had fun and games when you were down there and met my old friend Martin Adams.'

'You're very well informed Niamh,' said a surprised Clare

'It's my job to keep my ear to the ground. Just a social call is it?' Clare believed in being direct, it saved time in the long run and everyone knew where they stood.

'I know about Ruairí,' she announced, looking directly at Niamh.

'What do you know about some Ruairí person? I don't know him.'

'I know, and you know he's not a person, is he Niamh?' Clare said the last three words in a deliberate tone.

'Clare I am very busy and don't have time for riddles,' replied Niamh testily.

'When I stayed at your place, you and Donal were talking about Ruairí and you also let slip that you knew Mick, had spoken to him in fact.'

Niamh wasn't too sure what to make of all of this, where was this conversation going?

'You see Niamh, I've met Ruairí and he's filled me in on what's going on.'

'So you've met this Ruairí and you say he's filled you in what's going on, sounds very mysterious.'

'I know about Donal's plan for the sídhe,' said Clare softly. Niamh was in a state if total confusion. 'Apart from all his other little difficulties, you wouldn't want Donal to read about this in this in the press, would you Niamh?'

'Who in their right mind is going to believe any of this nonsense you're telling me?'

'I heard you and Donal talking about Ruairí when I stayed over and I also know that you knew about Mick being taken in by the Guards. In any case I'm your cousin, if I leaked that piece of information and that a source close to An Taoiseach thinks he's a loony, you wouldn't need a PhD to guess where I got it from. It's not the state of my mind that's going to be of interest when this sees the light of day. By the way, where did Donal get that flat cap he was wearing at Newgrange?'

'You and McCarthy were at Newgrange?' This added another dimension to proceedings. 'And you heard and saw what went on?'

Clare slowly nodded her head, 'Pretty much so yeh. You were both pretty nifty to get away before the Radio car turned up.' Niamh realised she had badly underestimated her cousin.

'Have you been speaking to The Phoenix?' shot back Niamh, her sources had told her that the magazine had a new angle on Donal and was going to run with it. The trouble was that Niamh didn't know exactly what the new angle was.

'Whose The Phoenix?' asked Clare puzzled. 'Is he some friend of Ruairí's I haven't met yet?'

'Never mind, it's not important' said Niamh. 'I assume you want something, I just can't figure out what it is.'

'Well now you come to mention it.'

'At last, cards on the table.'

'Mick is talented, undervalued and has huge potential, don't you agree.'

Niamh wondered if they were talking about the same person, 'Go on Clare.'

'I think he would make a perfect section head, if not

Head of Teach agus Tallamh itself. Fresh blood brings a new perspective.'

'I'm listening,' said Niamh. As Martin Adams and Brian Kelly had spent the morning sending her e-mails exonerating themselves and incriminating each other, a new possibility presented itself. McCarthy was amenable, and was unlikely to show much inclination towards empire building or nixers. He was a follower rather than a leader and would just do what he was told; the prospect was quite attractive on reflection. 'Well you know Clare, a vacancy has just arisen, leave it with me.'

Clare stood up and smoothed herself down, 'You stick to your side of the bargain and I'll stick to mine, he gets promotion and nothing leaks. By the way, in case you're wondering, Mick knows nothing about the Ruairí business. As far as he's concerned the Cavan assignment was what you said it was.'

'Have you ever thought of a career in politics Clare? You're a natural.'

As Clare left the office Niamh dialled, 'Get me Brian Kelly on the phone. I don't care where he is, this is urgent. Tell him to call me back immediately, I want to speak to him.' Niamh leaned back on her chair and looked at the wall clock, golden boy McCarthy should be arriving any minute.

'Good day at work?' asked Clare as Mick danced his way into the front room.

'You won't believe it Clare, I've been promoted!'

'No! really?' she feigned surprised and shock.

'Yes really!' said Mick sitting down in the front room. 'I went to see your cousin and gave her my preliminary report on the Black Pig's Dyke project. She listened and then said congratulations, you've passed. I had no idea what she was talking about, passed what I asked? You've passed the field initiative test she told me. It seems that the Department of the Taoiseach had been monitoring my progress and I'd been head hunted as a high flyer.'

'Go away!' said Clare in mock surprise, 'so what have you been head hunted for?'

'Only Head of Teach agus Tallamh, would you believe it! The people in the U.K. are delighted for me, said their loss was Ireland's gain. That's not all, I got back to my own office to find a real buzz. It seems the reason for my promotion is because Brian Kelly has been head hunted by The European Union! He's shipping out to northern Canada in a couple of days, very important assignment. He was so excited he couldn't speak, he just moaned with emotion.'

'Well this calls for a celebration, let's go out and eat, my treat,' said Clare.

Mick moved towards Clare, his eyes bright and shining, 'You know what this means don't you? I've got a full time post doing something I'll enjoy, no more mundane crappy holes in the ground to stare into.' He put his hands on her shoulders and gazed into her eyes; she looked up at him smiling, delighted he was so happy. He moved his face tentatively towards hers, their lips met and caressed as he gently stroked the back of her neck. 'It's a whole new beginning Clare and I want you to be part of it,' he said with feeling. She closed her eyes and slowly breathed out, it might have taken a long time, a time she never thought was coming, but they had finally got there.

'Maybe we should stay in and celebrate,' she said coyly, taking him by the hand.

'So is this it Donal, the end of an era?' asked Niamh mournfully. He put his head on her shoulder saying nothing as she stroked his cheek.

He stared in front of him, 'Nothing lasts for ever Niamh, it's probably for the best in the long run.' On the floor was a large cardboard box, overflowing with bits and pieces, they both looked at it sadly.

'I see you've made a start clearing your desk.'

'Yeh, just the personal things. I'll come back in tomorrow and make a proper start.'

'What about this Donal, are you leaving it?' asked Niamh picking up the old letter opener on his desk. 'You may as well, it was no good at slicing envelopes' she added. Niamh began to fight back the tears, dabbing her eyes with a paper hanky.

'You'd be surprised what that can do Niamh,' he said in a faraway voice. 'Ten minutes to go,' shouted an aide. Donal looked at the T.V. screen in his office, it was surreal really, watching something live that was taking place just a few hundred metres away.

'Come on Niamh, let's get it over with, I can see from that,' he said indicated the T.V. 'that they're chomping at the bit.'

'So are you sure resignation with immediate effect is wise Donal?'

'Ah yeh, everything's set up, the Tánaiste takes over on a caretaker basis until the Dáil reconvenes, everything's in place. I go up to the Áras after the bun fight down stairs to see An Uachtarán and that's it.'

'Five minutes An Taoiseach,' shouted another voice.

'They won't be calling you that much longer Donal.' He shrugged, he was a realist. The party's basic raison d'etre was power and holding on to it, he knew that.

'Taoiseach, I was just wondering,' said Máire hurrying in.

'Yes Máire?'

'Do you want those two by the fireplace, they'd look grand in my garden.'

'No you take them,' replied Donal in a melancholy tone.

Máire looked around her puzzled, 'Where are they Taoiseach, have they been moved?'

'No, they were there this morning, they must be around somewhere. Gnomes can hardly get up and walk out on their own.'

'Two minutes An Taoiseach.'

'Right, off we go.' Donal and Niamh left his office hand

in hand and picked up the rest of the group waiting in the outer office. Frank and Phil had raced into Government buildings and caught up with them heading towards the open double doors on the ground floor. The scene in front of Donal was reminiscent of a condemned man catching his first glimpse of the firing squad, moving to the podium at the top of the steps he cleared his throat and faced the sea of cameras. The Tánaiste flanked Donal to his right, the Minister For Finance to his left. The rest of the Cabinet, such as was available, fanned out behind them. Niamh stood near the back, too distraught to be seen on film.

Frank sidled up to Niamh, 'Great news,' he mouthed as Donal began his speech.

Niamh sobbed, 'What could possibly be good about today?'

'You know that book, well we've got it back. That Polish woman had it. Jesus, trying to separate her from that was like trying to open a tin of beans with a rusty knife. Anyway, it's in this bag here and we thought we could present it to An Taoiseach after he's resigned, cheer him up a bit you know.' Tears ran down Niamh's face, and she silently shook with emotion.

Donal had now reached the point where he was thanking all those who had nurtured and supported him during his time in office. Frank took a sideways step back to Phil.

'Well what did she say?' asked Phil.

'She didn't say no.'

Donal was now concluding his speech, emphasising that his decision to resign was his alone and that all he had ever done in his political life had been for the good of the country. There was silence when he finished and he seemed deflated and distracted as he turned away from the cameras.

'No questions,' said the Media Relations minders emphatically.

'O.K. let's go for it,' said Phil moving forward and muttering in Donal's ear.

Donal paused, looked at him and then down at the bag. 'Is it a parting gift?' shouted a voice from the pack around the steps.

'We even gift wrapped it for you An Taoiseach, the choice of paper was Frank's, very hard to find it was.'

'Very thoughtful,' said Donal, removing the book from the bag and examining it. There was a sharp intake of breath from the assembled throng, 'I never knew you could get swastika embossed wrapping paper,' exclaimed the woman from news talk radio.

'I wanted to come and visit you, but they wouldn't allow it,'

'I know,' said Donal as he waved goodbye to the staff on the steps, 'it's against the rules apparently.'

'So what was it like then?'

'The food was good, the rooms were grand, you had a T.V. and an en suite bathroom.'

'But what about the ...'

'Oh the sessions, they were gas. We all sat round in a circle and discussed things. There was a felleh in our group, sad case he is, raves about Guinness swilling transvestite soccer playing Roman soldiers. He reckons there's a second century Roman race track under Cork city centre where they used to ride Irish Elks in steeplechases. No way José I told him, doesn't everyone know the G.A.A. were there first, a hurling pitch is far more likely.' Donal paused for a second, 'He wasn't actually called José by the way, his name was Martin, he used to work for a newspaper.'

'Really, how very interesting,' said Niamh smirking to herself.

'So what's the press been saying since I went in, I bet The Phoenix went to town on this one.'

'No they didn't, I was able to do some horse-trading with them, Chinese horse-trading in fact. Anyway you're out now and we can start looking forward. So what's this surprise you said you had lined up Donal?'

'It's a holiday, seven days in Iceland.' There was a pregnant pause, 'Ruairí came to see me when I was in there,' said Donal cautiously. 'They'd have let me out sooner if it hadn't been for that, when they came in with lunch they thought I was talking to the pot plants.'

'And what did that little shite want? I thought he'd leave you alone now you're no longer Taoiseach.'

'Well that's the point Niamh. He's introduced himself to the Tánaiste and reckons that working with him, and whoever takes over after him, is going to be problematic.'

'So?'

'He had a proposal. He can't work with the new crowd like he did with me, they won't play ball, so he wanted to know if I fancied a comeback. In the meantime he has to make the best of a bad job, but he says he's been there before. I rise from the ashes, regain my rightful place as Taoiseach and its game on again.'

'I hope you told him where to stick his proposal,' said Niamh with emotion.

'Well now, no need to be hasty.'

'So the comeback kid deal from Ruairí is...?'

'I help him and he helps me, to begin with I'll show them all that the old Brady drive and initiative is still in gear and ready for action, I seize the opportunity that the deferred aviation transport Bill offers. I have an idea to revolutionise things,' he said smugly.

'And this revolutionary plan is?'

'What do people want in this life Niamh?'

'A steady job, nice house, reliable income, someone to come home to and of course....'

'Apart from that Niamh, what else?' said Donal cutting here off.

'Go on amaze me.'

'Cheap air fares,' he said triumphantly. 'You know how fast food places operate on a franchise basis, you just apply it to planes.'

Niamh pondered this concept for a few minutes, she

wondered if he'd banged his head whilst he was away or was it the effect of some the medication they may have slipped him?

'So let me get this right, the crew of an airplane are self-employed, or they work for the captain, or whoever it is owns the franchise for that aircraft?' said Niamh dumbfounded.

'Dead right, and if you add a profit sharing angle there's an added incentive to make it work. After a few years market forces kick in,' said Donal encouragingly, 'and they compete over the same routes.'

'But how can you have competition, more than one plane can't take off and land at the same time?'

'Second runways,' he said as if she was a simpleton.

She looked straight ahead concentrating on her driving, 'It's pure genius Donal, but why stop there? You could always go for corporate sponsorship of the Defence Forces or some other commercial angle,' the sarcasm was totally lost on him.

'How would that work?' he asked, interested and intrigued.

'It saves us money, more bangs and less bucks. Ireland's worldwide reputation in peacekeeping operations is second to none so they'd be falling over themselves to cash in. You could have Barbie on fashion patrol with the Naval Service.'

'What about the air corp and army?'

'Action Man, yeh that's it, Action Man for the army and

how about Rambo of The Rangers Wing?'

'That still leaves the air corp.'

'Ronal McDonald, he's yer man for the fly boys.'

'You could have something there Niamh,' said Donal pensively. 'It needs fine tuning, but I can run with that.' Donal produced a large envelope, 'I won't show you this whilst you are driving.'

'What is it?'

'It's my release papers, a certificate signed by a panel of three doctors. Do you know I'm unique in Dáil Éireann, the only one in the house who can actually prove they're sane, if some gobshite tries to tell me I don't know what I'm talking about I'll just wave this at them.'

The phrase lunatics taking over the asylum came into Niamh's mind. 'Back to our mutual friend, you never did tell me what you offered him to move to Cavan, what was it?'

Donal didn't say a word; he looked through the C.D's in the glove compartment and fished out an album.

'You're not going to tell me are you? asked a peeved Niamh.

Donal shoved The Book of Invasions by Horslips under her nose.

'I offered them that,' he said pointing at track seven, Niamh glanced to where his finger pointed.

'So what's so special about that?' she asked.

'It's one of their great treasures, there's four all together, but that's the one they want the most. Only the

Taoiseach of the day knows where it is, so I can't help them now even if I wanted to.'

'So you aimed to give it to them, I don't understand. Ruairí is nothing but trouble, why did you put up with him?'

'I never said I'd give it to them, I said I'd tell them where it was, there is a world of difference.' Donal looked sideways at Niamh, 'Do you think I'm the only one who's had enough of Ruairí, or that he's my only avenue of contact with the sídhe?'

'What are you getting at Donal?'

'There are those amongst Ruairí's kind who are not particularly enamoured with his way of doing things. These others think a change of leadership is long overdue, I agree with them and was prepared to give a helping hand.'

'How?' Niamh asked intrigued.

'Simple, it was a sting. Ruairí sells my deal to the sídhe, they move, I don't deliver, Ruairí is discredited and there's a palace coup. I'm then dealing with a more cooperative and amenable joint leadership.'

'So this whole thing, the Cavan project, Eoghan Dempsey and the offer, none of it was as it appeared. It was simply a plot to replace Ruairí?'

'But things didn't work out as planned. That gobshite queered the pitch and I'm no longer Taoiseach,' but he added with determination, 'don't you worry, I'll get the little fecker next time around.'

Time to change the subject thought Niamh, 'So when do

we go to Iceland?'

'At the end of the week, after I've been on retreat,' said Donal.

'What, you're going on a retreat? I am totally amazed.'

'It was Máire's idea, on the way out of the office to meet the fourth estate the day I resigned, she came up to me and said Taoiseach, if you never feel you need to switch off and have a restful break, I know just the place and just the man, a miracle worker he is, then she gave me this guy's phone number and I gave him a ring.'

'I can't wait to get away.' said Niamh enthusiastically.

'That's just what I told Father Peter Antheney when I booked my retreat. Mr Brady, he said, I'll be counting the days.'

There was a hesitant knock on Mick's office door. 'Come in, don't hang around out there,' he shouted. Into the room came Helen, the newest and youngest recruit to Teach agus Talamh, she smiled nervously. 'Mr McCarthy,' she began.

'Please just call me Mick, but if you're happier with Mr McCarthy then so be it.'

'Mick it is then. I have the field report from the Bord Na Móna Westmeath body in the bog and I'd like you to look at it.'

'Well if you like Helen, I will, finds like these may be rare but they aren't unusual.' She looked uncomfortable and fidgety.

'This one is a little different from the run of the mill. This particular mummified body was wrapped up in a woven linen cloth, found in a cedar wood sarcophagus and accompanied by statues of the god Osiris. The whole find was carefully and deliberately laid out on the deck of a papyrus boat.'

Glossary - Irish Language Words And Phrases

Word / Phrase	Meaning	Approximate pronunciation
Abhaile	Home	A Woll Ya
Agus anois	And now/ what next	Aw Guss Ane Ish
Amhrán na Bhfiann	The Soldier's song	Aw Ron Na Vee On
An aimsir	The weather	On Ime Sha
Arás an Uachtaráin	Residency of the President of Ireland	Aras On Oor Taw Rawn
Ard Fheis	Annual party conference	Ord Esh
As Gaeilge	In Irish (in the Irish language)	Oss Gale Ga
A stór mo chroí	Love of my heart	A Store Mow Cree
Beann sídhe	Wailing ghostly woman	Bann She
Bodhrán	Hand held goat skin drum used in Irish trad music	Bore On
Breith lá sonas duit	Happy birthday	Brea (as in bread) Law Soonas Gwit / Dit
Camogie	Women's hurling	Cam Oh Gey(like the ey in key)
Crathur	Creature	Cray Ther (like her, but with a th sound instead of a h sound)
Culchie	Red neck / chave	Cull Shee
Daíl Éireann	Lower house of the Irish Parliament	Dawl Air On

Word / Phrase	Meaning	Approximate pronunciation
Cumann	Constituency party branch	Come un
Faílte	Welcome	Foll cha
Fianna	Mythological elite Irish warriors	Fee Anna
Garsún	Boy	Gossen
Luas	Dublin city urban tram way – literally speed	Loo ass
Macra Na Feirme	Countrywide Irish youth / community organization	Mock Ra N Firm
Ráiméis	Nonsense / rubbish	Raw Mesh
Roisín Dúbh	Allegorical reference to Ireland – literally black rose	Row Sheen Do (Do is as in the English 'to do')
Seanad	Upper House of the Irish Parliament	Shan Add
Sídhe	Collective name given to Irish 'fairies'	She
Sláinte	Good Health / cheers	Slawn Cha
Tá Sé	It is / He is	Taw (aw like the aw in the English word saw) Shay
Taoiseach	Prime Minister – literally chief	Tea Shock
Taoisigh	Plural of Taoiseach	Tea She

Word / Phrase	Meaning	Approximate pronunciation
Teach Agus Talamh	House and Land	Chock Aw Guss Taw Luff
Co (Polish)	What?	Cho
Dziekujue (Polish)	Thank you	Gin kwee a
Dobry Wieczor (Polish)	Good Evening	Dob bree Vetch you
Tak (Polish)	Yes	Tack
Wodka Proze (Polish)	Vodka Please	Vodka Prosh A
Nazdrowicie (Polish)	Cheers	Naz drov ya